APACHE RAIDERS

Suddenly there was an eruption of noise from outside the building, and they all turned toward a window on the plaza. There were the sounds of hoofbeats, war-whoops, and screaming from the locals.

It took Dan'l and Rivera only moments to descend the wide staircase of the mansion and emerge onto the plaza below. What they saw there was chaos. The forerunners of an even larger Yellow Horse army were coming into the square, firing rifles and hurling lances at anybody on the street.

A young Spanish officer went down right in front of Dan'l, with a lance sticking out of him, front and back. Dan'l stepped forward and yanked a saber out of the officer's right hand, and moved out among the mounted warriors, who were yelling wildly in their attack.

"Damn it, Boone!" Rivera protested.

But Dan'l did not even hear him. He was surrounded by mounted Apaches. He wielded the saber recklessly, cutting and slicing with it in his right hand while he swung the Kentucky rifle like a club with the left. An Apache was almost cut in half by a saber swing. He sat surprised on his mount, then his torso doubled on itself and hung from the horse for a moment before falling to the ground. Dan'l swung his left hand then and brained a small pony. It fell sideways to the dirt, throwing its rider off. Dan'l moved up and beheaded the warrior on the ground.

Blood was everywhere, and a lot of it was on Dan'l's face and arms and chest. But none of it was his....

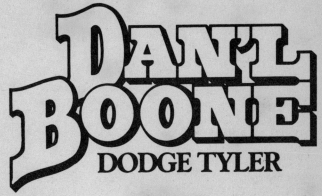

DAN'L BOONE

DODGE TYLER

DEATH AT SPANISH WELLS

━━━ △ ━━━

LEISURE BOOKS   **L**   NEW YORK CITY

A LEISURE BOOK®

August 1996

Published by

Dorchester Publishing Co., Inc.
276 Fifth Avenue
New York, NY 10001

Printed in the United States of America.

DEATH
AT
SPANISH
WELLS

Prologue

The bearded frontiersman sat on the narrow stoop before his cabin and carefully cleaned the Kentucky rifle that lay across his knees. As he worked, he watched the approaching rider. Gradually the horseman loomed larger, coming through the corn, rocking in his saddle. Finally the rider stopped just a few yards away. He wore a bowler hat and wire spectacles; he gave the impression of being a preacher.

"They told me in town where to find you. Are you really the great Indian fighter and explorer Dan'l Boone?"

The old man set the rifle aside and squinted up at the mounted stranger through clear, penetrating eyes. Boone was bareheaded; his hair was thinning and almost white. He had a tooth missing at the corner of his mouth.

"What if I was?" he asked suspiciously.

The rider dismounted, retrieved a large note-book from a saddlebag, and came up onto the porch, where the old fellow sat on a willow chair. The musket leaned against the log wall of the cabin beside the frontiersman, but Boone saw no need for it.

"I'm Adam Hollis. I've come all the way from Boston to find you, Dan'l. I'm pleased and mighty proud to finally meet up with you."

"I don't talk to newspaper people." When Hollis smiled, Dan'l liked the eyes behind the glasses.

"I'm just a library clerk. Mind if I shake the riding cramps out on your porch?" Hollis asked.

When Dan'l motioned grudgingly to a second chair not far away, Hollis slumped onto it and stretched his legs. The aroma of cooking food came to him from inside. He looked out past the cornfield to the woods and admired the view.

"Thanks," he said wearily. "People have been coming to me for years, selling me bits and pieces of your life story because of my special interest."

Dan'l grunted. "Most of them is selling swamp fog."

Hollis grinned. "I figured as much. But all those stories got my curiosity up, sir, and I came to realize your own story could be one of the great untold legends of the frontier. So I spent my life savings to get out here, hoping you might talk to me some about yourself."

The old hunter regarded Hollis sidewise. "You want to write down all that stuff? Hell, ain't nobody'll want to read about them times. We're in a whole different century, by Jesus. Nobody gives a tinker's damn about that early stuff no more."

Hollis shook his head. "You'd be surprised, Dan'l. You're already something of a legend—even in Europe, I hear. But I think that's just the beginning. If you let me document your life while it's all still in your head, generations to come will know what wild adventures you had."

The great hunter rose from his chair. He no longer enjoyed the renowned robustness or grace of his youth, but he still looked as hard as sacked salt. Dan'l went to the far end of the porch and stared out into the green forest beyond the fields, the kind of country that had been his home for all of his life. He finally turned back to Hollis.

"What would you do with these stories once you got it all writ down on paper?"

Hollis shrugged. "Publish them, but only if you wanted me to. At least we'd have them all down. For safekeeping, you might say."

Dan'l shook his head. "I can't say I'd want them in no book. Not in my lifetime. Not the real stuff. Most of them are too damned private. There's too many people out there who might not want them told. Or they might be moved to correct them, so to speak. Come out with their own versions so they would look better."

A resolve settled over Hollis. "All right. It can all be hidden away till long after you're gone if that's what you'd like. Then if the stories don't get lost somewhere down the line, maybe they will all come out later, at a better time, and be given over to some book people. That's what I would hope for."

Dan'l thought for a long moment. "You'd promise that in writing?"

Hollis nodded. "I will."

A laugh rattled out of the old man's throat. "I guess you'd want even the bear mauling and the wolf eating and the nasty ways some redskins liked to treat a white man when they caught him?"

"Yes, everything," Hollis said.

"There's treks into the West, the far side of the Mississippi, that hardly a man alive now knows about," Dan'l said, reflecting. "And these eyes have seen things that nobody's going to believe."

Hollis was becoming excited. "I'd want it all."

Dan'l took a deep breath in and called, "Rebecca! You better put a big pot of coffee on! Looks like we got company for a spell!"

As Hollis relaxed and smiled, Dan'l heaved himself back onto the primitive chair and closed his eyes for a moment. Finally, he said, "I reckon we might as well get going on it then."

Hollis was caught off guard. He fumbled in a

pocket for a quill pen and a small ink pot, then opened up the thick but empty notebook. Hollis dipped his pen into the ink and waited.

"Most of it happened in about thirty years," Dan'l said quietly. "The important stuff. The stuff most folks don't know nothing about. That's when I got this raw hunger for the wild places, the far-off country where no settlers had been.

"I was just a stripling when I first started hearing about the land west of the Alleghenies," Dan'l said, his gaze wandering off toward the woods.

Hollis did not hesitate or interrupt with any questions. As the old man talked, he just began writing steadily in the thick book with an urgency he had never before experienced. He had to get every sentence down exactly as Dan'l said it. He could not miss a single word.

Chapter One

The peones that were crowded into the central plaza at Santa Fe that warm spring morning had no hint, as their governor spoke to them from a raised podium hung with brightly hued bunting, that raw violence and death would soon descend on them from the surrounding buttes and mesas like a high-country storm.

One man, though, seated behind Governor Alvarado on the high platform with a group of dignitaries, felt the hair rise on the nape of his neck for no obvious reason, and he kept looking past the crowd, toward the edge of town, with hard, suspicious eyes.

He was the Kentuckian Dan'l Boone.

Governor Luis Alvarado, descendant of conquistadors, stood proudly before the gathered throng. As he addressed them in rolling Spanish, his speech rising and falling eloquently, he was interrupted regularly by the tumultuous shouts of approval among the locals, mostly mestizos, with mixed Spanish and Indian blood.

"And we know," Alvarado was saying loudly, over the whisper of breeze through plaza cottonwoods, "that when our illustrious visitors from St. Louis have seen with their own eyes the richness of mineral deposits around Santa Fe, they will rush to stake their claims to some of the wealthiest ore-producing sites in the great territory of New Mexico."

Behind Alvarado on the platform were seated his aides, the local garrison commander, the investors Dan'l had guided from St. Louis—named Jameson and Douglas, and Dan'l himself. Beside Dan'l was an interpreter who was called Dura Cabeza, an alias. Nobody knew his real name, not even the authorities. He had been one of the first traders to the area, and had spent some time in Boston as a young man, even though he was Mexican.

There was more cheering for Alvarado's remarks, and hats were thrown into the air and a few guns were fired. Alvarado was popular in Santa Fe because he paid little attention to the authorities in Mexico City, and because he gave the locals freedom to make money and prosper.

Dan'l listened to Cabeza's translation distractedly, still watching the horizon beyond the brown adobe buildings and dwellings that encroached upon the square. There was not really much of substance to trouble him. A brief flash of light on a distant butte, the almost-indiscernible yelping of coyotes from afar that others had not heard. And something Alvarado had mentioned yesterday about a possible movement north of an Apache army, led by the belligerent Chief Yellow Horse. Dan'l put all that together, felt again the hair on the back of his neck, and could not keep his attention on Alvarado's speech. He sat there tight-coiled in his buckskins and black, wide-brimmed hat, and hoped his feelings were unfounded and that all was fine on this spring morning in the Great Southwest.

"We welcome investment from outside our borders," Alvarado went on. "From our neighbor to the north and east that has just recently thrown off the yoke of European domination, and is even now forming a new, democratic government that will undoubtedly become our best trading partner!"

The crowd liked that. They looked upon the recent American Revolution as a prelude to one of their own, after which Mexico City would govern itself. Colonel Pedro Rivera, the garrison commandant sitting behind Alvarado, gave him a sour look at those last remarks. Rivera was a staunch Spanish loyalist, and understood that Alvarado had the political courage to make such comments only because he was far from Mexico City.

Jameson and Douglas applauded loudly after Cabeza's translation, and beside them Dan'l nodded absently and fixed his attention on the hills beyond town, where he thought for a brief moment he could see riders. He recalled a day in Kentucky when the Shawnee had come quietly to Boonesborough, and he suddenly felt very uneasy. On the other hand, danger was what he had always gone out looking for. When Kentucky had finally become too civilized, about a year ago, he had moved his family to Missouri, to continue doing what he did best. Exploration, and guiding parties of men into wilderness areas, like the one between St. Louis and Santa Fe.

Samuel Douglas, a rather small, wiry man, rose and shook Alvarado's hand enthusiastically, and then Will Jameson, tall and gray-haired, followed suit. Dan'l applauded from his seat, but then he looked down a side street leading away from the plaza and saw an Indian on horseback cross the narrow way quickly and disappear behind a dwelling.

Now Dan'l was convinced. What he had seen were Apaches. Chief Yellow Horse had orchestrated a sneak attack on the town during its celebration, while it was otherwise occupied. He would bring his warriors in like demons from hell, with the intent of destroying the Spanish settlement and driving the white man from New Mexico.

Dan'l rose from his seat and interrupted Alvarado.

"Mr. Governor . . ."

Alvarado smiled warmly at him. "A wonderful reception for you, yes?" he asked in good English. "Just a moment, amigo, I must dismiss our large audience."

Alvarado turned back to the crowd, which cheered him loudly again. A rather tall, elegant-looking man in a dark suit with silver buttons, Alvarado looked the part of a governor. Dan'l stood behind him frustrated as Alvarado said his last words.

"Now we will return to our homes, *compadres*," he announced in Spanish, with a big grin. "But I ask that you make a special effort to offer friendship and hospitality to our guests while they are in Santa Fe!"

As the wild cheering filled the square, Dan'l stepped up beside Alvarado and whispered into his ear. Alvarado's face changed subtly, then dramatically. "What?" he said.

As a reply, Dan'l pointed down a wide street leading into the square, and when Alvarado looked, he saw a mounted Indian there alone, looking as elegant as Alvarado in an eagle-feather headdress and bright war paint. It was Yellow Horse.

"Dios mio!" Alvarado breathed.

16

"I think we're under attack," Dan'l said to him.

Now many of those gathered in the square were turning to look, too, and a hush came over the gathering like an invisible blanket being thrown over the plaza.

"What is it?" Sam Douglas asked from behind Dan'l. He was still smiling, still basking in the warmth of their reception.

Colonel Rivera, though, and a captain of his named Salazar were both staring fiercely toward the lone Indian facing them boldly on the lonely street.

"It's Yellow Horse!" Rivera shouted out hoarsely.

"Dios mio," Alvarado repeated in a half-whisper.

Rivera stepped forward, beside Alvarado. "We're under attack! Everybody take cover! If you have guns, find them!" He turned to Salazar. "Captain, call out the garrison!"

Now, as other Apaches showed themselves in the merging streets, gathering like a swarm of locusts and beginning to shout out war cries, the crowd in the plaza panicked. Men and women ran in all directions, wild looks on their faces, serapes flying. In just seconds, the streets leading into the square were choked with Yellow Horse's cavalry and there was a din going up from them and the locals.

"Take cover! Take cover!" Alvarado was shouting.

17

Dan'l turned to Jameson and Douglas and their several associates. "Get back to the Governor's Mansion! Now!"

"It's Apaches?" Jameson said. "How do we know they're hostile? Can't we talk to them?"

Dan'l scowled fiercely at him. "Get the hell back to the mansion."

In the next moment, Chief Yellow Horse, now surrounded by his mounted warriors, raised his arm in a signal to his troops, and then brought it down swiftly.

There was a wild yelling by the Apaches from all points around the plaza, then a thunderous pounding of hoofbeats as they came roaring toward the square, wielding lances, bows, and primitive rifles.

The investors and their people ran toward the two-story, brown-adobe Governor's Mansion at the edge of the plaza, as locals dispersed for cover, yelling and screaming. The podium was abandoned by those on it, then used for cover. On the opposite side of the square from the mansion a bugle sounded, and Dan'l knew that troops would soon flood the area. There were a few soldiers out in the square already, to keep order in the crowd during the speeches, and they now crouched behind trees and other cover, firing at the attacking hordes as they came roaring into the open plaza.

Dan'l found himself beside Rivera and one of his soldiers, but without a weapon. The Apaches were streaming into the area, firing at anything that moved. Dan'l saw men and women both go down under the hooves of the savage mounted attack, with arrows stuck in backs and chests, heads destroyed by hot lead from rifles. There was a lot of whooping and yelling among the Apaches, who seemed to enjoy their work greatly. Yellow Horse rode in among his warriors, exposing himself to death or injury, to participate in the bloodshed. It was a large war party, more like an army, and every man was mounted on a fast horse. The Apaches were everywhere, their faces painted in bright colors.

Rivera and his men had begun firing back, and in the first moments a wild-looking Apache, muscular and tall, rode right up to the podium and hurled a lance at those huddled behind it. The weapon hit the soldier beside Dan'l square in the chest, and sliced through him until half the lance stuck out through his back. Rivera fired at the young, tough-looking warrior, but missed completely as the Indian's horse reared up nervously. Then the warrior rode off, readying his rifle for firing.

"Diablo!" Rivera swore, re-loading. *"Eso es El Perro Corriendo!"*

Dan'l grabbed the soldier's flintlock repeating revolver, and saw that only one shot had been fired. It was an eight-shot, .40-caliber weapon, a gun Dan'l had seen often back in Carolina. He quickly primed it, glancing at Rivera. "What?"

"It is Yellow Horse's son that killed my private. Running Dog, in English. He has a reputation for ferocity and cruelty. The Taos Indians fear him greatly. I had him in my sights!"

"Then you ought've killed him," Dan'l said evenly. He had not liked Rivera from the moment they had been introduced upon Dan'l's arrival two days ago, when Rivera had treated him with arrogance and disrespect.

As Rivera turned to glare at Dan'l, Dan'l fired the handgun and brought down one of Yellow Horse's warriors, who had been riding right at the podium. The Indian crashed onto the wooden platform, breaking through its fragile flooring. Dan'l primed and fired quickly, over and over, and killed an Apache with each shot. Rivera took notice of his accuracy as he killed a couple of Apaches himself.

The plaza was filled with death and bloodshed. Most of the celebrants had not found cover before the Apaches arrived, and the Indians were mowing them down like wheat in an open field. Yellow Horse had now retreated to the edge of the fighting, and was urging his men on from there. Running Dog, his only son, pulled out a saber, probably stolen from some Mexican officer in an earlier battle, and was lopping off heads and arms with it. He wore a tight grin throughout the slaughter.

Women and children who could not get to cover were being killed, too, without mercy. That was one reason the great horse warriors of the Southwest were so feared by the Comanches and Kiowa before the Mexicans came. They killed all in their path. Soon the square was littered with the corpses of women and children, as well as men.

But as Dan'l fought back from the podium, he saw that Running Dog was much worse than the others. He went out of his way to maim and hurt before killing the enemy. Dan'l saw him run a dark-haired mestizo woman down and cut off both arms before she could hit the ground. Then he crushed her under the hooves of his mount.

"That son of a bitch!" Dan'l growled. He aimed for Running Dog, and started to fire, but another Apache came between them, and Dan'l killed the nearest man instead.

Now the garrison soldiers were streaming into the plaza, aiming their fire at the mounted Indians. The crackle of gunfire increased dramatically, and the acrid odors of gunsmoke and spilt blood filled the air. Soldiers were being felled with arrows and hot lead, but now the Apaches were taking losses, too. The battle was no longer one-sided. In the melee, Dan'l saw Captain Juan Salazar, the one who had gone after Rivera's troops, firing into the attackers with two pistols blazing. Dan'l, too, came out from the cover of the podium, and was priming and firing. He killed an Apache with each shot fired, but there were so many that none of it seemed to make a difference.

The garrison soldiers, though, were making a

difference. They were outnumbered, but they had many more targets to shoot at. Dan'l leaned against the podium to re-load, and an Apache came at him with a lance. He thrust it at Dan'l's chest, but Dan'l stepped aside, caught the lance in his free hand, and hauled the Indian off his mount as he went past. Dan'l then threw the fellow to the ground, placed the revolver against the side of his head, and blew away half his skull.

"Keep firing!" Rivera was yelling from behind the podium. "Keep killing them!"

Dan'l reloaded now and ready to fire, got another glimpse of Running Dog across the plaza. He was carrying a lance and heading toward a baby that had been dropped on the ground in the chaos, separated from its mother. Dan'l saw what was about to happen and started toward him.

"Don't, you bloody bastard!" he yelled.

But the Apache did not even hear him. He made a violent thrust of the long lance, impaled the baby and lifted the lance into the air.

Yelling wildly, Running Dog waved the baby in the air, impaled on the long pike. The child was still alive.

"You bastard!" Dan'l screamed. A vision of his own youngest child, back in St. Louis, flashed across his mind. "You goddamn demon!"

At that point, Running Dog finally heard the Kentuckian, and turned and glared at him, the baby now dead on his pike. Yellow Horse, over at the perimeter, also heard Dan'l's epithet. He focused hard on Dan'l and his eyes widened slightly. Then he recalled his warriors, and one by one they turned their mounts and galloped out of the plaza. Governor Alvarado now stood in the doorway of his mansion. He had just fired an old musket at the attackers, and had brought one down. Now he watched, stunned, as Dan'l strode out into the square among the disbanding Apaches, firing with two pistols, felling Indians on all sides. Jameson and Douglas had found shelter inside, and cowered behind Alvarado. Jameson had a gun out, but had not used it.

Rivera came out from behind the podium, too, and was taking last shots from behind Dan'l. The Apaches streamed out of the area, but a last one, emulating Running Dog, had picked up the decapitated head of a Spaniard, and waved it above his head on a short lance as he left the plaza, yelling obscenities at his enemy in his native tongue.

Dan'l saw Running Dog at the end of the plaza, preparing to follow his father out. He had discarded the dead child, and now screamed out his hatred at the survivors of the attack. Dan'l took careful aim a second time, but again lost his target in the melee. Two departing Apaches fired rifles at Dan'l at the last moment, as he stood boldly in the center of the square. Both missed.

"Senor Boone!" Alvarado yelled. "Get down!"

Yellow Horse took one last look toward the plaza, and saw Dan'l missed by the two well-aimed shots. Then he urged his son and his other warriors to leave quickly, since the garrison soldiers were now taking a toll among them.

In another couple of moments they were gone, as quickly as they had come, like a spring storm, galloping back down the dry streets to the southwest, raising a great wall of dust between themselves and the plaza.

Dan'l stood there amid the dead and dying and felt a strong loathing inside his chest. Rivera came up beside him, stuffing his gun into a holster. Dan'l glanced at him.

"That young one. The one you called Running Dog. I wish I'd killed that son of a bitch."

Rivera nodded. "He is a prince of the Apache nation. His atrocities in the south country are well known to us."

Dan'l had seen atrocities with the Shawnee, too, back in Kentucky and Tennessee. But these warriors were more dangerous. The Shawnee had usually been on foot in an attack. These Apaches, mounted and mobile, were much more efficient in their killing. And some of them seemed to enjoy it too much.

"Will they come back?" Dan'l wondered.

Rivera shrugged his shoulders. "There is no way to tell. They never seem to act in the same way twice. But their message to us is clear: Get out of Santa Fe, leave our territory. They have never tolerated intrusion by any tribe or people into an area they think is theirs."

Dan'l nodded. "That part sounds kind of familiar."

Rivera caught his eye and scowled slightly. "Incidentally, you did not act wisely. You should be dead. Then I would have to answer to the governor. I hope you exercise more common sense the rest of your stay here."

Dan'l turned to him, a sober look on his bearded face. "How many of these fracases you been in, Rivera?"

The colonel stiffly raised himself up to his full height. "I have been in three other great battles. With the Apache, the Kiowa, and with peasant revolutionaries in my own country. I have been twice decorated by the viceroy himself in Mexico City," he declared in an arrogant voice.

Dan'l remained somber. "Well, I got you twice over, mister. I fit Shawnee and Cherokee, mounted and on foot. I went against the French twice at Fort Duquesne, and then I had to fight the British, too, 'cause of that lunatic George. General Washington hisself offered me one of them medals you're talking about, and I refused it 'cause I don't think a man ought to be rewarded for killing."

A new look had come into Rivera's swarthy face.

"So don't be telling me that I acted stupid, Colonel, when I was under fire. That's a thing a man's got to figure out for hisself."

Rivera did not respond. Instead, he turned and stalked away, stiff-backed, toward the Governor's Mansion.

Dan'l watched him go for a moment, then turned back to the square. There were wounded to tend to.

It was over an hour later when Dan'l finally made his way into the mansion at the edge of the square, after helping get many wounded locals off the plaza and into the compound of the garrison, where they were being tended by the two doctors who were available. When Dan'l entered the mansion, he soon found Jameson and Douglas in a crowded corridor, sitting at a table and drinking coffee, looking very scared. They had come across hundreds of miles of wilderness to get there, but had never seen anything like what just happened.

Dan'l walked over to them, and they eyed him glumly.

"You didn't say it would be like this," Jameson said. "We thought Santa Fe would be civilized." His graying hair was mussed, his lean face pale. Sam Douglas, beside him, looked particularly small and weak.

"Well, maybe we seen the last of them," Dan'l said wearily, sitting on the corner of the table before them. "It could be a long time before Yellow Horse tries this again. He didn't expect so big a garrison."

"I don't want to be here if he decides he

doesn't care," Douglas said in a quiet voice. "And I sure as hell can't bring my family to a place like this."

Just as Dan'l was about to reply, Governor Alvarado came down the long hallway with murals on its walls and glistening floor tiles. With him were his top aide, a couple of Rivera's soldiers, the omnipresent Cabeza, and a scared-looking Senora Alvarado, in a floor-length, frilly gown. They all came up to the table where the investors sat.

"Ah, here are our guests! I am so sorry, senores, that you were put through this horrible experience. I assure you this is an extraordinary event. Yellow Horse has never strayed so far from his home territory. And we will now hope that he does not do so again."

Dan'l was surprised to see Alvarado's arm in a sling. It turned out that he had received a flesh wound while shooting from the doorway of the mansion. He was no coward, Dan'l decided.

"Frankly, Mr. Governor, this gives us something to think about," Jameson said soberly. "There must be a hundred dead in your plaza out there. And many others injured. We thought Santa Fe would be a safe place for investors." He let his gaze drift along the corridor wall, where wounded men and women were awaiting treatment.

Douglas had risen to his feet, in deference to Mrs. Alvarado. "We have to talk about this, Mr. Governor."

Isabel Alvarado stepped forward. She was slim and elegant, and quite attractive with dark hair piled up on her head. She spoke English without an accent. "Please, gentlemen. Come into my husband's private office and let me serve you a relaxing drink. It will be my personal pleasure."

The two investors looked at her, and Jameson also rose. "All right, Mrs. Alvarado. That might be best."

"Mr. Boone," Alvarado said, turning to Dan'l. "Will you please join us?"

Dan'l thought for a moment. "I hear we took a couple of prisoners, Governor. Where would they be?"

Alvarado raised his eyebrows. He was bareheaded now, and his silver hair shone in the dull light of the hallway. He was a handsome fellow, fair-skinned and Castilian-looking, just the type that people would look up to for his leadership, Dan'l thought.

"Why, I believe Rivera had them taken into the garrison," Alvarado replied. "For possible questioning, I suppose."

"I reckon I'd like to see them, if the governor don't mind," Dan'l said politely.

"Of course," Alvarado said. "Just tell Rivera I sent you."

"Thanks, Governor," Dan'l said. "I'll just walk over there now, if you'll oblige."

"Yes, *cierto*," Alvarado said. He turned to a rangy, broad-shouldered man who had just

28

walked up to them from across the corridor. The fellow was obviously not Spanish, and he wore a dyed-black rawhide tunic not unlike Dan'l's. His trousers were dark cloth, decorated with silver buttons in the Spanish style. Dan'l thought he looked like a hunter, a mountain man.

"Before you leave," Alvarado said, "I would like to have you meet Senor Stefan Kravitz, a Polish immigrant to our Santa Fe. He often hunts for our troops and guides them on small expeditions."

"Pleasured," Dan'l said, extending his thick hand.

Kravitz grinned broadly, and showed a gold tooth at the corner of his mouth. He had a long, bony face and a brown mustache. He carried a beaded, wide-brimmed hat in his hand. He took Dan'l's hand in his free one, and Dan'l felt the strength in his grasp.

"I been hearing about you for years," Kravitz said in a deep voice. He was an inch taller than Dan'l, but not so broadly built. In his thirties, he was also a decade younger than the Kentuckian. "It's an honor and a pleasure, Dan'l."

Alvarado looked surprised. "Do we have a celebrity in our midst, then?"

Jameson spoke up. "Dan'l has quite a reputation back East. As an Indian fighter. That's why we hired him."

"Ah," Alvarado said. "Now I see why I was so

impressed with the way you handled yourself in the plaza, Mr. Boone."

"Hell, that waren't nothing," Dan'l said quietly.

"I'd like to go with you to the barracks," Kravitz said to Dan'l. "If you don't mind." Kravitz had spent time in New York and Mexico City, and spoke both English and Spanish with a slight accent.

"Fine with me," Dan'l said.

As they left the others and went back out onto the plaza, Cabeza trailed after them. Since he spoke fluent Apache, he thought he might be needed.

Inside the garrison walls there was a lot of activity. Men and women were laid out on the ground, some with their faces covered. Others were being tended by doctors and medics, and there was a lot of blood and groaning.

At the headquarters building, Dan'l and the others were stopped by a sentry, who called over Juan Salazar, the broad captain who was Rivera's next in command. He recognized Kravitz and Cabeza, then frowned when he saw Dan'l.

"Yes? What do you want here?"

"We would like to observe the interrogation," Kravitz told him.

Salazar smiled smugly. "I'm afraid that is impossible. This is a military matter," he said in Spanish.

"What did he say?" Dan'l asked Kravitz.

But it was Cabeza who replied sourly, "He says we cannot participate."

Dan'l looked into Salazar's dark eyes. Salazar was shorter than Colonel Rivera, but just as swarthy, with a small mustache that looked painted on. "Governor Alvarado sent us. Do you want to question his authority?"

Salazar understood most of it, but Cabeza translated anyway. Salazar glared at them for a long moment, then said, "All right," in heavily accented English. "You may go. Second *puerta* across the corridor."

When the three of them entered the white-washed room, they found a tough-looking sergeant with two private soldiers. The soldiers had been working the prisoners over, and one Apache lay dead on the floor, his face bloody. The other one was chained to the opposite wall, and had been cut and slashed across his torso.

"What the hell," Dan'l growled.

"Que pasa?" the sergeant said with a frown, turning to Dan'l and the others. Salazar came in behind them and closed the door.

"Is this your notion of questioning?" Dan'l said in a hard voice to the sergeant, gesturing to the dead Indian on the floor.

"You complain about our methods?" Salazar said. "Did you not see what these savages did to our women and children?"

Kravitz decided to keep out of it, but Dan'l turned a somber look on Salazar. "You mean we got to act this way 'cause they do?"

"We?" Salazar hissed. He had to look up a couple of inches into Dan'l's eyes. "You have nothing to do with this, Boone. It has nothing to do with you. You may watch, but you may not interfere."

Salazar nodded to one of the privates, and the fellow returned to the Indian on the wall, holding a hunting knife.

"We wish to know whether Yellow Horse has moved his village, and whether he has reserve warriors back there," Salazar said firmly. "Hopefully, this man will tell us."

The soldier raised the knife to slice the Apache's chest some more. Dan'l made a sound in his throat, went over, and grabbed the fellow's arm in an iron grip and twisted. The knife fell to the floor. The sergeant, standing nearby, uttered an obscenity in Spanish and rushed Dan'l.

Dan'l turned just in time, threw a hard fist, and knocked him to the floor.

The sergeant lay on his back with a look of complete shock on his square face. The second soldier raised a rifle and aimed it quickly at Dan'l.

Salazar stopped him with a quick command, then stood scowling fiercely at Dan'l. The tension in the small room was almost palpable.

The sergeant swore darkly, and rose to his feet. Dan'l returned Salazar's angry look.

"What do you think you are about, damn you!" Salazar said through clenched teeth.

"I'm stopping the torture of another human

being, by Jesus," Dan'l replied evenly. "I reckon if you want to make a thing about it, we'll go to the governor. Right now."

The Apache hung there, his vision blurred with pain. But he had noticed what had happened.

"Dan'l's right, Captain," Kravitz said finally. "This is not right."

Salazar was fuming. "You damn foreigners and your crazy ideas! You don't know how to treat these people! If you are soft with them, they take it as a sign of weakness! You have no idea what you are doing!"

Dura Cabeza moved over to him and spoke softly. "It is not important, Captain. The Indian will lie to you anyway."

Salazar looked as if he might hit Cabeza for a moment. Then he let himself cool down. "This is an outrage."

"If one of your soldiers won't shoot me in the back," Dan'l told him caustically, "I'd like to make a try at it."

"What?" Salazar sputtered.

Cabeza asked, "What is the harm, Captain? The governor wants the goodwill of these men, yes?"

Salazar fumed, but relented. "Colonel Rivera will hear of this," he warned Dan'l. Then he turned and stormed out of the room, taking the sergeant with him. The two soldiers remained watching Dan'l carefully.

"You won't get anything, Dan'l," Kravitz told him.

Dan'l went over to face the Apache, who was a lean, athletic looking warrior with a bare chest and legs. Cabeza came up beside Dan'l for translation. The Apache looked defiantly at Dan'l, and then his expression changed subtly, just as Yellow Horse's had earlier upon getting a glimpse of Dan'l's bearded face across the plaza.

"We're not going to harm you further," Dan'l said to him. Cabeza translated.

The Indian looked him up and down, as if he had never seen a white man before.

"Was this all of your army?" Dan'l asked him. "Or is there more?" Cabeza translated again.

"Ancient Bear!" the Apache hissed.

Dan'l turned to Cabeza. "What did he say?"

Both Kravitz and Cabeza were smiling slightly. "He called you Ancient Bear," Cabeza said. "Very interesting."

"That's right." Kravitz grinned. "I think he's got you mixed up with a tribal deity, Dan'l."

"Ancient Bear!" the Apache repeated in a whisper. Then he bowed his head reverently to Dan'l.

"I know the story," Cabeza explained. "Thousands of years ago, a great chieftain ruled the Apache, and he turned into a god in the form of a bear. He said he would watch over his people through the centuries, and if the time came when they did not live up to their heritage

34

of courage, he would come back in the shape of a bear-man, with a pale face and a golden beard. He would depose all current chiefs and resume his place as head of their nation."

"I'll be damned," Dan'l muttered.

"I've seen pictographs. Ancient Bear does look a lot like you, Senor Boone."

The Apache was eyeing Dan'l warily, his expression a little wild. He was now in the grip of abject fear.

"Use it, Dan'l," Kravitz advised him. "Maybe he'll talk to an Apache god."

Dan'l shook his head. "It ain't right, Kravitz." He looked into the Indian's face. "Look at me. Ancient Bear." He used the warrior's Apache word, pointing to himself. Then he shook his head. "No. No!"

The Apache's face did not change.

"He does not believe you," Kravitz said, enjoying it.

"How many warriors does Yellow Horse have?" Dan'l asked the Apache.

Cabeza repeated it in Apache. The Indian eyed Dan'l and licked dry lips. "You know there are over two hundred, Ancient Bear. Please. Do not send me to the Netherworld."

Cabeza translated, and Dan'l shook his head. He asked if Yellow Horse had moved his home village. The response, after another translation, was a vigorous shaking of the head. The Apache was sweating profusely now, wanting only to be out from under Dan'l's intense gaze.

Dan'l was satisfied. He turned away from the Indian. "That should help them some, if it's the truth."

"It is the truth, senor," Cabeza told him. "He would not dare lie to you. There is a recent addition to the legend that makes it more real to him. That Ancient Bear has already reappeared across the wide Mississippi and knows all the Indian languages, and is coming west to reclaim his natural tribe. Now they may have heard about your presence here, and that you led these other men from the East."

Kravitz was also shaking his head, smiling. "I like it. You are a god, Dan'l!"

"Goddamn nonsense," Dan'l muttered. He opened the door to the corridor and stepped out, followed by the other two. He called over the sergeant he had hit earlier. The fellow looked at him bitterly.

"He told us what we wanted to know. I'll report it directly to Rivera. Don't touch him until you hear back from us. I'm going to ask the governor to release him."

Cabeza looked quizzically at Dan'l before translating, but told the sergeant what Dan'l had said. The sergeant looked at Cabeza as if he was crazy, then said, "Sure, sure. We wait."

Dan'l and his companions left the building, returning to the Governor's Mansion across the square.

When they were gone, the sergeant returned to the room where the Apache still hung, bleeding, on the wall. The two soldiers looked at him questioningly. "Are they gone?" the one with the rifle asked.

"Yes, they are gone."

"What do we do with him?" the other one asked, jerking his head toward the chained Indian.

"Him?" the sergeant said casually. "Oh, yes." He pulled a primed revolver from its leather holster, aimed it at the Apache's impassive, defiant face, and squeezed the trigger.

The gun exploded loudly in the close confines of the room, and the Indian's head disintegrated, hurling gray matter, bone, and blood all over the wall behind him.

The sergeant re-holstered the weapon with grim satisfaction. "Now clean up the mess," he said in a low snarl.

Then he returned to his other duties.

Chapter Two

The Governor's Mansion in Santa Fe was not much to look at from the street, but inside, it was decorated sumptuously. There were corridors with glass chandeliers from Madrid, and potted plants from Mexico City, and ornate, polished furniture from various craftsmen of the viceroyalty. Large portraits of Carlos III, the governor himself, and other dignitaries hung imposingly in quiet halls and intimate libraries. The Great Hall was bedecked with rich tapestries and striking wall arrangements of arms and armor.

Governor Luis Alvarado's private office, where he met with Dan'l and Colonel Pedro Rivera on the morning after the Apache attack, was no less splendid. Alvarado sat imperiously behind a long, beautifully carved desk, surrounded by portraits of several of his noteworthy ancestors, including Pedro de Alvarado, who had been one of Cortez's lieutenants.

Alvarado waved a hand toward the latter painting, as Dan'l and Rivera sat on straight chairs before his desk.

"Have you heard perhaps of Alvarado's Leap, Mr. Boone?"

Dan'l furrowed his brow. His face was rough and coarsened by his recent trek to New Mexico, and he had a tough, physical look about him. He was one of the few men from the other side of the Mississippi that Alvarado had ever seen. Alvarado thought he looked like a mountain man.

"Can't say as I have, Governor," he said, staring at the oil painting with its cracked surface. "Sounds like it must've been something special, though."

Colonel Rivera smiled tolerantly at Dan'l's ignorance of Mexican history, and smugly caught Alvarado's eye.

"Oh, it was," Alvarado said. "Pedro de Alvarado, my lineal ancestor, was a great Spanish hero. Hernan Cortez picked him personally for the military expedition into Mexico. He fought bravely and well against the Aztecs, and when the Spaniards were forced temporarily out of Mexico City, the Aztecs had cut holes in their causeways leading across Lake Texcoco, to keep the Spaniards from escaping. Pedro leaped across one of these breaks in the masonry on his white stallion, awing the Aztec soldiers who surrounded him with his equine skills and bravery, and rallied Spanish forces on the far shore. His leap to safety, and survival, became legend."

"I guess we could've used him at Fort Duquesne," Dan'l offered, grinning.

Rivera laughed softly in his throat, and the governor gave him a hard look. "I have heard of your battles with the French," he finally responded. "I understand you fought alongside your great George Washington."

"Yep, we had ourselfs a time," Dan'l replied. "Then we had to do it all over again with King George."

Alvarado looked pensive. "Yes. Your people fought bravely for independence. Unfortunately, the fire of revolution has been ignited in our own country now, because of what the American colonies did. But it is a very different situation. These *Indios* are not ready for self-rule."

"They are like children," Rivera said harshly. "Not much better than these wild Apaches in the territory."

"I reckon you ain't seen the last of old Yellow Horse," Dan'l said to the governor, ignoring Rivera. Rivera had shown only arrogance toward Dan'l, and Dan'l had disliked him from the first.

"That is quite certain," Alvarado said. "He has been harassing settlements in New Mexico for a couple of years. But he never had the effront-ery to attack Santa Fe. He has made it clear that he wants all Spaniards out of this area. Unlike the Taos Indians, the Apache is resolutely hostile toward settlement here."

"That sounds like the Shawnee in Kentucky," Dan'l said. "But they was finally outgunned by sheer numbers. I reckon that will happen here."

"Eventually, yes," Alvarado agreed. "But they could cause much trouble in the meantime. I am very sorry this outbreak had to occur just when your people arrived."

Dan'l sighed slightly. "I have to admit that they're some spooked. I talked to them last night, and Jameson wanted to return to St. Louis. I asked him to take some time to think about it."

"If they scare that easily, they should not have come to New Mexico in the first place," Rivera said gruffly.

Dan'l turned to him with a sober look. "That was quite a show that Yellow Horse put on yesterday. I reckon I can understand Jameson's feelings. He's thinking of putting a lot of money into land here, and mining claims. That money could be lost if Yellow Horse gets his way."

"Yes, of course, Mr. Boone," the governor said. "We have had the same trouble with Mexican investors. And that was before Yellow Horse came here yesterday. What I am hoping is that we can convince you, and you can convince your investors, that we can handle the

Apache. Santa Fe is here to stay, Mr. Boone."

"I'm right sure of that, Mr. Governor," Dan'l said.

"Maybe we could talk with your people together," the governor suggested. "Sometime today or tomorrow."

Dan'l nodded. "I'm sure that can be set up."

The governor clasped his thick hands in front of him on the long desk. "I have heard a story about you, Mr. Boone."

Dan'l met his gaze, but said nothing.

"One of the colonel's men has reported that an Apache prisoner mistook you for an Apache deity."

Rivera grunted out a laugh again, and both Alvarado and Dan'l ignored him.

"That's what I was told, too," Dan'l said. "Damn strange. Looked like a good warrior. And since you mentioned the Apache, I want to request he be released."

"Released?" Alvarado said.

"Yeah, turned loose. He told us what we wanted to know. Yellow Horse would be impressed."

"Who gives a damn what Yellow Horse would think!" Rivera blurted out.

Dan'l looked at him.

"I think what the colonel means," Alvarado said hurriedly, "is that pleasing Yellow Horse would have a low priority here after yesterday."

Dan'l nodded. "But having his respect could influence the way he fights you, Governor. If

42

he's anything like the Cherokee or Shawnee."

"He is nothing like anything you have ever seen back in your colonies," Rivera said stiffly. "He is a brute, and you deal with brutes in a brutish way. Anyway, the savage you speak of is dead."

Dan'l frowned at him. "Dead?"

"He apparently resisted further questioning, and succumbed to . . . physical pressures applied to him."

Dan'l remembered the fear in the Apache's face. "Damn," he said heavily. "I asked your people to spare him."

The colonel glared at him. "You are not in the chain of command, Mr. Boone. My men are not trained to heed the requests of civilians." He tried a smile, but he was not good at it. "Of course if you had come to me, I could have considered your request and possibly intervened."

"I am truly sorry, Mr. Boone," the governor put in. With his elegant look and silvery hair, he made a sharp contrast to Rivera. Rivera was stocky and dark, and rather athletic looking. He was in a bright dress uniform, had a shako hat on his knee, and had his brass buttons polished. The governor ran a hand through his hair. "Your request signifies an understanding of the red man that is not easily come by. And because of that, I have a request of my own to make."

Dan'l was still thinking about the death of the Apache warrior. "Yes, Mr. Governor?"

"I suspect Yellow Horse may be back. Their

attacks often come in pairs. If that happens, it would be helpful if we had the support of the local Taos Indians. They despise the Apaches. I would be very pleased if you could accompany the colonel to their nearby pueblo, and maybe also take Stefan Kravitz with you. He knows the Taos chief Morning Star personally. Morning Star should be asked to volunteer his braves to help in defending Santa Fe in the event of a second attack by Yellow Horse. If Santa Fe is destroyed, the Apache would reign supreme here. Also, the Taos tribe would lose us Spaniards as trading partners. Morning Star should be reminded of all of that." He paused. "Would you undertake such a mission for us? The Taos people probably know of the Apache legend. You might greatly impress them."

Dan'l glanced at the colonel, and saw that the whole notion was as much a surprise to him as to Dan'l himself.

"Well, Governor. I ain't got a lot to do in the next few days, until my people decide what they want. I'll ride out to the pueblo."

The governor smiled and rose from his ornate chair. "Excellent! I knew I could count on you, Mr. Boone. Your reputation precedes you. We will be most grateful. Isn't that right, Colonel?"

Rivera looked at his superior as if the governor belonged in a madhouse. "Uh. Why, yes, of course, Governor. The Army is always willing to accept help from informed civilians in negotiations with the Indians."

"Then it's settled." Alvarado smiled again. He proffered his hand to Dan'l, and was surprised by the iron in Dan'l's grip. "I'll set up the meeting with Morning Star."

It was later that same day that Dan'l rode out to Taos Pueblo with Rivera and the likeable Kravitz. Kravitz had a heavier accent than either Alvarado or Rivera, but he was an outgoing, friendly fellow whom Dan'l already liked, and who made the trip out to the pueblo much easier for Dan'l.

By mid-afternoon the threesome and several Spanish soldiers had arrived at the pueblo. It was built on both sides of a small stream, in several levels of brown adobe, and legend had it that the village had been there for eight hundred years, and that the first people there used to trade with the Toltecs of Mexico.

Unlike the Apaches, the Taos Indians were rather civilized, with cultivated gardens and substantial, permanent houses. They had welcomed the Spaniards with open arms when they first came, but now they merely tolerated them because the Spaniards traded things the Taos wanted.

There was a kind of town hall in the village, a separate adobe building with a large hall inside for palavers and meetings of the elders. It was in that room that the chief met with the entourage from Santa Fe.

They all sat around a fireplace that was a ring

45

of stones with a low fire inside, the thin smoke lofting to an opening in the tall roof. They sat on benches, with Dan'l, Rivera, and Kravitz on one side of the fire, and Morning Star and his medicine men on the other.

The big room had a low door and four size-able windows that let the sunlight in. Around its perimeter were built shelves at head height, containing sculptures and pottery of Taos arti-sans. Battle axes and lances hung on a back wall, but were not prominently displayed.

Morning Star was clothed in rawhide pants and cloth shirt, and had a headband with one eagle feather in it. The two shamans wore only rawhide vests above the waist, but both had an-telope headdresses, with a length of fur falling down their backs.

Surprisingly, Morning Star spoke not only fluent Spanish, but quite good English. He had spent some time with traders as a boy.

When Dan'l had entered behind Rivera and Kravitz, the three Indians immediately had fixed their stares on him, and the shamans had begun whispering quietly but urgently between themselves. Now that they were all seated and a pipe was being passed around, Morning Star broke with protocol and spoke directly with Dan'l, bypassing Rivera.

"So you are the one the Apache calls Ancient Bear."

Dan'l was surprised by the remark, and the

importance obviously placed on it by his host. He laughed quietly.

"That was one Apache that got confused," he said. "I'm sure Yellow Horse would know better."

Morning Star frowned. "If Yellow Horse sees you, he will have fear. But he will not give up his power to an ancient god so easily. He will want to kill you, to show you are mortal."

"Such nonsense!" Rivera spat.

"Not if Yellow Horse believes it," Kravitz pointed out.

Rivera looked over at him.

"The man is right," the chief said to Rivera. The shamans did not speak English, and had little idea what was being said. Dan'l noticed that one of them was reluctant to meet his eye. "If the Apaches believe it, it becomes true. To them. Maybe it is not the Apache warrior who was confused, Long Hunter. Or must I call you Sheltowee?"

Dan'l stared at the chief in disbelief. Morning Star had used both of the names Dan'l had been known by in the land of the Cherokee and Shawnee.

"Most folks call me Dan'l," Dan'l told him quietly.

Morning Star smiled. "We are an ancient people, my friend. We know many things."

"I'm honored that you know my Shawnee name," Dan'l said.

"We are honored by your presence here," the chief replied.

Both Rivera and Kravitz turned to stare at Dan'l, seeing him in a new way. But while Kravitz's face showed wonder, that of Rivera revealed resentment.

"Perhaps we might get on with the purpose of our visit," Rivera suggested icily.

Morning Star spoke to his advisors in their native language, explaining about Dan'l. He now turned to Rivera somberly, ignoring his rudeness.

"Yes, of course, Colonel. But we know your purpose. You want to arm my braves to help you repel the Apaches."

Rivera looked embarrassed. "Well, yes. We have always been your friends, Morning Star. And friendship has its loyalties."

He had spoken in Spanish, and Dan'l did not understand much of it. The shamans did, though, and clucked their tongues. They were not interested in sending their people to fight for the Spaniards. Dan'l watched their faces as Kravitz translated the exchange for him.

"I spoke with my people," the chief said after a long moment. "Before you came. They are not pleased to fight under Spanish command."

"There must be a chain of command," Rivera told Morning Star. "In any fighting. You know me personally, and I would treat your men well. If you could spare a hundred, we would billet them outside Santa Fe until this crisis is over.

You could have your own leadership under our officers."

Dan'l saw the chief's continued reluctance, and after Kravitz translated Rivera's statement for him, decided to intervene. "The French was bothered with the same problem when they was fighting the English," he said. "At Duquesne, they agreed with the Shawnee on a general strategy of battle, then let the Indians fight it their own way, under their own leaders."

Morning Star raised his eyebrows, showing surprise and approval. Rivera, on the other hand, was suddenly furious. He turned angrily to Dan'l.

"It is not your place to recommend an arrangement with the Taos that goes against what we have done here for over a century!"

All present were embarrassed by Rivera's outburst. The shamans lowered their eyes discreetly, while Morning Star just stared stoically at Rivera. A restrained smile appeared on the face of Kravitz.

"I am sure Dan'l meant to cause no trouble," Kravitz said gently to Rivera. "He merely points out that the French made a special effort to treat their Indian allies as equals. I know this to be true, and that it helped form a powerful alliance against the English."

Rivera gave Kravitz a blistering look. Kravitz operated closely with the military at Santa Fe, and went on special missions with them, and Rivera considered him a subordinate under his command even though he was a civilian.

"I am not an idiot, Kravitz! I know what is suggested, and that the method met with some success. But it has been my experience with these people that they need a strong Spanish leadership in battle, and that can only occur if their people are subordinated to our officers." He said all of this in English, so Dan'l would know exactly what he was saying.

"Colonel, I am just trying to point out—"

"Silence, damn it!" Rivera said loudly to Kravitz.

Kravitz held Rivera's stony look. "As you wish. Colonel."

Another embarrassed hush fell over the group. Morning Star glowered at Rivera. One did not dispute with underlings in this kind of meeting. It was not polite to one's counterparts across the fire.

"Perhaps we must take this up at another time, Colonel," the chief suggested to Rivera in Spanish.

Rivera got himself under control. "I must take some kind of reply back to the governor. If you wish continued friendly trading with Santa Fe, I recommend you send a favorable one."

Dan'l shook his shaggy head slightly, listening to Kravitz's translation of the exchange. Alvarado had made a mistake in appointing Rivera to head talks with the Taos. He was too heavy-handed, too arrogant.

Morning Star caught Dan'l's eye, then turned

to Rivera. "The last time we fought beside your people, Colonel, neither you nor I were involved," he said in English. "But we remember well as a tribe. Our people were badly deployed under Spanish command, and a number were taken prisoner by the Arapaho with no support from your troops. Later, one of our people escaped and returned here to tell what had happened to the other prisoners.

"One of them was my great-uncle. He was tied to the ground, and a very sharp knife was used on him. He was slowly skinned alive, Colonel. His chest, his belly, his thighs. There was so much blood that the man doing the cutting slipped and fell into the pool of it that had gathered under my great-uncle. When they found him not quite dead after that, they gouged out his eyes, cut him open from throat to groin, and pulled out his internal organs."

"Shit," Kravitz said under his breath.

"And the Apache are worse than the Arapaho," Morning Star concluded.

Dan'l looked into the chief's grave face and saw the pain there. These Apaches sounded very much like the Shawnee he'd met when he first went into Kentucky. Only worse.

"Sheltowee gives us much to think about," Morning Star said in English. Rivera glanced at Dan'l darkly. "We will confer among us, Colonel, and send our reply to Governor Alvarado within two sunrises. This meeting is finished."

They all rose and left the building, with Rivera acting disgruntled. But Morning Star caught Dan'l's arm as he started to leave and held him for a moment. He looked deeply into Dan'l's blue eyes.

"You are not really Ancient Bear, are you, Sheltowee? Come here to cause discord between us and the Spaniards and help your people, the Apache, to dominate this land?"

Dan'l saw the slight smile move the chief's mouth, and he returned it. "If I was, would I tell you?" he said.

Morning Star held his gaze for a long moment, assessing what was behind Dan'l's eyes. Finally he said, "No," widening the smile.

"I hope to see you in Santa Fe," Dan'l said. A moment later, they were all saddling up to ride back to the settlement.

On the way back, Rivera told Dan'l that he had in effect spoiled the chance of a quick agreement, and asked him pointedly to keep out of future negotiations, no matter what the governor asked him to do. For the good of the colony.

"I'm not sure what's good for Santa Fe," Dan'l replied. "And I'm not sure you know either, Colonel."

That put an end to the conversation for the remainder of the ride back, and Rivera reported privately to Alvarado that evening. Dan'l knew that meant Alvarado would hear only a very biased version of what had occurred at the pueblo, but he did not care.

This was essentially the problem of the people who lived here, and not his. His was to give assurances to his investors that they and their capital would be safe in Santa Fe, or reasonably so, and that their long trek from St. Louis had not been in vain.

Dan'l had a meeting with Jameson and Douglas and their small entourage early that evening, and advised them that there was a danger of another attack, but that the Spaniards would be ready for this one if it came, and that they might have the help of the friendly Taos tribe. Douglas was convinced, and persuaded Jameson to stay on, too, for a while at least, and go ahead with their plan to look over some claims to the west of Santa Fe, where silver and other metals had been successfully mined from the dry ground.

The following morning, Chief Morning Star arrived with a dozen mounted warriors, and met privately with Governor Alvarado. When the meeting was over, the governor announced a defensive treaty had been concluded that was a compromise between Rivera's position on command and the one suggested by Dan'l. Alvarado was very pleased, and announced to a crowd in the plaza that Morning Star would bring almost a hundred warriors to Santa Fe the very next day, to be encamped just at the edge of the town for the duration of the crisis. Alvarado then declared a day of celebration in honor of the agreement, and by mid-morning the plaza was crowded with celebrants: Spanish soldiers, townsfolk, and Indians. Morning Star and his men stayed on to help celebrate, as did some Taos Indians who had come for trading. There was dancing and singing, and some drinking. The governor and Morning Star were seated on a small raised platform looking out over the square, attended by two bodyguards each. When Dan'l arrived at the square, walking with Kravitz, the governor spotted him and called him up to the platform.

"Morning Star tells a different story about your meeting with him than I was told by Rivera, Mr. Boone. I sense that this treaty would not have occurred without your help. Am I right, Chief?"

Morning Star nodded. "Exactly so, Mr. Governor."

The governor spoke loudly, above the clamor of shouting and singing in the square. "You have our gratitude, Mr. Boone."

"It weren't nothing much, Governor," Dan'l told him.

"The chief was just telling me that Yellow Horse is not the worst of the Apaches at the moment. That his son Running Dog is really behind this military move by the chief. And that he is a hateful and cruel young man."

Dan'l nodded. "I saw him in action when we was attacked. Looked like a deadly soldier. And a real bastard."

Morning Star smiled. "I agree." He was a middle-aged man, with a broad face and intelligent eyes. Dan'l figured him to be smarter than a lot of the Spaniards who treated him like a savage.

There was a lot of shooting of muskets and rifles into the air now, which the governor tolerated during a celebration such as this. He looked toward the noise, then back to Dan'l. "This taller fellow standing beside Morning Star is his son Wind in Trees. He was just telling us that bows are more effective than our guns, and that his men would prefer to use them if a fight comes."

Dan'l nodded. "I can understand that. Bows is right deadly in a fight. Especially against a long gun that has to be reloaded regular. A side arm is better against bows. But there ain't nothing beats the accuracy of a Kentucky rifle."

Morning Star turned and translated for his son and the other bodyguard on the platform. There was a brief exchange between them.

"Our troops are outfitted with the same rifles your colonials used in your revolution," Alvarado told Dan'l. "The Charleville flintlock. Rifled, of course."

"It's not a bad gun," Dan'l said. "But it misfires some."

"We have had some trouble with them, I admit," the governor replied. "Do you have this Kentucky rifle with you?"

"It's on my mount's irons, over at the edge of the plaza."

"Ah. I would like to examine it at your convenience," the governor said.

The chief turned toward them. "Maybe we can do better than that, my friends. My son and his friend would like to demonstrate the effectiveness of the bow in accuracy against Sheltowee's long gun. We could set up a target in the plaza."

Kravitz was standing at the base of the platform, and Colonel Rivera had come up beside him just in time to hear the chief's suggestion. He knew how good these Indians were with the bow, so a smile lighted his square face.

"What a good idea, Boone!" he said from the ground. "Don't you agree, Kravitz?"

Kravitz turned to him and nodded slowly. Unlike Rivera, Kravitz knew of Dan'l's reputation with guns. He had known it before Dan'l had ever arrived in Santa Fe. Most mountain men and trappers had heard of Dan'l Boone and his exploits back East.

"Yes. I believe it might be very entertaining."

"Good!" Alvarado said. "Will you accept the challenge, Mr. Boone? Your rifle against the Taos bows?"

Dan'l sighed inwardly. He did not like shooting exhibitions. A gun was made to kill with, not play with.

"If you want it," he finally said.

Rivera cleared the near side of the plaza beside the raised platform while Dan'l went to get his rifle. Wind in Trees and his companion, Soaring Hawk, came down to a hastily inscribed shooting line, and an ordinary circular target was set up fifty yards away, at the other end of the square. The celebrants saw what was developing, and many of them crowded around the shooting area to see the competition. It was decided that Kravitz and Dan'l would shoot against the two young Indians, both of whom had brought their beautifully carved longbows and quivers of arrows, with razor-sharp iron tips. They were both very athletic looking, and very self-assured.

Kravitz owned a heavy Charleville rifle, the same kind used by Rivera's troops, and he was good with it. He had hunted and trapped all his life, and was considered one of the most experienced mountain men in that area.

When the shooters were all ready, the governor gave the order to proceed. Kravitz went first, firing three shots. The first one hit the edge of the bulls-eye, and the next two went dead center. There was a lot of yelling and applause from the spectators, and the governor smiled broadly. He knew Kravitz was good, but he really wanted to see the Kentucky rifle in action. So did Morning Star.

Dan'l insisted that the Indians fire next. Wind in Trees put two arrows into the bulls-eye, and one just outside, and was disappointed with himself. Kravitz had edged him. There was more yelling from the crowd.

When Soaring Hawk stepped up to the firing line, Dan'l sensed that he was the best they had.

He hurled a brittle look at Dan'l and Kravitz, then took his turn. The first arrow hissed to its mark and sank deeply into the bulls-eye. Hushed exclamations rose from the crowd. The second one hit just barely inside the bulls-eye. The third one, flying straight and true, hit the dead center of the target.

There was scattered but restrained applause. Soaring Hawk had beaten both of the previous shooters. Morning Star tried to hide his pleasure, but a faint smile touched his face.

"Excellent!" the governor said to him. "It appears your son was right, Chief."

The plaza fell silent as Dan'l stepped up to the shooting line. He had three balls and flints ready. The Kentucky rifle looked ten feet long as he raised it to fire. In the next forty seconds, Dan'l fired, reloaded, fired, reloaded again, and fired a third time.

The three shots were so closely centered that they split Soaring Hawk's center arrow in shards, and made only a one-inch hole in the dead center of the bulls-eye.

The crowd exploded into wild applause and cheering. None of them had ever seen shooting like that. Kravitz whistled between his teeth.

"Dios mio!" Alvarado hissed.

Morning Star was stunned. Maybe this was Ancient Bear after all. Rivera, standing near-by, narrowed his eyes at Dan'l, making a new assessment of him. Dan'l turned to Kravitz, who was wearing an Annely repeating revolver on his belt.

"Can I borrow that?" he said to the mountain man.

Kravitz agreed readily. Dan'l took the gun, made sure it was loaded, and then put two extra primers in his left hand. "You got some Spanish coins handy?" he asked Kravitz.

Kravitz acknowledged that he did.

"Take two dollar-size ones, and a smaller one, and throw them up in the air," Dan'l said. "Throw them high."

Kravitz nodded and got the coins out as the governor and Morning Star sat forward on their chairs. Soaring Hawk, Dan'l noticed, was watching Dan'l with a dark scowl.

Dan'l nodded to Kravitz. He had done this once before, at Boonesborough, but it required the most perfect timing. Maybe it would impress Morning Star, and help bind his allegiance.

In the next moment, Kravitz hurled the three coins high into the air.

They sailed up and up, glistening in the morning sun, sending sparkles of it back into the eyes of those in the plaza. While the coins were still rising, Dan'l aimed quickly at the lowest, a big one, and put a hole through its exact center. While the coins were still aloft, Dan'l re-primed and aimed and fired a second time. The second large coin went zinging through the air, a hole also in its center.

Now Dan'l had to work fast. The smaller coin was on its way down as Dan'l calmly but with lightning speed re-primed a second time and cocked the pistol. The coin was already at head height. He fired and caught it at waist height, and put a hole through that third, smaller coin.

The shots were still echoing through the plaza when the coins kicked up dust on the ground, only thirty yards apart. Gun smoke assailed the nostrils of the crowd as they watched wide-eyed while a Rivera underling went and collected the coins. The man's jaw dropped as he stared hard at them, then held them up for all to see.

"Three perfect hits!" he shouted in Spanish.

"*Carramba!*" Rivera muttered under his breath.

Each shot had hit in the center of the silver disc. While they were all in the air.

"Holy Jesus!" Kravitz said quietly.

Alvarado crossed himself, looking stunned. "It is black magic!"

Suddenly, Soaring Hawk yelled out hysterically, "He is Ancient Bear! He must be destroyed!"

Catching everyone, even Dan'l, by surprise, the Taos warrior came rushing toward Dan'l, wielding a thin dagger, intent on driving it into Dan'l's chest.

Dan'l saw him at the last second, sidestepped the wicked thrust, and grabbed the Indian's arm. The blade ripped into Dan'l's rawhides and nicked his rib cage; then Dan'l brought the pistol down onto the side of the fellow's head. Soaring Hawk was thrown to the ground, dazed and bleeding, kicking up a great deal of dust.

Two Spanish soldiers rushed him and pulled him to his feet, holding him fast. Morning Star was on his feet, his face livid. He shouted something at Soaring Hawk that left little doubt as to its meaning.

"Oh, Christ!" Kravitz said from somewhere near Dan'l.

Rivera was just a few feet away. "Put that crazy Indian in chains!" he yelled at his men.

"He is Ancient Bear!" Soaring Hawk repeated in Taos.

Morning Star spoke quickly to him again, then turned to the governor, who was still reacting to all of this. "He thinks Boone is the Apache god," he said in perfect Spanish, so all in the plaza could hear.

"Take the idiot away!" Rivera shouted angrily.

There was a moment of raw tension in the plaza as the Spaniards and mestizos assessed the situation and began looking at the few Taos Indians present with hostility. Dan'l knew there could be big trouble if he did not intervene.

"Wait!" he called to the soldiers.

All eyes turned to him. The Taos chief looked down at him, hoping for some miracle that would end this peaceably.

"Colonel, Mr. Governor," Dan'l began. "This man ain't responsible for his actions. He thinks

I was practicing magic. If there's any fault, it's mine. I ask you to release him, Mr. Governor, into his chief's custody."

Rivera looked at Dan'l quizzically. The governor glanced toward Morning Star as if for help, but the chief could not give it. The decision had to come from Alvarado.

"I . . . appreciate your frankness, Mr. Boone. And insight. The fellow seems calm now. Why don't you release him, Colonel? Everything should be all right."

Rivera hesitated, but finally realized the importance of the moment. "Oh, very well. Release him."

The soldiers did so, and Soaring Hawk stood there alone for a tense moment. Then he slowly moved back toward the platform, accompanied by Wind in Trees. He gave Dan'l a wide berth, watching him fearfully every moment.

"Take him to our wagons," Morning Star instructed his son.

The twosome left the square, and the crowd resumed its merry-making. Rivera asked Dan'l, "Are you all right?"

Dan'l nodded. "Right as rain, Colonel. But thanks for asking."

Morning Star came to the edge of the platform. "I apologize to you and the governor, and all assembled here," he said balefully. "We are dealing with powerful forces. I hope you all understand."

"It was nothing, Chief," Dan'l told him.

"I believe, Mr. Boone, that you have just become a legend in New Mexico," Alvarado said, grinning at him.

Dan'l grunted, and turned toward Kravitz and smiled. "If I'd let him stab me, they might have even heard about it in Mexico City," he offered.

Kravitz laughed very loudly at that.

Chapter Three

When Morning Star left town later that day, he had committed himself to sending about eighty men to billets at the edge of the settlement, for an undetermined period, until the threat from Yellow Horse had dissipated. It was a timely arrangement, too, since one of the garrison's scouts, a half-breed named Scarface Charlie, returned from a brief foray to the southwest and reported that Yellow Horse had moved closer to Santa Fe once again and was preparing for battle. Charlie, who was half Apache and half Mexican, worked for the army off and on when he needed money, and was considered a necessary evil by Rivera. He reported big palavers in Yellow Horse's camp, and the sharpening of many weapons. Also, the presence of boxes of round balls to use in the Apaches' few muskets.

Dan'l could not keep this news from Jameson and Douglas, so he met with them that evening at the local cantina, and bought them whiskey. He broke it to them as gently as possible.

"Oh, for God's sake," Jameson complained, sitting at the small table with Dan'l and Douglas. "This is becoming a dangerous situation. I wish to hell I'd never left Missouri, frankly." He sat sideways because his long legs would not fit under the table, and his lean face with its gray sideburns looked very somber.

A bar ran the length of the room, with a painting of the desert hanging on the wall behind it. At the rear of the room, where other customers sat, mostly meztisos, a hired guitar player was strumming out a soft Latin melody.

Not far from Dan'l's table sat three military personnel, including the right-hand man of Colonel Rivera, Captain Juan Salazar, who had deigned for the moment to sit with two of his enlisted men, a Sergeant Torreon and a Corporal Gomez. Dan'l noticed that these men spoke in hushed tones and kept looking toward him and his investors.

"I'm not so sure Jameson is wrong about that," Samuel Douglas said to Dan'l. "Maybe our timing was wrong in making this trip, Boone."

Dan'l sat there nursing a glass of whiskey. He was reluctant to drink when he had serious business to discuss. Sitting there in his rawhides, with his thick hair and heavy beard, he looked as wild to the men with him as any Apache. They had come to Santa Fe on his recommendation, and now they wondered whether this man's judgment was sound.

Dan'l looked much older than he had on those campaigns to Fort Duquesne those many years ago. There were lines in his face, and graying in his brown hair, and a kind of hardness in his eyes. The Revolution had aged him, as had the years of hardship out in the wildernesses of Kentucky and Tennessee, and more recently, Missouri. But it was apparent to all who knew him that he was still strong as a grizzly, the most skillful hunter on either side of the Mississippi, and had the fire for adventure in his gut. Now that the Revolution was a success and constitutions were being drafted back East, he was not needed anymore there. These days he felt that that adventure was to be found out here in the West.

"I think," he finally replied, "that the worst timing would be to leave Santa Fe now."

They both scanned his rough face. When Dan'l spoke, it was as if each word were loaded with meaning. With importance.

"Yellow Horse ain't the future of this country," Dan'l said slowly and evenly. He looked around him. "And the Mexicans ain't, either."

Jameson shot a glance at Captain Salazar, who was looking directly at him. Jameson looked down quickly.

"Americans will be coming out here," Dan'l said. "Just like they come clear across the ocean for a new chance at life. If you're here first, you'll do the best."

"You could be talking a hundred years from now," Jameson argued. "Even the Mexicans are scared. I talked to a couple of them."

"The Mexicans ain't got the fire in their bellies like the Americans," Dan'l said. "They'll be here, all right. And it won't be no hundred years. Then the Spaniards can stop worrying over the Apache and Comanche, and think about their paleface competition." He grinned slightly.

Jameson took a deep breath and thought about that.

"You put on a good show out there with your guns," Douglas admitted to Dan'l. He was a rather small, wiry fellow with mustache wax in his long sideburns and wire-rimmed spectacles on his nose. He did not appear as nervous about all this as his tall, lean partner. But he had the same misgivings. "I guess you were born for this kind of thing, Boone. Well, all of us weren't. Even if Yellow Horse is subdued, I just wonder whether I want to bring my family out here. It's very . . . primitive. I don't even speak Spanish."

Dan'l shook his head. "Look, boys. I don't want to talk you out of nothing, or into nothing. It ain't my place. But if you want to make your fortune, I reckon this is as good a place as any. The land here is rich in minerals and metals. Some of it's even good for grazing. You can build your own kind of house here, and you can learn their language. You'd be pillars of the community." Another smile. "But it's your call. Frankly, I like what I see here. I just might stake a claim out west of here in silver country myself. It's the future, boys. It's the by-God future!"

"Hey, Boone! *Como está!*"

They all looked toward the nearby table where the soldiers were sitting. Dan'l recognized Salazar, and also the sergeant, who was the one Dan'l had knocked down to keep him from torturing the Apache prisoner. The sergeant was glaring toward him, but it was the corporal who had called out to Dan'l. He was an experienced soldier, and a big, beefy man.

"*Oye!* How did you make the gun *engaño*—the *fraude?* The *monedas* already have the holes in them, *sí?*"

Dan'l did not know the Spanish words, but he got the idea. The corporal was accusing him of trickery in the shooting.

"Pay no attention to them," Jameson said stiffly. "They've been drinking the cheap tequila."

"I shot the holes in them," Dan'l said easily. "On the spot."

The corporal and sergeant laughed between themselves, as if Dan'l had made a joke. Dan'l recalled his fracas with the sergeant in front of the prisoner, and figured the odds were good that it was he who had ordered the execution of the Indian.

"*No creo que si,*" the sergeant said. He did not believe Dan'l.

The captain did not like Dan'l either, but kept aloof from the exchange with the other table, a smug smile on his square face. He was a slightly smaller version of Rivera, with a wide mustache. Very erect, very spit-and-polish.

"Maybe we should leave," Douglas said to Dan'l.

Dan'l turned to him. "All's well, Douglas. I been through this before. I shouldn't done that shooting just to impress Morning Star. Alvarado won't arm the Taos, anyway."

"They know you hit those coins," Jameson said.

"Hey, amigo!" the corporal persisted. "I can do that trick, too." The sergeant had given him a new English word. "You understand trick, senor?"

"I reckon you got a lot of them," Dan'l said sourly. "Ain't that how you made corporal?"

The corporal did not understand. The captain leaned over and explained the remark to him, and they all saw the corporal's face color slightly.

"*Ching a tu madre!*" the corporal swore under his breath. "You damn *cabron!*" He reached for the sergeant's holster and pulled out his gun, surprising both the sergeant and the captain. He quickly primed and cocked it.

"Now I shoot. No *engaños*—no tricks." He aimed the gun at Dan'l's face. "Put that whiskey glass on your head, *cabron,* and I will shoot it off."

"Good God," Jameson muttered.

Douglas crouched down at the table, as if he might crawl under it.

The sergeant looked suddenly tense, and the captain got a dark look on his face. "Corporal! Give the sergeant his gun back," he ordered in Spanish.

"*Un minuto, Capitan,*" the corporal growled. As they said in Mexico City, the Indian had climbed into his head because of the liquor. He aimed the gun more carefully at Dan'l's face. "The whiskey glass, *por favor*. Or I practice on the ears, yes?"

"Gomez!" the captain said loudly.

Jameson, closest to Dan'l, eased out of his chair and backed away from the table. Dan'l was not carrying a side arm, and his faithful Kentucky rifle was back at his billet in the garrison quarters. But he always wore a broadbladed skinning knife on his belt in a leather sheath. He slid that knife out of its resting place, and showed it to the corporal.

"You better be good with that thing," he said slowly and carefully. "'Cause if you don't kill me with that first shot, you're going to have cold steel sticking outen your back."

Stefan Kravitz had just entered the cantina, accompanied by the rough-looking Dura Cabeza, who wore a Spanish uniform but without any insignia or markings.

"I'll be damned," Kravitz muttered. "Look at this."

The corporal's finger whitened over the trigger of the gun. Captain Salazar, whom Dan'l recalled now as the officer who'd given him permission to interrogate the Apache, suddenly stood up and drew his own side arm.

He aimed it at Gomez's head.

"Put that goddamn gun down, Corporal!"

Gomez glanced at him quickly, then looked at the gun. He hesitated, then slowly dropped the sergeant's pistol to his side. The sergeant quickly took it from him.

"He wouldn't cooperate. He wouldn't put the glass on his head," Gomez complained in Spanish.

Sergeant Torreon pulled him back onto his chair and re-holstered his pistol. The captain did likewise, just as Kravitz and Cabeza walked up to Dan'l's table.

"*Lo siento,*" the captain said quietly to Dan'l. "Accept my apology, Boone. It is the alcohol, you understand. You were never in any real danger."

Kravitz laughed in his throat. "I don't think we can say the same for your corporal," he said deliberately, looking at the big knife Dan'l was just now sliding back into its resting place.

The captain did not respond. Kravitz and Cabeza joined Dan'l's group at their table, and Dan'l ordered them drinks.

"Now. Like I was saying," he said.

* * *

The next morning, bright and early, Dan'l took the two investors out to inspect a mine site. He had convinced them to stay on awhile before they made any decision regarding their investing in mining or land.

Dan'l asked Kravitz to accompany them because he knew the territory so well, and Kravitz invited Cabeza because he was so proficient in translating from Spanish to English. Rivera had insisted they take two armed soldiers with them.

Kravitz and Cabeza were both tough-looking, outdoors types, but were quite different physically and in their personalities. Kravitz was quite tall, standing somewhat above Dan'l, and loose-jointed. Cabeza was shorter than Dan'l, had a potbelly, and was rather light-complexioned for a Spaniard. Also, whereas Kravitz was a quiet fellow, fairly reserved, Cabeza was very outgoing and, at times, loud in his speech. They knew each other well, and had both worked for Rivera and the Army on many occasions. Cabeza, in fact, was on a retainer with the military, and had little other income. Kravitz made a living in various ways, much of it importing goods from Mexico City on an irregular basis.

The seven of them rode out to the west that morning, and inspected a couple of small mines first. One had been abandoned, and the other was being worked by a thickset Spaniard, but it was for sale. The third mine they visited was a large one, with deep shafts, and also was not being worked. Kravitz knew it well, and led the others into the main shaft to point out the layered strata of rock that contained the silver ore. It looked good to Jameson and Douglas, and seemed to buoy their spirits.

Kravitz led the way as they explored, with Dan'l just behind him, and the soldiers, who did not like going into the mines, reluctantly brought up the rear. As they rounded a corner in one of the lesser shafts, while Kravitz was talking about the yield per ton, he suddenly stopped in his tracks and jumped back, knocking into Dan'l. A small, thin snake, muddy in color, slid past Kravitz and Dan'l and disappeared into a crevice.

"Damn!" Kravitz exclaimed. "I heard this mine had a few snakes. I hate them, personally. And these are quite venomous."

"Jesus!" Douglas whispered.

"It is only a snake," Cabeza said with a wry look of distaste.

The taller soldier nodded. "Yes, just a snake," he said to his comrade in Spanish.

A couple of moments later they all stopped at the juncture of an even smaller shaft, and again Kravitz showed the investors the look of the strata. The shorter of the two soldiers turned into the small shaft while Kravitz was talking, and walked a few paces down its dark length, the light from Cabeza's oil lamp flickering along beside him.

At the juncture, Kravitz kept talking. "This mine has potential, there is no doubt. I almost bought it myself. I can't imagine why the owner wants to sell. Maybe he got homesick for Mexico City."

Just at that moment, a scream came from the small shaft, then another one.

"What the hell!" Dan'l exclaimed.

"It is Garcia!" the second soldier said tightly.

The six of them started into the shaft, with Dan'l in the lead. As they rounded a curve, the light from Dan'l's lantern fell on the soldier.

He was on the floor of the shaft, his rifle on the ground beside him. He was grabbing at his right leg, grimacing in pain.

All around him were snakes, slithering on the dirt floor.

Kravitz was at Dan'l's shoulder. "Sidewinders," he said.

"We have to get him out of there," Dan'l said.

"Good God!" Jameson muttered from behind them.

"You can't get to him," Cabeza said, sighing. "They will kill him."

"To hell with that!" Dan'l said. He walked up to the snakes and kicked a couple aside before they could strike him. He was just a few feet from the fallen soldier. "Reach for me!"

The soldier raised his arm, his face all screwed up in pain and shock. Dan'l leaned toward him, and Kravitz grabbed Dan'l's free arm to hold him in place. Dan'l reached and just barely grabbed the soldier's hand. Then he dragged him free from the snake nest, and onto open floor.

The snakes were writhing about agitatedly now. "Son of a bitch," Kravitz mumbled. "I hate the little bastards."

"Let's get away from them," the second soldier said in fast Spanish.

"Jesus!" Sam Douglas whispered again.

"Let's get him outside," Cabeza said. "He's been bitten twice."

"Get him out of here," Dan'l agreed.

The second soldier and Cabeza picked the wounded fellow up by the shoulders and dragged him out of the shaft. Douglas followed them with a lantern. Dan'l, Kravitz, and Jameson stood there watching the snakes move defensively into a pile at the center of the shaft. Kravitz had a lantern, too, and when he held it up in front of Dan'l, Dan'l nodded. Kravitz hurled the lantern into the midst of the snakes.

The lantern broke on the shaft floor, right beside the pile of snakes, and fire from it spread quickly over the surface of the dirt, and through the snakes. The flames soon engulfed them, and black smoke rose from the writhing mass.

"That ought to do it," Dan'l said. "Let's get out of here."

Jameson and Kravitz were coughing as they moved out to the larger mine shaft, and then to the outside. The smoke from the fire followed them out, and Dan'l was coughing, too, as they emerged.

The others had gotten the bitten soldier onto his horse, and he was leaning heavily onto the saddlehorn.

"We lanced the bites," Cabeza told Dan'l. "And we've got a tourniquet on the leg, as you see. With a little luck, he will be all right. You probably saved his life, Boone."

Dan'l sighed. It seemed that nothing was going well for him and his people. "Let's get him back to town," he finally said.

Jameson and Douglas were shaken by the incident at the mine, and an outing that Dan'l had hoped would convince them of the wisdom of going ahead with their investments had done anything but. Now it seemed to them that the very land was hostile to them.

They promised to go out to the north and inspect some grazing land, as scheduled, before making any final decisions. Dan'l enlisted Kravitz to take them, but Cabeza had other duties at the garrison, and would not be going. Also, Kravitz was fluent enough in Spanish that Cabeza was not really needed, except for additional defense. Cabeza had reported Dan'l's action in pulling the soldier to safety at the mine, and when it was found that the fellow was past the worst and would survive, Dan'l's stature rose even higher in Santa Fe.

Death at Spanish Wells

A couple of days after the mine tour, Dan'l took his people on a long ride north, overnight, into grazing country, and decided to combine the venture with a hunting trip, since Kravitz told of small herds of antelope in the area. They rode up into some rather green country, not as dry as Santa Fe, and into grassland. They passed several herds of antelope, and Kravitz and Dan'l both shot two animals to take back to the garrison for meat. Kravitz was once again very impressed with Dan'l's shooting when Dan'l brought a large buck down at almost five hundred yards.

There were six of them on that trip, including two new soldiers armed with rifles. The soldiers did no hunting, nor did Jameson or Douglas. The two investors were pleasantly surprised by the change of scenery and the obvious richness of the land to the north. Kravitz told Dan'l that if a hunter headed even farther north, he would begin running into the biggest herds of buffalo anywhere on the continent. That thought intrigued Dan'l, and he stored it in the back of his head for future reference.

In early morning of their second day, just as they had begun heading back to Santa Fe with the carcasses of the antelope secured onto pack animals, they met a friendly Indian. The young Kiowa brave greeted them openly. He was mounted on a beautiful pinto.

Kravitz returned his gesture. He knew some Kiowa, but suddenly wished Cabeza, who was fluent in several Indian languages, was there.

"Who is he? What does he want?" Will Jameson asked Dan'l anxiously. He had had a bad night and was jumpy.

The soldiers had raised their weapons, but Kravitz waved them down. Dan'l liked the way he handled the situation.

"It is all right," Kravitz told them. "The Kiowa are very tolerant of our presence at Santa Fe." He noticed that the brave was now staring intently at Dan'l. "He asks for water. I will share mine with him."

Kravitz gave his canteen to the Kiowa, and the Indian guzzled some of its contents. Kravitz asked him, in his few words of the Indian's language, whether trapping was good in the area. The Kiowa, still watching Dan'l rather suspiciously, indicated that there were abundant beaver on a small stream to the north and east of them, near the Indian's home village. He said he was on the beginning of a long hunt, and asked Kravitz where they had found their antelope. Kravitz told him of several locations where the herds had been.

The Kiowa pointed at Dan'l. "Your friend. Is he the one the Taos are calling Ancient Bear?"

Dan'l recognized the name, even in this new language. "What did he say?" he asked Kravitz.

"He doesn't look friendly to me," Douglas offered.

"He wants to know if you're the one called Ancient Bear," Kravitz said to Dan'l.

"Jesus," Dan'l growled. "If he knows about that, Yellow Horse probably does, too."

Kravitz grinned. "The Apache may come back just to get a better look at you, Dan'l." He turned to the Kiowa. "This is the man. But he is not Ancient Bear. He is a great hunter from Kentucky."

"Ken-ta-ke," the Kiowa repeated, and his face went quite straight. When his mount whinnied nervously under him, he grabbed the rawhide reins tightly. "I thank you for your water." Then the Indian wheeled his mount without another word and rode off.

"I'll be damned," Dan'l said.

"I told him you're not an Apache god," Kravitz said. "But he didn't believe me."

Sam Douglas, looking very small on a large horse, laughed softly. "Maybe we could use this," he said to Dan'l. "If we buy any land. Tell them it belongs to Ancient Bear and they'll keep off it."

Dan'l gave him a dark look. "Let's get back to Santa Fe," he said quietly.

When they arrived back at the settlement without further incident later that day, the investors told Dan'l that they might each purchase a parcel of grazing land on this visit, and then decide later whether to move their families out there. Dan'l felt the real money was in the mining, but did not try to dissuade them from their plan.

The Taos warriors on loan from Morning Star

were now encamped on the southern edge of town, but Governor Alvarado was beginning to think his plans for a second attack might have been unwarranted.

"In my opinion, Yellow Horse would have come back by now, if he planned another assault in the near future," the governor said to Dan'l, Rivera, and Salazar in the privacy of his inner office the morning after Dan'l's return.

The governor was seated on the corner of his long, darkly polished desk, and the other three sat on straight chairs around the room facing him. Colonel Rivera had been told that this would be a military council, and had brought his favorite captain with him. He resented the governor's inclusion of Dan'l.

"You may be right, Governor," Juan Salazar said, running his fingers through his well-groomed mustache. He looked rather diminutive, sitting between thickset, wild-looking Dan'l and ramrod-erect, stern-looking Rivera. Rivera turned slightly to him and gave him a reproachful glare. Captains did not speak before colonels, especially about policy.

"We know Yellow Horse is poised, Governor, and ready. I can't imagine what would cause him to delay what he considers to be the inevitable," Rivera said in Spanish. Then he turned to Dan'l. "Excuse me, Boone. I speak so much more fluently in my own language."

Dan'l knew it was an intentional slight, and so did Alvarado, who cast a stony look at Rivera.

"Please, Colonel. Keep it in Mr. Boone's language, if you please."

Rivera sighed obviously. "Very well, Mr. Governor. I think Yellow Horse is coming. I think it is in his nature."

The governor respected his commandant's opinion. He sat there, his hands folded before his handsome face. "And you, Mr. Boone?"

Dan'l looked past him for a moment, then focused on him. "I have to agree with the colonel, Governor."

Rivera was surprised. He turned and stared at Dan'l.

"I've talked with Kravitz and Cabeza," Dan'l went on. "They think a second attack is coming, and soon. And if the Apache is anything like the Shawnee, I'd agree. Most Indians have to be shown twice. They'll tend to think luck went against them the first time."

Rivera nodded. "Also, there is this Ancient Bear thing. Yellow Horse will have heard about it by now. He will want to return, just to convince himself that the notion has no basis in reality."

"I agree again," Dan'l said.

Salazar looked embarrassed. "Well, that does seem reasonable," he said quietly. He had not mentioned the cantina incident to Dan'l.

Alvarado, the silver-haired descendant of conquistadors, pursed his lips, looking worried. "Well. I trust your judgment, gentlemen. We will keep the garrison on alert, Colonel. I presume the Taos contingent is posting sentries so that—"

There was a loud knocking on the closed door. Alvarado and Rivera exchanged curious looks, and Alvarado called out, "Yes, come in!" He had asked not to be disturbed.

The door opened and an excited secretary called Sanchez came in, leaving the door open. He was middle-aged and obese.

"Senor Governor!" he said quickly. "It is Cabeza! He says he must see you *en seguida!*"

Alvarado sighed. "Oh, all right. Send him in."

Rivera turned rather angrily toward the door. Cabeza was under his command, and knew better than to interrupt an important meeting. Cabeza came hurriedly into the room, in his Spanish uniform, looking ruffled. The half-breed called Scarface Charlie followed him. Cabeza waited until the secretary had gone and closed the door again before he spoke.

"*Señor Gobernador!*" Cabeza said loudly. "*Tenemos que preparar! Los Apaches venimos!*"

Alvarado rose slowly from his chair, the color draining from his face. Rivera rose, too.

"*Hable en Ingles,*" Alvarado said numbly.

Cabeza glanced at Dan'l, who had turned toward him.

"The Apaches are coming!" Cabeza repeated with quiet urgency. "Charlie has been out there!"

Scarface Charlie, Cabeza's assistant in scouting, was almost sixty years old, with heavy lines in his weathered face. He wore rawhides not unlike those of Dan'l, and mocassins on his feet. A small dark hat with an osprey feather in the band decorated his head. He spoke English and Spanish haltingly, and had a thin scar running across his right cheek and mouth, on a diagonal line. His father had been Mexican meztiso and his mother full-blooded Apache. He was a heavy drinker, and used only occasionally by Cabeza, when a special need arose. Neither Rivera nor Alvarado had really ever trusted him completely.

"True," Charlie said in English. "Yellow Horse ready. He come now. Now!"

"*El diablo!*" Rivera grated out. "*Capitán. Despierte el guarnición.*"

"*Sí, Coronel.*"

Captain Salazar hurried from the room, with Cabeza and Charlie close behind him. Dan'l was on his feet, too. "They might be here already," he guessed.

"Governor, I recommend—"

Suddenly noise erupted from outside, and they all turned toward a window on the plaza. There were the sounds of hoofbeats, and war whoops, and screaming from the locals.

"They are here!" Rivera said loudly.

It took Dan'l and Rivera only moments to descend the wide staircase of the mansion and emerge onto the plaza below. What they saw there was chaos. The forerunners of an even larger Yellow Horse army were coming into the

square, firing rifles and hurling lances at anybody on the street. Dan'l could hear yelling
coming from side streets, too, and a great
clamor from out at the edge of town, where the
Apaches had been surprised by the force of
Taos defenders. Part of Yellow Horse's assault
force was still caught up in battling these front-
line fighters, while the rest of his force had ridden on into the city.

Fortunately, people were not crowded into
the central plaza, as they had been on the previous occasion. Garrison soldiers were pouring
onto the plaza this time, and in moments the
gunfire was heavy in the square. A lot of the
Apaches, though, were in side streets, shooting
at anything that moved, and surging through
doorways to kill citizens in their homes.

Captain Salazar emerged from the garrison
gate on a horse, and was followed by a company
of cavalry, waving sabers and firing side arms.
They rode right through the square and headed
for the streets of the city, where most of the killing was taking place. Foot soldiers fought in the
plaza, firing back at mounted Apaches, knocking them off their horses. A few local citizens
had been caught in the square in the attack, and
now their bodies littered the broad expanse of
the square. One meztiso hung on a lance impaled on a cottonwood tree, and another, near
Dan'l, had been hit with so many arrows that
he looked like a big pincushion.

Captain Salazar rode right through all that.

"Follow me!" he was yelling in Spanish. "Cut them down in the streets!"

Rivera and Dan'l had taken cover behind a nearby tree, and Dan'l had his rifle, which he had retrieved from the main reception area of the mansion. Both men's weapons were now loaded and primed, so they both stepped out and returned fire to the enemy.

"Shoot their horses!" Rivera shouted through the gunfire. "Put them on foot!"

Rivera fired and hit an Apache in the chest, sending him plummeting off his mount. When Dan'l stepped out to fire, an arrow hissed past his left ear and buried itself in the tree next to him. He fired the long rifle, and an Apache warrior's face was blown away.

A young Spanish officer went down right in front of Dan'l, with a lance sticking out of him front and back. Dan'l stepped forward and yanked a saber out of the fellow's right hand, and moved out among the mounted warriors, who were yelling wildly in their attack.

"Damn it, Boone!" Rivera protested.

But Dan'l did not even hear him. He was now surrounded by mounted Apaches. He wielded the saber recklessly, cutting and slicing with his right hand while he swung the Kentucky rifle like a club with his left. An Apache was almost cut in half by a saber swing. He sat surprised on his mount, then his torso doubled on itself, and hung from the horse for a moment before falling to the ground. Dan'l swung his left hand then and brained a small pony. It fell sideways to the dirt, throwing its rider off. Dan'l moved up and beheaded the warrior on the ground.

Blood was everywhere, and a lot of it was on Dan'l's face and arms and chest, but none of it was his.

Just at that moment, Running Dog rode wild-eyed into the square, and his father, Yellow Horse, came right behind him. They stopped their mounts at the far edge of the plaza, and the young Running Dog saw Dan'l immediately. He had a lance in one hand, and a rifle in the other. His face darkened when he spotted Dan'l. He yelled something to his father in Apache, and then pointed the lance right at Dan'l.

"It is Running Dog!" Rivera yelled at Dan'l. "Find cover!"

Dan'l met Running Dog's fierce gaze, and realized in that moment that Running Dog and his father knew the rumor about him. Across the plaza, Yellow Horse nodded to his son. "Yes, that is the one! I saw him the last time!" he said in Apache.

"He is an impostor!" Running Dog yelled back. They had had quite a discussion about it, with Running Dog giving no credence at all to the story. But Yellow Horse was worried. Running Dog now aimed the rifle right at Dan'l's chest. "We will prove that he is mortal, just like us!"

Dan'l saw the exchange and heard it, but had no idea what they were saying.

"He is coming for you!" Rivera yelled. "Take cover!" He was sure he would be blamed somehow if Dan'l or one of his investors were killed while in Santa Fe.

But Dan'l was not in a mood to hide from Running Dog. He remembered him from the last time, when he had impaled the baby on a pike and butchered others wantonly. Now the Apache dug his heels into his mottled mount and headed right at Dan'l. Yellow Horse sat his white mount at the perimeter, held his breath, and watched.

The Apache came at Dan'l in a melee of thunder and dust, right through Spanish soldiers and Apaches alike, focused entirely on his opponent. Like a demon from hell he came, rider and horse as one, flowing across the plaza like unbridled death itself, the long gun ready to fire.

Dan'l stood out in the open, no one near him. When he saw Running Dog, he squared his body and resolved to meet the attack openly, armed only with the saber and unloaded rifle. Halfway across the square, with nothing between him and Dan'l, the Apache fired right at Dan'l's chest. The hot slug whistled under Dan'l's arm, between his arm and his torso, and missed him completely. Dan'l saw the look of consternation cross Running Dog's hard face as he reined in twenty feet away. He could not believe he had missed. Across the plaza, Yellow Horse sucked in his breath, and concluded that

Dan'l's magic had protected him, that the bullet had gone right through him without harming him.

But Running Dog was not finished. He now spurred his mount again, his lance out in front of him, with its war ribbons and feathers fluttering out behind. At ten feet, he hurled the deadly weapon at Dan'l's body.

Dan'l saw the move coming and sidestepped the throw, and the lance tore his tunic in passing. It thumped into the ground just behind him, and then the Apache was on him. The mottled mount hit Dan'l full in the chest, even though Dan'l tried to avoid it, and knocked him to the ground, and he lost the Kentucky rifle for the moment. Running Dog turned the horse as Rivera fired at him and missed. A nearby soldier also fired at the Apache and narrowly missed. Running Dog drew a long dagger from his belt and held it so Dan'l could see it. "You are not Ancient Bear! I will show that your blood runs free, just as ours!"

Dan'l was on his knees, then got to his feet. "You son of a bitch," he muttered under his breath, not understanding the warrior's words.

Running Dog could not hear what he had said, but he saw the dark look in Dan'l's eyes, and was momentarily afraid. Dan'l swung the saber savagely, sliced a wound across the mount's throat, and cut the reins.

Running Dog saw the blood flow from his

mount, and did not want to be put on foot in this melee.

"The gods damn you, you fake!" he yelled into Dan'l's face in surprisingly good English. "If I see you again, I will kill you!" Then he repeated it in Apache as he kneed his mount into another run across the square.

Dan'l never got another good try at him, and swore under his breath because of it. On the far side of the plaza, Yellow Horse already knew that this attack was a failure, and despite a loud argument by his son, they both headed back out of the plaza and called their troops into a retreat from the city.

In another twenty minutes it was all over. Salazar came riding back into the square with blood on his saber.

"They are gone, Colonel! The day is ours!"

Rivera was out of ammunition. He leaned against the cottonwood tree near them, and wiped perspiration from his brow as Dan'l went and retrieved his rifle. Then Dan'l turned to him.

"I damn near got him."

The colonel grunted. "He damn near got you, Yankee. If he had, I would be in disgrace."

Dan'l regarded him narrowly. His full beard was stained with sweat, and there was blood on his side where the lance had grazed him. He came wearily to the tree and leaned against it beside Rivera.

"Well, I'm mighty glad I didn't cause you no

trouble, Colonel," he said acidly.

The colonel met his look. "You fought well, Boone. But do us all a favor. Take your businessmen back to St. Louis before somebody is hurt."

Dan'l made a sound in his throat. "When we're ready, Colonel. When we're damn good and ready."

Chapter Four

The Apaches had killed almost fifty Taos Indians in that whirlwind attack, twenty-odd garrison soldiers, and about as many civilians. Others were badly wounded, and many houses were burned to the ground.

But Yellow Horse had failed.

He knew now that he could not destroy Santa Fe or its will to survive.

Through the next twenty-four hours, his battered army headed back southwest to home ground. But the Apache chief was not finished with the white man.

On his way south he detoured to two tiny settlements of Mexican ranchers and slaughtered everybody he could find. He killed livestock and burned buildings.

Near the end of his journey back he attacked a larger community. It was a trading post called Spanish Wells, or Fuentes Españoles. The warriors massacred thirty-three Spaniards, meztisos, and foreigners in that last attack, including an official from Mexico City, and the incident soon spread terror throughout the entire territory.

Word reached Governor Alvarado about the atrocities within two days, while Dan'l and his people were still debating when to leave Santa Fe. Jameson and Douglas had definitely decided to buy some grazing land to the north, under grants from Mexico City, and then return to St. Louis with Dan'l guiding them. There they would go back to their businesses and wait for things to settle down in New Mexico. If things looked quieter next year, they might take their families there. Douglas had even purchased a potential home site on the outskirts of the settlement.

While Dan'l was making plans to leave, and allowing his slight side wound to heal under newly purchased rawhides, the governor called him in again.

Always willing to accommodate Alvarado, Dan'l responded immediately to the governor's call. When he arrived in Alvarado's private office, though, he was surprised to find Rivera and Salazar there. Also present, standing alone in a corner, was the ubiquitous Dura Cabeza.

"Morning, Governor," Dan'l said. "Gentlemen."

This morning his thick, wild hair was wet and slicked back, and his new trousers were stuck into high hunting boots. His fringed rawhide shirt, which had been made by Taos craftsmen, looked stiff and clean. He held his black Quaker hat in his right hand, and his rifle had been checked downstairs.

Alvarado rose to greet him. "Mr. Boone. How kind of you to meet again with us. I know your people expect you to be with them, and we promise not to keep you long."

"It's all right, sir," Dan'l said politely. Alvarado offered him a chair, and Dan'l sat down. His side hurt when he moved much. He looked over at Rivera and Salazar, who were both scowling at him more sternly than usual. Cabeza wore a small, enigmatic smile.

Alvarado paced behind his desk. Not far away, a wide window let sun in from behind the mansion, and the rays fell obliquely across the desk, the governor, and the carpeted floor.

"We have had some bad news, Mr. Boone," Alvarado began, still pacing. "Yellow Horse has avenged his loss here at Santa Fe, it seems. He has gone rather wild in the south."

Dan'l frowned. "I'm right sorry to hear that, Governor."

Alvarado looked at him. "He has wiped out a settlement called Spanish Wells. The place is in ruins. There may be no survivors."

"The son of a bitch," Rivera muttered, rather to himself.

"It is a terrible tragedy," the governor continued. "This whole Apache uprising. We obviously must do something to stop Yellow Horse and his son for good."

"As long as that Running Dog is on the loose," Dan'l offered, "you ain't going to have no peace."

Alvarado nodded. "We, too, think he is the dark force behind his father. Something must be done about him."

"It's about time!" Rivera mumbled.

Alvarado cast a sour look toward him. Salazar lowered his gaze to his knees, and Cabeza's smile widened slightly.

"Maybe we should have acted sooner," the governor admitted. "But none of us wanted unnecessary war, Colonel."

Rivera wisely kept his silence.

Alvarado came around the desk and walked over to Dan'l. "We are sending an army south, Mr. Boone. Most of our garrison, and a few Taos. Colonel Rivera will head it up."

"A good idea," Dan'l said.

"We want to wipe out Yellow Horse's army once and for all, so he will never again be a threat to this royal city, or to the territory."

Dan'l wondered why he had been called in to hear all this. He searched the governor's face.

"I've been watching you since your arrival, Mr. Boone," Alvarado went on. "Your have impressed me greatly, I am pleased to say. I mean your fighting ability, your ease with the red man. Your natural feeling for the country and the wild places here."

Dan'l was embarrassed. "Mr. Governor—"

"No, please. Allow me to finish. I think your presence on an expedition to the south would be invaluable to our forces. You understand the red man. Maybe better than any of us here ever will."

Rivera glared darkly at the governor, but said nothing.

"Would you consider joining our small army for this military action, Mr. Boone? I would be personally very grateful."

Dan'l shook his head. "This all comes as a real surprise, Governor. Jameson and Douglas are ready to return to Missouri. I owe it to them. They depended on me to get them here and back safely. I can't desert them now."

"I would not ask such a thing," Alavarado said quickly. "This expedition would require perhaps a couple of weeks to complete. Perhaps less. Yellow Horse is undoubtedly holed up in his usual canyon, off to the southwest. Our force can be there in two or three days, the colonel tells me. Your people would merely be delaying their trek back. For a very good cause."

"Boone's first duty is to his investors," Rivera put in. He had disagreed with the governor from the outset about this proposal. He did not need an outsider in his little army, with his own ideas of command. Someone else to protect from the Apaches, an important person to the governor. He had made his feelings known to Alvarado, but to no avail.

Alvarado eyed him coolly. "Of course, Colonel. None of us is suggesting otherwise."

"I'd have to talk with my people," Dan'l said.

"Yes, I understand."

"If they won't stay on, I can't."

"Yes."

Dan'l looked over at Cabeza. "The half-breed. Will he be going?"

Cabeza raised his brows. "We haven't requested his enlistment."

"I'd want him to go," Dan'l said. The breed was the one of them he trusted most. "He knows the Apache."

"*Jesus y Maria!*" Rivera spat out. "Do you understand now the difficulty, Mr. Governor?"

"We choose our own guides!" Salazar protested. "Mr. Cabeza has not reported the need for the Indian's assistance."

The governor turned to Cabeza. "Would you have any problem with taking the breed along, Cabeza?"

Cabeza glanced quickly at Rivera before he replied. "I would welcome his presence, Mr. Governor. He is my close friend."

Rivera was scowling hotly at Cabeza.

The governor shrugged his wide shoulders. "I don't see an issue, Colonel. Please arrange it, if Mr. Boone can go."

Rivera hesitated. "Yes, Mr. Governor," he said stiffly.

Dan'l was surprised at the hostility, but not concerned. Rivera was not one of his favorite people.

"You would be paid, of course," Alvarado said. "And you would be equal in rank to Captain Salazar."

Salazar made a low sound in his throat, but Alvarado ignored it. Dan'l sighed.

"I'll talk to my people."

Alvarado smiled widely. "That is all I ask."

Down at Spanish Wells, in the *tierra caliente*, a few survivors of Yellow Horse's savage assault had gathered in what was left of their once-proud settlement and trading post.

Elvira Lucas had run off into the underbrush with her two children when the attack came. They had huddled there for hours after the Indians had gone, and on through that night, before they felt safe to come out into the open. What they saw on their return to the settlement stunned them. The place had been burned to ashes, and corpses were everywhere, beginning to smell in the heat. Only one end of the trading post building remained standing, with charred wood all around it, but Elvira found the remains of some dry meat there, and some hardtack, and she fed her children with it and then sat dazed through that next day, trying to understand what had happened. Elvira was a widow who had stayed on at the settlement after her husband had died from a fever, and now she thought that maybe she and the children would die, too, out there alone.

Partway through that day, though, Pedro Rueda showed up. He had lived at the post, but had been off hunting when the Apaches came. Now his house was a heap of ashes and his dog was dead. A boy named Robi, who had also survived the attack, adopted Rueda as his savior. In early afternoon of that day, Rueda also found Elvira and her two children, and together they verified that there were no more survivors. With all three children under eight years of age, and no obvious way to feed or shelter them for more than a few days, Elvira was very glad to find Rueda, even though she knew him as an eccentric bachelor. With Elvira's help, over the next two days Rueda dug a mass grave for the corpses and covered them with the dry soil of Spanish Wells.

But after that, they had no idea what to do next.

"The governor at Santa Fe will hear about this," Rueda told Elvira in his accented English. "He will probably send a military force here. We must wait here for rescue. I will clean out the well, and we will have fresh water. We can survive."

And so it was that a forty-year-old potter from Michoacan in southern Mexico holed up in a desolated heap of ashes and rubble with a young blond woman from New Orleans with three children to care for, and waited and prayed for help to come. The nearest civilized oasis, now that Yellow Horse had wrought his havoc and death, was over a hundred miles distant.

Almost as far as Santa Fe.

Almost fifty miles to the west, Yellow Horse had once again settled into his favorite red canyon, a sometimes-green place with high buttes all around, and a good place to defend in case of attack by Comanches or Mexicans.

Yellow Horse had a large village of tipis and wickiups. He had consolidated various groups under his leadership until most Apaches of southern New Mexico were sworn to his allegiance. Now most of them lived at his large village and participated in his continuing war against the hated Spanish and Anglo invaders.

The village itself took up most of the mile-long canyon, but many of its inhabitants were gone much of the year, during more settled times, because the nomadic Apaches moved about the region, following wild harvests and hunting.

The Apaches had always been warlike, viewing life as a deadly contest fought against their environment and other tribes. Even though they hated the Spaniards, however, they had gotten their horses from them originally, almost two hundred years before and, because of that, had become some of the most feared mounted warriors of the West. Besides the Spaniards and other white and near-white men, their enemies had always been, and still were, the Pawnee and Comanches. Yellow Horse's band was primarily Lipan Apache, and called themselves the Tinneh—simply, the People.

On that sunny morning when Elvira Lucas and Rueda were trying to think of what to do next, Yellow Horse was ensconced in his Great Tipi in a palaver with his son and his top shaman advisor.

The tipi was larger than most, forming one large, circular room with an open fireplace in its center. The structure itself was constructed of long poles covered with thatch, and then hides over the thatch. The floor was dug out to a distance of two feet, and its perimeter reinforced with fieldstones. Light entered through the big opening that served as a doorway, and through a hole in the roof where smoke exited.

Yellow Horse sat cross-legged on a short length of beech log, to elevate himself above the others present. Because Apaches traditionally did not wear elaborate headdresses, he was adorned only with a headband with one falcon feather affixed to it. He had an antelope skin draped over his broad shoulders for this occasion. His cloth trousers, taken from a Mexican in battle, were tucked into knee-high boot-moccasins.

Across the low fire sat Running Dog and the

shaman. Running Dog wore a brightly beaded headband with no feather or other decoration, and his long, black hair hung to his shoulders, loose and free. He was bare to the waist, showing a heavily muscled torso, with beaded bands around his biceps. At the hips he wore only a breechcloth with beaded edges, and he also wore the knee-high moccasins. His square face held his usual scowl, because Running Dog was almost always displeased with one thing or another. To remind the shaman beside him of his importance, he had stuck into the dirt near him, just off the edge of the blanket on which he sat, a tribal war shield of buffalo skin. It was an elongated oval, with painted animals decorating its surface. He also wore a thin knife in a rawhide sheath at his waist.

The rather young shaman beside him would have looked very exotic to a visitor. He wore a gaudy straw mask on his face, giving him a monstrous look, and above that a fox-head cap, with the hide of the animal hanging down his back. His chest and arms were brightly painted with natural dyes. He also wore rawhide leggings that were worked with beads, depicting Apache deities such as Child of the Water, White-Painted Woman, and Ancient Bear, the mythological founders of the Apache nation. His feet were bare.

The shaman was singing in a high, singsong manner, and throwing black powder onto the fire occasionally to make it flare up so that he might read the future in the white smoke. He cast a handful of slender bones onto the blanket he sat on, studying them carefully, his face and eyes hidden from view. His power, taken from the sun, was always in a duel with the unseen forces around them, wielded by human enemies, animals, and gods. Before they all sat down at the fire, Yellow Horse had personally marked the shaman's body with cactus flower pollen to enhance his natural powers. Then the shaman had lighted a twist of peyote, blown smoke in four directions, and chanted four times, "May it be well."

Now, quite suddenly, the shaman, called White Medicine, stopped his chanting and stared across the fire silently at Yellow Horse.

"Well?" Yellow Horse said in athapaskan.

White Medicine lifted his eyes toward the hole in the ceiling. "You failed at Santa Fe because of Ancient Bear."

Running Dog turned a hostile look on him. "This is not true!"

"Silence!" Yellow Horse told his son. Running Dog was becoming more and more difficult to control. Some even said he was now the real leader of the People.

"Proceed," Yellow Horse told the shaman.

"The man you saw in battle was Ancient Bear," the shaman said quietly, avoiding Running Dog's hard look. "It is in the smoke. Also in the bones."

"To hell with the bones!" Running Dog growled.

Yellow Horse glared at him, and he fell silent again.

"In ancient times, you remember, Killer of Enemies slew monsters like Owl-Man Giant to make the Earth safe for the People. Ancient Bear was the human son of Killer of Enemies, and he himself became a god. He told us he would return from where the sun rises if our nation needed new leadership and lead us to greatness again. This man-thing called Boone comes from across the Great River to the east, and fits the description given to us."

"Then why would he fight us and kill our warriors, if he has come to save us from destruction?" Running Dog said angrily.

The straw mask turned to him. "It is in the legend. We must fall from grace before our deliverance. Ancient Bear will cause that fall, to reveal our weaknesses to us. Then and then only will he step in and show himself to our people. He will eat all chiefs and their progeny, and proclaim himself leader of all the Tinneh everywhere."

Yellow Horse swallowed hard. "He will kill all chieftains?"

"It is written," White Medicine said carefully. "Also, Great Chief, you will remember that one year ago I had a vision in the night that Ancient Bear was coming out of his long hibernation into the Upper World. A messenger came to me

103

in the shape of an owl. The owl said Ancient Bear would look like the First Spaniard, Cabeza de Vaca. This Boone apparently does." He paused. "The next night, I heard the Thunder-bird."

Yellow Horse sighed deeply. He was not able to sleep because of this Ancient Bear thing. There were young Apaches who had little belief in the old legends, including his son, and he almost wished he were one of them.

"I saw with my own eyes," Yellow Horse said quietly. "Bullets pass through him."

"I made him bleed!" Running Dog yelled. "He is human!"

"He shows you what he wishes," the shaman said. "Metal cannot touch the body of a god. He made himself bleed to fool you."

"Aagh!" Running Dog spat.

"The smoke also tells me that he is coming," the shaman went on, ignoring the chief's son. "He will come here, leading a Spanish army. Soon."

Yellow Horse swore under his breath. "I have made the People strong. Why would he want to rid the world of me?"

The shaman shrugged. "He represents an ancient force. We cannot know its ultimate purpose."

"This is all buffalo dung!" Running Dog hissed.

"Can I . . . rightfully resist this force?" Yellow Horse asked tentatively.

Again the shaman shrugged. "It is not clear if this force is good or evil. You can do what you will. If I could be placed close to him, I could call on White-Painted Woman to intervene and wield her great powers over him to send him back to the Netherworld. But I fear his magic is much greater than mine."

"If you place *me* close to him, I will kill him with a dagger to his heart," Running Dog declared. "Then you will see that he is an impostor."

"In the old days," White Medicine said, ignoring the comment once again, "the identity of gods was tested by boiling the oil from various fruits, dropping a stone into the oil, and then having the subject pick the hot stone out of the liquid. If he was not burned, he was a god." He paused. "He lived in a different sphere of existence, in the Luminous Cocoon."

"Luminous Cocoon!" Running Dog barked out. "All of that old business has been disproved!"

Yellow Horse met his son's hard look. "Beware, Running Dog, that you do not offend too many ancient spirits with your reckless talk. We will see what this Boone is made of, if White Medicine's prediction is correct. In the meantime, we will keep our warriors on the alert, and I will pray every night to Moon Woman and Star Children to send the Sun Father over the horizon each morning so that our future, whatever it is, remains assured."

"It is a worthy thought, Great Chief," the shaman told him.

Running Dog rose to his feet, ignoring all protocol, and stood towering over both of them like a subtle threat.

"Read your smoke and rattle your bones," he said in a low, brittle voice. "But the next time I see this hunter from the east, I will personally cut his liver out and eat it for breakfast. I will put his head atop a tall pole and ride with it through the village, to reveal his deception to all our people. Then this Ancient Bear silliness will be finished!"

Before either of them could respond to that, he stormed out of the tipi.

Chapter Five

Santa Fe was preparing for all-out war.

Guns and ammunition were assembled and dispersed, horses shod, and gear repaired.

The Mexicans were ready to fight. Rivera had announced that they would ride out the following day.

When they had left the Governor's Mansion the morning that Alvarado had invited Dan'l to accompany the expedition, Rivera had gotten Dan'l aside. He'd told Dan'l in no uncertain terms that he did not want Dan'l along, that he would not tolerate any interference with command, and that he expected Dan'l to keep out of his way. The only reason he was allowing Dan'l to go, he'd explained, was to appease Alvarado.

Dan'l had thanked him for his warm welcome to the command.

It was arranged that afternoon for Scarface Charlie to accompany the expedition, and that pleased Dan'l. He had also gotten Alvarado's permission to bring another outsider of his choice, and that evening he sought out Stefan Kravitz.

Dan'l found the Polish immigrant in the cantina on the plaza, drinking by himself. Dan'l joined him at a corner table, and ordered a strong Mexican mescal. The waiter came and went before Dan'l mentioned the coming expedition.

"The governor has asked me to go south with Rivera, to find Yellow Horse," he said after swigging the liquor. Dan'l never got drunk, no matter how much he drank. His father had been the same way.

"A smart man," Kravitz said with a smile. "You can teach Rivera a thing or two, I'd wager."

"Rivera doesn't want me," Dan'l said. "He told me so."

"If I was Rivera, I wouldn't want you," Kravitz said. "Did you accept the governor's offer?"

Dan'l nodded. "I talked to Jameson and Douglas just a couple hours ago. Told them there could be survivors at Spanish Wells that need our help. That seemed to convince them it was the right thing to go. They say they'll wait for me to get back from there."

"I imagine they will not leave their quarters in the garrison. When do you leave?"

"Tomorrow morning, before dawn," Dan'l said. He looked over at Kravitz's bony face with its handlebar mustache, and liked what he saw in this mountain man-turned-business trader. "How would you like to go, too?"

The gold tooth at the corner of Kravitz's mouth showed as the grin widened. "You need a drinking partner, Dan'l?"

Dan'l returned the grin. "I need somebody I can trust to use some common sense in an emergency. I don't think Rivera is that man. He seems too hotheaded to command an expedition. And he thinks the Apaches are dumb animals. I don't like that either."

Kravitz grunted and took a sip of whiskey. "The Apache fools you. He tends no seed gardens and makes no permanent home anywhere. So you think he must be stupid. But he isn't, Dan'l. He's still hog-tied with superstition, but he can outmaneuver most armies and he knows how to live in comfort in this arid land. I have much respect for him."

Dan'l nodded. "So do I, Kravitz. And that's why I'd mighty like to have you with us. You got a feeling for things out here. Rivera don't. I can't get you a commission, but you can join up on the same pay as Cabeza. He said he'd be proud to have you."

"I and Cabeza go back beyond Santa Fe," Kravitz told him. "We both hunted and trapped

109

east and north of here before the garrison came. He's kind of noisy sometimes, but I always liked him."

"Then you think you might go?"

Kravitz hesitated, then nodded. "I think my small business will survive without me for a while. I would go just to get to know you better, Dan'l."

Dan'l smiled through the thick, graying beard. "I'm much obliged."

"*Niema za co,*" Kravitz mumbled.

Dan'l regarded him quizzically.

Kravitz caught the look. "Ah. *Przepraszam.* I am sorry for lapsing into my native tongue. Sometimes I do that with a person who makes me very comfortable. It is a bad habit."

Dan'l laughed softly. "Pissing on a grizzly's foot is a bad habit. Bartender! Bring us more of the same!"

Kravitz smiled and leaned forward, his long face going somber. "You know you will have to deal with this Ancient Bear thing, Dan'l."

Dan'l shook his shaggy head. "Hell. The Shawnee thought I was a goddamn devil from the depths of hell for a while. Then they give me a special name and tried to adopt me. I been through this kind of stuff before, Kravitz. It never bothered me none."

"The Ancient Bear legend could be different from anything you've run into before," Kravitz said quietly. "Emotions run deep in that kind of thing among these dry-country red men. It could be very dangerous for you."

Dan'l fixed him with a steady stare. "Life without risk ain't hardly worth living, Kravitz," he said in a low, deliberate tone.

Kravitz did not reply.

Any response would have seemed inappropriate.

Dan'l left the cantina in the early evening to get himself a meal and to make sure Charlie had been contacted by Dura Cabeza.

He found the half-breed in his tiny hut on the outskirts of town. It was a brown adobe place, one room, with one lantern to light the interior and a straw mattress to sleep on. Charlie had eaten not long before Dan'l's arrival, and the odors of cooked meat and fried *tortas* hung in the air inside. Charlie opened the door looking a little tired, and Dan'l wished he had not disturbed him.

"Maybe I come at the wrong time," he said in the doorway. "I just wanted to make sure Cabeza has been here."

"*Sí.*" Charlie nodded. Yes, he come. I will go with you, Senor Boone."

"That's good," Dan'l said. "You know the Apache. How he thinks. That could be important."

"Please. Come in," Charlie said, his facial scar glowing pink in the soft light from the hut. He was bare-chested and wore only soiled cloth trousers, his brown feet bare. His black hair looked stringy and unkempt, but Dan'l did not smell liquor on his breath.

Dan'l stooped low to enter the place, and the air seemed close inside. There was a rough-hewn table and two straight chairs, and when Charlie invited him to sit, he did, and Charlie took the other chair. A dirty tin plate sat on the table.

"It is not a mansion." Charlie grinned through the scar. "But it is mine."

Dan'l was amazed at how youthful Charlie's body looked, despite the gray in his loose hair and the wrinkles in his brown face. "It's a good house," Dan'l said. "Kind of like my first one in Kentucky."

"It serves me well," Charlie offered, watching Dan'l's face closely.

There was a half-full bottle of tequila sitting on a small wall shelf. Dan'l recalled Charlie's reputation for drinking, and cleared his throat before he spoke. "Charlie, I got this job for you. I'll feel kind of responsible about that, if you understand."

Charlie frowned slightly, making his face even more wrinkled. "Yes?"

"You can't drink after you leave here," Dan'l told him. "Not till you get back to Santa Fe."

Charlie stiffened slightly. "Yes? Who says this?"

"I say it," Dan'l said evenly.

"You are not the colonel," Charlie reminded him. "You are not even Cabeza." His English was good when he was sober.

Dan'l smiled. "I reckon not. But if you take a drink out there on the trail, I'll send you back. Rivera will back me."

Charlie turned away from him. "Then I will not go."

"You'll go," Dan'l said easily. "Because you've always gone when they needed you. Now we need you even more than before."

Charlie turned to him. "You are from Kentucky. You do not know what is needed and what is not."

"I know more than you think," Dan'l said.

Charlie regarded him with a scowl. "Another man came. Said he was a god of Aztecs. Over two hundred years ago. They called him Malinche. But his magic was not real. They drove him from their city."

Dan'l had had little schooling, but he knew the story of Cortez. "But then he come back with a bigger army and conquered the mighty Mexicans. And not because he was a god."

Charlie grinned drily. "Maybe because he did not drink the tequila?"

Dan'l grinned, too. "That's right. And because he used his knowledge of the enemy against them. Like you can do."

Charlie sighed. "I grow too old for this, Sheltowee." He saw the look on Dan'l's face. "Yes, not just the Taos know your name. That is why Yellow Horse worries. He has many words fall in his ear about the white warrior from the

East. If he believes or not, you become a worry. Because many of the Tinneh believe. This makes big medicine. Do you understand, Sheltowee?"

"Yes," Dan'l said soberly. It was his second cautioning in one short evening. But Charlie had already demonstrated his value to the expedition with such insight. "Now. Will you go with us? I'd feel a mite better if you did."

Charlie thought for a long moment. "I have the whiskey fever. If there is firewater among the soldiers, I will find it."

"There won't be none. Unless you bring it."

Charlie stared past Dan'l with concern. Then he said, "All right. I make this deal with you. I will go to Spanish Wells with you, and to the People of Three Buttes. But I tell you this, there are many who will not return to Santa Fe."

Dan'l returned Charlie's somber look. "I know."

When Dan'l left the hut shortly thereafter, his head was busy with thoughts and plans for the foray south, and he could not think of sleep. When he got back to the central plaza, therefore, he picketed the appaloosa he was riding to a hitching post outside the cantina and went back inside, hoping Kravitz was still there. But Kravitz was gone, so Dan'l sat at a table and ordered a tequila to help him sleep.

Just after the bartender had delivered the drink, though, Sergeant Torreon and the beefy Corporal Gomez came in, saw Dan'l, and seated themselves at a table just a few feet away from his. When Dan'l saw them, he groaned inwardly. They already looked as if they had had a few drinks off the premises.

"Hola!" Torreon said loudly as soon as he had sat down. *"El Capitán Boone! Que afortunado!"*

Torreon was beaming giddily, but Gomez, his big face flushed, looked belligerent as he focused on Dan'l. Dan'l nodded to them curtly, and swigged half of his drink.

"Capitán!" Gomez said with open disgust. He spat on the floor between him and Dan'l.

Dan'l just shook his head slowly.

"Senor Boone," Torreon said in a pompous voice. "We have been talking. How much do you pay *el gubernador* for to make you Spanish officer? Heh? You must be *muy rico.*"

Dan'l glanced over at him. "Maybe you ought to let it go, Torreon."

"What?" Gomez said to his sergeant in Spanish. "What did he say?"

Torreon ignored him. *"No comprendo, Americano.* I don't understand this. Maybe you say it different way, *sí?* For us poor dumb peones?"

"I said, drink your own stuff, and leave me be," Dan'l told him in a low voice. "I ain't in no mood for drunks."

"Drunks?" Torreon said fiercely, his happy look gone. "You call us drunks? I know that word, senor!"

"Then keep it quiet over there," Dan'l suggested.

"He says we are drunkards," Torreon explained to Gomez.

Gomez's swarthy, meaty face grew even more grim. "What?" he said to Dan'l. "You think we are *pellejos*, yes?"

Dan'l was beginning to remember why he preferred the loneliness of the wilderness over the companionship of men. He looked over at Gomez, but said nothing.

"The captain does not wish to speak with us," Torreon observed. "Maybe he likes to speak only with officers, yes? Because he is a high-ranking captain?"

"I think he must remember he is just a *ciudadano*," Gomez said gutturally. "We must return to him this memory."

Dan'l looked at him. "You don't seem to listen very well, mister. You must be kind of thick between the ears."

"Que?" Gomez said to Torreon.

Torreon was irritated. "Do you speak no Spanish, *cabron?*"

The bartender had been watching the exchange. He was a rather small, rotund fellow, overfed and greasy-looking, with slicked-back hair and brows that grew together over his nose. He came over to the tables now with a worried look on his olive-hued face.

"Please, gentlemen," he said in English, in deference to Dan'l. "We want no trouble inside here."

"Then tell them two to let a man have a drink

in peace," Dan'l said icily to him. "I pay the same pesos as them for my liquor."

The bartender sighed, turned to Torreon and Gomez, and spoke to them in fast Spanish, requesting them to drink their drinks quietly and leave the American alone. It was Gomez who answered him, shouting loudly in Spanish. He told the barkeep to go wash his glasses and mind his own business.

Dan'l did not understand any of it, except the tone of Gomez's voice. He knew, too, that the bartender was not about to give a soldier the size of Gomez too much trouble.

The bartender turned to Dan'l, shrugged, and returned to the bar across the room, where two other customers, both local civilians, had begun watching the tables with increasing interest. Many Santa Fe citizens disliked the garrison soldiers because they often got drunk and caused trouble in the otherwise peaceable town. But since the recent attacks by Yellow Horse, when the soldiers had had to put their lives on the line to defend the settlement, feelings had become more benign toward these uniformed men who served the crown of Spain.

"You are *mudo!*" Gomez now hissed at Dan'l. "Dumb. Even little children speak Spanish with fluency. You are dumber than a small child."

Dan'l was slowly becoming riled. "You're going to push that saucy line too far, Corporal," he said evenly. "You better cool down while you can."

Now Torreon got back in it. He rose from his chair, and pushed it backwards. He still wore the pistol that Gomez had threatened him with before, but he made no move for it. "You threaten us, damn you? You tell us to be quiet?"

"That's right," Dan'l said. He swigged the rest of his tequila, and wiped his sleeve across his mouth.

Gomez rose, too. He was suddenly breathing hard. "You dumb *cabron!* We will teach you a lesson, yes?"

He looked over at Torreon, who nodded his acceptance of the challenge. Gomez stepped away from their table, widening the distance between himself and the sergeant, so that Dan'l could not confront both of them face-to-face.

Dan'l sighed, rose from his chair, and kicked it over behind him. Then he took hold of the table, and hurled it across the room, where it crashed heavily into another table.

"You want me?" he growled. "You got me."

When Torreon saw the look on Dan'l's face, he ran a hand across his mouth in indecision. Dan'l looked a little like an aroused grizzly, with his arms out at his sides and his feet set wide apart. Neither of the other men had armed themselves, so Dan'l kept his hunting knife in its sheath.

Torreon act as if he wanted to back off, but Gomez had lost all control of himself. In the next moment, he charged at Dan'l.

Dan'l waited. Gomez hurled his massive body

at him, swinging his right ham of a fist as he came. The fist came right at Dan'l's head, but Dan'l ducked easily under it, and threw a vicious right into Gomez's ribs as he sailed past.

Gomez uttered a low grunt of raw pain as he went to the floor beyond Dan'l, hitting like a boulder and making the floorboards creak.

"Por favor, señores!" the barkeep was pleading from across the room.

"Madre de Dios!" one of the civilians at the bar muttered.

Torreon figured they were committed now, so he also hurled himself at Dan'l, intending to hit him bodily and take Dan'l down with him. Then Gomez would come to his aid, and they would beat this interloper senseless. Maybe the governor could find a way to send him to Spanish Wells with his arms and legs broken and his insides mashed. But Torreon doubted it.

Dan'l was just turning back from the big man as Torreon came. He did not have time to side-step him, and in the next half-second Torreon hit him hard in the side and head, taking them both down.

"Gomez!" Torreon yelled out desperately as he grabbed onto Dan'l to hold him down.

Dan'l swung the back of his forearm into Torreon's face, fracturing his long nose, and Torreon went flying, hitting the floor on his back.

Gomez had struggled to his feet, grimacing in pain as he felt two cracked ribs biting into his chest. But he was far from through. He gnashed

119

his teeth and snarled at Dan'l, who also rose to his feet.

"I will kill you, *Americano!* I will break your back, then I will crush you under my foot like an insect!"

Dan'l shook his shaggy head. "You just can't teach some people nothing," he said.

Gomez came at him again, flailing his big arms. Dan'l avoided the first blow, but Gomez managed to strike a glancing hit with his left hand. Dan'l staggered back a step, pain rocketing through his head, and something awoke deep in his gut, some animal thing that was always there, just waiting. Dan'l swung a hard fist into Gomez's big belly, and doubled the Spaniard over, air whooshing from Gomez's throat. Then Dan'l punched him in the side of the head with such force that everyone in the room heard Gomez's skull crack under the impact.

Gomez went down like a felled tree and rolled onto his face. Torreon was still down and had decided not to get up. It was much safer on the floor.

Gomez scrabbled there, with Dan'l breathing hard over him, his eyes like those of a cougar. Gomez got up onto his knees groggily, not knowing where he was.

"I will . . ." he muttered. Crimson ran from his left ear and down across his jaw.

Dan'l walked deliberately around him, determined to finish Gomez off.

The barkeep was suddenly tugging at his elbow.

"No, senor," he said to Dan'l. "You will surely kill him!"

Dan'l turned and stared hard at him. Slowly, reluctantly, the thing inside him crawled back where it belonged, and he could think again.

"What?"

"You have beaten them. You do not have to carry it any further."

Dan'l looked down at the dazed and bleeding Gomez, and then over to where Torreon cowered on the floor.

Dan'l stepped away from the big soldier and nodded. "Yeah. I'm done."

The two civilian customers at the bar were staring wide-eyed. They had never seen a bar fight quite like this one.

Dan'l glared down at Gomez. "How do you say asshole in Spanish?" he growled at the dazed soldier.

Then he stormed out of the place, busting a slat in the swinging doors as he exited.

Chapter Six

When the garrison left the next morning, Corporal Gomez was not with it. He was in the infirmary in heavy bandages. He had regained full consciousness, but had no memory of what had happened to him. He thought he must have been run over by a supply wagon. It was Torreon who took a quick look in on him before the troops rode out and told him what had occurred in the cantina. Then Gomez remembered, and his face filled with raw terror.

"He will . . . be gone at dawn?" Gomez asked Torreon.

"Yes."

"Good," Gomez said, and breathed more easily, despite his busted ribs.

Torreon smiled weakly past the bandage on

his broken nose. "Rest well, Corporal. At least you will not have to face Yellow Horse."

Light was just creeping into the eastern sky when the mounted troops began moving out. There were two hundred enlisted men, officers, and Taos warriors, with the Indians bringing up the rear of the long column. In the front rode Colonel Rivera and his four other captains, each the commander of a company of cavalry. Then came Dan'l, with Kravitz and Cabeza alongside him. Behind them were the color-bearers, with unit flags flying in a light breeze, and then the long column of mounted soldiers, four abreast. They wore plumed hats and blue dress uniforms with brass buttons and insignia, and short sabers on their belts. Each soldier also had a rifled Charleville musket on his mount's irons, in a fancy, leather scabbard decorated with silver. Ammo pouches hung on their waists, and in saddlebags, holding oiled paper cartridges of ball and powder. There was also a small pouch for extra flints, which were needed to ignite the priming powder in firing the gun.

The cavaliers were well aware that they would not get more than a shot or two off with the Charlevilles in close combat, so they depended heavily on their ability to kill with the sabers, and trusted those weapons more than the more modern ones. The Apaches used lances and bows to supplement their guns for the same reason. The officers were better off, since each of them, down through noncommissioned sergeants, carried an Annely repeating revolver, which contained eight balls, although priming was still necessary. Dan'l had been given an Annely when he met with Rivera that morning, and he now wore it in a holster on his wide belt. He also carried his "Ticklicker" Kentucky rifle in a saddle boot.

Scarface Charlie, who had been the first one in the compound before leaving, now rode out a mile ahead of the column. Cabeza would join him there later.

The flag of Mexico was carried proudly in the banners, signifying the authority of Governor Alvarado, and ultimately of Bernardo de Galvez, Viceroy of Mexico, who answered to the king in Madrid, Carlos III.

Dan'l remembered his expeditions to Fort Duquesne, with colonial and British troops, under the leadership of British officers. The French were the enemy then, and the Shawnee. Now it was the "deadly Apache," so called by their Indian neighbors because of their ferocity. The Zuni, the Navajo, and even the powerful Comanches acknowledged that when the Apache was in full fighting force, he was practically unbeatable in open battle.

The column rode south and west all through that first morning. At first it was all open ground, sometimes red in color, sometimes gray. Because it was spring, they crossed a couple of small streams where the water ran clear over rocky terrain. In the fall, these would have been dry riverbeds. There was vegetation along the streams, including cottonwood and aspen trees, all leafed out in subtle shades of green. Away from the rivers, though, there was little flora other than sagebrush, Spanish dagger, and prickly-pear cactus. Occasionally, they would see beaver tail with its crimson blossoms, or jumping cholla.

Small herds of antelope were seen standing short distances off their route every few miles or so, and Dan'l spotted two gray coyotes, running side by side very purposefully, as if late to some kind of rendezvous. He knew, also, even though none were seen that day, that this terrain was home to the diamondback rattler and the horned toad. The locals even saw an occasional cougar slinking along the crests of the high buttes.

It was all very different from Kentucky and the Carolinas. Dan'l missed the thick forests, the cool ferns underfoot, but he had to admit that this dry country was exciting. When the desert and arid grasslands were in bloom, as they were now, they were rather spectacular.

"If you come back one day," Kravitz told Dan'l as they rode along together, "I can show you things that make men stop and stare. Up north, the great buttes that thrust into the sky from a flat plain, looking like monuments to some Indian deity. Farther west, the ancient hole in the ground that the locals call the Cañon Grande."

Dan'l nodded, stirred up inside. It had been stories like this one, told by another, earlier friend, that had gotten Dan'l to dreaming about exploring wild Kentucky, when it was inhabited only by Shawnee.

"I'd like to see all that," he said.

Kravitz pointed skyward at several turkey buzzards that were floating lazily above the column, circling and lofting on a small breeze.

"Look. They are smarter than we think. They know that if they are patient, there will be death among us. They have seen this kind of thing before."

Dan'l squinted into the brightness above them. It was a harsh world here, outside the settlements. He admired the Apaches for making it their home. Maybe they deserved to keep it.

"I've seen them like this back East," he said. "They know what's coming. Some soldiers used to shoot them down, because of what they stood for. But it ain't got nothing to do with them. It's us."

Kravitz looked over at him and said nothing.

"I kind of like them," Dan'l finally added. "They keep the woods and plains clean."

Kravitz sighed. "When I first got here, I rode out with an officer to find a couple of soldiers that got lost west of Santa Fe. One was still alive when we found him, but the other one was dead. When we asked about it, the survivor told us that they were both thrown from their horses and injured, and the horses had run off.

Spooked by a cougar, I believe. The survivor had gotten to his gun, the other man not, and neither could walk or even move about. The vultures came quickly, and kept their distance from the survivor because he managed to fire off the gun regularly. The other man, several hundred yards away, but in clear sight of the survivor, could not keep the birds off him as he weakened from the injuries. According to the survivor, they ate him alive. Pecked his eyes out first. Then went for his vital organs, opening him up like a package of meat. His screams echoed off the nearby buttes, and it took a long time. Because he had seen and heard all that, the survivor was never the same man again. He resigned from the army shortly thereafter, and returned to Mexico City."

"That happened to a Shawnee I come on once, in a clearing in the woods," Dan'l said. "It was pretty clear he'd died slow." He guided his mount around a bristling cactus. "But them birds was just doing what comes natural. It's their world, after all, ain't it?"

Kravitz smiled. "That is an interesting point of view, my Kentucky friend."

"It's just a fact of life," Dan'l told him.

They stopped at midday, and Cabeza rode out ahead to bring Charlie in. The four companies set up separate messes, and ate a small meal from mess kits. Kravitz and Dan'l took their dry food under a mesquite tree, and when Cabeza and Charlie returned, they joined them there.

When they were about finished, Colonel Rivera came past and stopped.

"Well, Boone. We are getting into Apache country slowly. How do you like it?"

Dan'l nodded. "Just fine, Colonel. I think I could get used to this in a hurry."

Rivera's blue uniform was already dusty, and there was a dew of perspiration on his upper lip. "Don't get too comfortable with it, my friend. There are dangers out here you can't imagine. You may know your Kentucky woods, but this is all very different. Please exercise caution. You are in my charge."

Kravitz could not believe that Rivera would lecture the great Dan'l Boone like some raw emigrant. He regarded Rivera sourly. "I have advised Dan'l of our special dangers, Colonel," he said. "I am certain he is quite capable of taking care of himself. Here or anywhere."

"Perhaps," Rivera said arrogantly.

"It's all right, Kravitz," Dan'l said. "The colonel is just doing his job."

"I am glad you see it that way," Rivera told him brusquely. Then he moved on to speak with one of his captains.

"He is such an offensive man!" Kravitz said when he was gone.

"What he needs is a little humble pie." Dan'l grinned. "I just try to ignore him."

"I don't know how you will be able to do that, on this kind of expedition," Kravitz said. "It makes me wonder why you would volunteer to come."

"The governor asked me as a personal favor," Dan'l said slowly. "He's worried about Yellow Horse, and about there maybe being survivors at Spanish Wells. I couldn't say no to him. He's been good to me."

"You owe Alvarado nothing," Kravitz said. "He should not have asked you. You will be at the very top of Yellow Horse's death list."

Dan'l grinned at him. "I been there before," he said.

"All right, let's move out!" came the call in Spanish from one of the captains.

A few minutes later, the big column was on the move again.

They did not cross any streams in the afternoon, and the ground underfoot became drier and dustier, and high buttes rose on both sides of them, gray-white and rather foreboding, perfect places for an enemy to ambush the column. But Rivera knew that Yellow Horse was holed up in his canyon now, preparing to meet Rivera's army head-on.

They finally did arrive on the bank of a small river at the end of that day, and the small army encamped on an open area running along it for a half mile.

The area was a real bivouac for the night. Tents were thrown up for shelter, and a command tent for Rivera and his officers. Water was gathered from the stream, and tested, and food was cooked over open fires. The fire lighted the night and reflected in the water of the stream.

In mid-evening, Rivera gathered his four captains in the command tent, and also called in Dan'l, Kravitz, and Cabeza. As it turned out, the governor had instructed Rivera in no uncertain terms to include Dan'l in briefings, and as little respect as Rivera had for Alvarado, he feared to go against his wishes, because Alvarado was almost as powerful as the Deity Himself in New Mexico. Rivera would have included Cabeza anyway, and he figured it could not hurt to have Kravitz there, since Kravitz knew the country and operated as a guide for them from time to time.

The eight of them sat around a small table in the center of the large tent, on straight chairs. Rivera scanned a primitive map before him on the table, and ran a hand through his dark, slicked-back hair. He was a rather handsome fellow, like Alvarado, but his skin was swarthier, and his face more square than the governor's. He looked very much like a military man, sitting there poring over the map.

"A couple of you captains have been this way before," he said after a long silence. "And Cabeza. Didn't you come with us a year ago, Kravitz? When we marched to the Little Colorado?" He had to speak in English in deference to Dan'l, and even Kravitz, and that nettled him deep down.

"Yes, Colonel," Kravitz said. "This area is familiar to me. I also own a small mining claim just to the west of here."

A captain sitting next to Salazar grunted acidly. Some soldiers did not like civilians among them on a mission.

Dan'l glanced at Salazar, who commanded Torreon and the disabled Gomez. He had had a full report on the fight in the cantina, and how Dan'l had almost killed Gomez, and had not spoken to Dan'l once on the trek. He returned Dan'l's look now with a surly one.

Rivera went on. "My plan is to march directly south for the next couple of days, and that should bring us very close to Devil's Canyon, the place of Yellow Horse. We will make a small detour then to Spanish Wells, to look for possible survivors of the Apache attack. It is the governor's wishes."

All sat silently.

"Any questions or suggestions?" Rivera asked confidently.

Cabeza cleared his throat. "*Dispenseme, Coronel,*" he said quietly.

Rivera glared at him. "Yes?"

"I was speaking with Charlie this afternoon. Sir."

"Yes, yes?" Rivera said irritably.

"Charlie says that when we arrive in the territory of Yellow Horse, we must not delay in our attack. He knows we are coming, and any delay will give him time to assemble his forces."

Dan'l hesitated, but spoke up, too. "He told

me the same. He thinks we got to go to Devil's Canyon first, and bypass Spanish Wells. Attack Yellow Horse and then look for survivors at Spanish Wells afterwards."

Rivera's eyes sparked fire. "Bypass Spanish Wells? Leave any possible survivors on their own, maybe to die during our delay in rescuing them?" He looked smug as he turned to his captains. "Is this the way things are done in your new country, Boone? It appears you agree with this half-savage in his recommendation."

"Charlie ain't no more savage than most of us," Dan'l said, crossing his arms on his chest.

Cabeza, Charlie's friend, grinned slightly, but said nothing.

"Do I agree with him? Well, I reckon I do. Anybody what survived that massacre probably ain't going to die in the couple of days it'll take for you to have it out with Yellow Horse. But if Yellow Horse beats you to the punch, Colonel, you could lose a lot of men. A lot more than a few Spanish Wells survivors."

Rivera scowled fiercely at Dan'l. "We are soldiers! It is our duty to think of civilians first, and ourselves second. Even if it does cost lives."

"*Exacto!*" Salazar said loudly.

Dan'l looked at his boots. "People is people, Colonel. Uniform or not. You can't jeopardize a whole command on the off-chance of saving a few settlers. You take on some wounded or sick people at the Wells, and then lose to Yellow Horse because you give him the advantage, you could cost the lives of soldiers *and* survivors."

"That does make some sense, Colonel," Kravitz said.

Before Rivera could react, one of his own captains added fuel to the fire. "Also, there might not be any survivors, Colonel. Perhaps we must give thought to the Indian's words."

Rivera turned and hurled a white-hot look at the officer that made his face go pale.

"The Indian's words?" Rivera hissed. "Jeopardize my command?"

A heavy blanket of silence descended on the group, and tension crackled like sheet lightning in the tent.

"Is there any other officer here," Rivera thundered, "who feels that I jeopardize the safety of this command if I do not heed the words of a drunken Indian?"

The silence grew even more oppressive as Rivera turned from the indiscreet young captain to each of the others in turn. One by one, except for Salazar, they averted their gaze.

"Would you like to go on the record, Mr. Kravitz, as recommending that we ignore the survivors at Spanish Wells, if there are such there, hoping and praying for our arrival?"

Kravitz shot a quick look at Dan'l. "Colonel, I did not say that—"

"Ah, I see. So it is really only the outsider—a first-time visitor to this territory—who takes it upon himself to dictate strategy to the commander of this expedition."

Dan'l felt like getting up and leaving. But he knew that that would look bad for him. "I'm just giving you another opinion to think on, Colonel," he finally replied. "I hear tell that even Viceroy de Galvez has his advisors."

Kravitz grinned at that, despite himself, but Rivera did not think there was any humor in the remark.

"My officers are my advisors, Mr. Boone. And I have listened to them. Please do not think it strange that I do not solicit the advice of any Apaches, including our current guide, or a complete alien to our world out here in the territory such as yourself. I told you before you embarked on this mission: Do not intrude yourself into affairs that you do not understand. Keep the Apache and Cabeza entertained, if you wish, and try to keep out of trouble. But do not presume to intervene into discussions of military strategy. You will only embarrass yourself, and the governor."

Kravitz could remain quiet no longer. "Damn it, Colonel! You demean the governor's judgment in your treatment of this man! Alvarado is very impressed with Dan'l's military credentials, and so are a lot of us. He was fighting the French in Pennsylvania when some of us was just learning what end of a gun to shoot with. And he knows more about how the red man thinks than any of us in this tent, I'd bet my life on it. Maybe you could learn something, if you'd just let him talk."

Once again, Rivera was angry. "If you were a regular, Kravitz, I would court-martial you for that outburst! As it is, I will only insist that you leave this tent at once, and take this Alvarado emissary with you, now that we have had his opinion of how we are to conduct our campaign."

Kravitz stood up in a huff. "I would resign from this duty, Colonel, if it were not for Boone."

Dan'l rose, too, and was surprised to see Cabeza get up with him.

"Sorry we spoiled your little palaver," Dan'l said easily to the emotional Rivera. "But I thought I ought to mention how I feel about this. Alvarado made it clear he wanted me to help your people advise you. As a courtesy. I reckon you better remember you have to answer to him—and to the viceroy—when this thing is all over."

Rivera glared icily at him. "Thank you for reminding me of my responsibility, Mr. Boone," he said deliberately. "Now, if you will excuse us."

Dan'l, Kravitz, and Cabeza left the tent without any further comment, aware that they had lost any chance of making an impact on Rivera's thinking about the campaign.

He did not want their opinions.

He would obviously proceed without them.

* * *

Dan'l kept away from Rivera for the next couple of days, and things went quietly within the ranks. Dan'l now wondered if Kravitz were right, and if he should have refused Alvarado's invitation to join the expedition. It seemed at the moment that the only way he might contribute would be to shoot a few Apaches, possibly in a losing battle.

Dura Cabeza was out of favor with Rivera now, too, after getting up and leaving with Dan'l. But Cabeza had weathered storms with Rivera before and was not concerned. When the disagreement filtered down through the troops, most of them sided with Scarface Charlie and Dan'l,. and wanted to go directly to Devil's Canyon to find Yellow Horse, and maybe catch him unprepared.

On the second day after that briefing in the tent, Dan'l rode out ahead of the column with Cabeza, who had temporarily relieved Charlie as scout for part of the morning. Dan'l and Cabeza were watching for signs of the enemy, studying the butte crests and the ground underfoot. But the morning was uneventful. The multilingual Cabeza had come to like Dan'l, even though they were from different worlds. Actually, they had a lot in common, just as Kravitz and Dan'l did. Riding along beside Dan'l, Cabeza told him of his brief time in Boston as a child, when he had learned most of his English. Dan'l described Carolina to Cabeza, and Kentucky, and Cabeza thought he would like to return to Dan'l's new country some day.

About mid-morning Cabeza went up into some rocky terrain off the main trail, to get a better vista of the surrounding countryside, while Dan'l kept on the trail, expecting to meet up with Cabeza about a mile farther along.

Cabeza had not been on that detour more than ten minutes when the jaguar found him.

It was a very big, mature animal, and very hungry. Also, a few months previously, it had fed off the remains of a Kiowa Indian, and had tasted the flesh of a human, and found it palatable. On this bright spring morning, it had scented Cabeza and his pinto mount, and decided to investigate. It came into high rocks overlooking Cabeza's trail while Cabeza was busy studying antelope tracks in the hard soil underfoot. Cabeza decided to report the spoor to Dan'l. Maybe they would obtain permission to go hunting for table meat for the column.

The big cat spotted him at fifty yards, and crouched low on a high boulder that Cabeza would pass just underneath.

Cabeza was still concentrating on the spoor when his horse whinnied softly, scenting the cat. Cabeza reined in and looked around him, but saw nothing. He urged the pony onward.

Up on the rock, the jaguar waited, almost eight feet long from head to tip of tail, weighing well over three hundred pounds. Its floral-shaped spots looked like dappled leaves in the jungle of its main habitat to the south, but afforded little cover up here in the dry country. So it pressed its great body flat against the boulder until just the ears and eyes were visible from below. Because the jaguar was so seldom encountered at this latitude, in comparison with its smaller cousin the cougar, men like Cabeza never even thought of meeting one on the trail, and did not watch out for them. So Cabeza rode slowly forward, wondering if the horse had smelled a cougar, which rarely attacked a man.

When Cabeza was exactly below the animal, he heard its claws on the hard surface of rock, as it got its back feet under it to spring. He looked up, and suddenly there it was, looking huge.

"Madre mia!" he gasped, eyes going wide.

He reached for the rifled musket in its scabbard just as the jaguar leapt down on him from above.

He never got the gun out of its sheath. The heavy weight of the animal hit him and he and the horse both went down.

Cabeza hit the ground hard, and the horse began scrabbling wildly to its feet in sheer terror. While the jaguar pinned Cabeza to the rocky ground, the horse regained its feet and galloped off into the rocks. Cabeza tried to defend himself with his arms, but the cat's strength was enormous, and it ripped him with its razor-sharp claws. It opened him up at the chest and belly in a moment, and he went quickly into shock. But he was still very much conscious of the animal tearing his innards out and devouring them. He screamed once, and then again, but then he died silently as the jaguar painted its muzzle with his blood.

It was about that time that Scarface Charlie rode up to Dan'l on the trail to take his place as scout. He immediately looked up ahead when he saw Dan'l alone.

"Where is Cabeza?" he asked in his Mexican-Apache accent.

Dan'l was already looking toward the higher terrain above them, off the trail to their right. "He went up there to get a better look ahead. I could swear I just heard something from up there. Like maybe a yell from him. I reckon we better have a look."

Under his black hat with its osprey feather, the weathered face of Charlie showed quick concern. Cabeza was his friend. "Yes, we will," he agreed.

As they rode up into the big boulders, their mounts began acting nervous.

"I bet we got us a cat around here somewhere," Dan'l said as they reined in. "Maybe a cougar?"

Charlie wrinkled his nose. "It is a different smell," he said slowly.

Dan'l slid his rifle from its scabbard quietly, watching the rocks around them, then quickly loaded and primed the big weapon. Charlie took a slim war dagger from its sheath.

"It's up ahead there," Dan'l said. "Go slow."

Just a moment later they came upon the site of the attack. The jaguar had gone, hearing them approach. All they saw now was Cabeza's mangled body, partially devoured, lying in a big pool of blood.

Charlie uttered a low profanity in Apache.

"Oh, Jesus," Dan'l said.

It was a gruesome sight. Cabeza's insides had been largely eaten in the brief moments the cat had had, and his face was smeared with crimson.

Charlie dismounted, but held the reins of his guffering pony. He knelt over Cabeza and shook his head slowly.

Dan'l stayed aboard the appaloosa, watching the rocks, both hands on the rifle now. "That's a hard way to go," he said grimly. "Damn!"

Charlie sighed deeply and looked at the tracks beside the dead Cabeza. "Jaguar," he said.

"By God," Dan'l murmured. "I didn't know you had them up here. That's a big cat, ain't it?"

"It is a Devil cat," Charlie said darkly. "Twice as large as a cougar, and twice as deadly." He rose to his feet, still looking about. "There are two."

Dan'l nodded. "That's what I figured."

"The female came to join him after the kill, but did not get to feed. We scared her off."

"I'll go look," Dan'l said.

"No, you will not find them."

"So what do we do?" Dan'l said.

"The jaguar is intelligent," Charlie said, "and

bold. They will probably strike again, because this hunt was successful. They must be found. We will arrange with Rivera to form a hunting party. There must be several guns. They are very dangerous."

Dan'l nodded and slid the long gun back into its holster. "Let's get this poor bastard buried."

Rivera showed little concern about the jaguars. But when Kravitz agreed with Dan'l and Charlie that Rivera could lose several men along the way to the animals if they did nothing, including all their scouts, Rivera reluctantly agreed to bivouac the troops for a few hours until a hunting party could go out after the cats and destroy them.

Dan'l volunteered immediately, and Rivera gave him an argument, but finally relented. Kravitz thought they should have five or six guns, but Dan'l realized that most of these men were not hunters and would just get in the way in case of real trouble, and thought three or four men would do. So after Kravitz nominated himself to go with Dan'l and Charlie, Rivera appointed Captain Salazar as the fourth man, because he was a good shot.

"Salazar will be in charge of the hunt," Rivera said severely, "and you will follow his orders without question."

The three hunters knew that that decision was flawed, but they all kept quiet. Dan'l figured Salazar would probably defer to them, anyway, when they got out there.

It was almost noon when they set out. The four of them rode to the place where Cabeza was buried, and Dan'l and Charlie started the tracking from that point. After they had established the cats' trail away from the site, Salazar turned to the others. He looked quite bulky on his long-legged mount, and his mustache made him look very Latin.

"The Apache will take the lead. If the tracks diverge, I suggest he and Boone follow one set, and Kravitz and I the other. Any problem with that?"

Dan'l shook his head, because Salazar was looking right at him. "Sounds like a good plan, Captain." Salazar seemed much more reasonable than Rivera.

"Then let's head on out," Salazar said. "We will hope to recover Cabeza's body on our way back from Spanish Wells."

Five miles ahead, to the west, the pair of jaguars rested on a rock outcropping. The female was only slightly smaller than her mate, and a beautiful golden-and-black animal. She had fed on the remains of an antelope earlier, so neither cat was hungry now. The male, though, liked the ease with which he had brought the man down, and he was getting accustomed to the taste of human flesh. He was in no hurry, therefore, to leave the area, because they both had smelled the presence of many more of these humans, not far away, and heading toward them. This meant, to the male, a ready supply of food in the foreseeable future. Antelope were scarce in this area, so the big cat was pleased to see the introduction of another food supply.

"They are smart as foxes," Kravitz told Dan'l as they rode along watching for spoor, Charlie and Salazar behind them. "They have been known to double back on their trails and ambush hunters. If there are dogs, they kill them first. There is no smarter animal."

Dan'l shook his head. "I'm glad we didn't have them in Kentucky. Bears is bad enough."

"These animals have killed young grizzlies," Charlie said soberly. "The Apache avoids them." Charlie tipped his hat farther down over his eyes to cut the glare of the sun. His cloth shirt seemed to have been washed since the last time Dan'l had seen it, and he also wore rawhide trousers and a pair of knee-high Apache moccasins.

They rode through some high country, among the red buttes, and passed through some yellow-blossoming palo verde and yucca. Occasionally there would be a juniper tree, gnarled and twisted, hanging onto the rocks for dear life. Over an hour passed before Dan'l finally stopped them.

"Whoa!" he said, raising his hand to halt the small procession. "Looky here, these tracks is looking real fresh."

"It is true," Charlie said, getting off his mount

and kneeling over them. "The cats are very close now."

"Well, we have four guns," Salazar said grumpily. "Proceed up the trail until we see them."

Kravitz pulled up beside him, looking a little worried. He had seen a jaguar kill a steer once, south of there, on a ranch, and he would never forget it. He could still see that spotted pelt thrashing on its prey in the tall grass, and the yellow eyes, and the heavy jaw. It was the most fearsome hunter in the Americas. "Isn't that taking a lot for granted?" he said to Salazar.

Salazar looked at him curiously.

"I think he means that the cats already know we're here," Dan'l said. "And they'll be waiting for us, if our numbers ain't drove them off."

"Well?" Salazar said. He wanted to get this done with and get back to his military duties. "What do you recommend then, hunter of bears?"

Charlie glanced quickly at Dan'l, but he was smiling. "What do you think, Charlie? Are our jaguars still close by somewhere?"

Charlie wrinkled his rather flat nose again, and Dan'l's smile widened. He was glad Charlie had come. He might have been too old for real military duty, and he might be a drunk, but he knew this country.

"They are still here," Charlie finally announced. His pinkish scar shone in the sun. "This happens sometimes. When there are more than one of them—and they have just killed a man—they get very bold. They have thought about it, and believe they can take us."

Dan'l nodded and turned to see Salazar's reaction. Salazar took a deep breath, but said nothing.

"Maybe we ought to split up, two on each side of their trail," Dan'l said, thinking as he spoke. "'Cause there's two of them. That way they can't flank us."

"I'd agree with that," Kravitz said.

"This is not a band of Apaches!" Salazar said disgustedly. "Oh, very well. We will do as you say. But let us get this finished, this cat hunting, and get back to the column."

Dan'l and Charlie took the left side of the trail, and Kravitz and Salazar the other, and the two pairs rode on into the rocks about twenty feet apart, scanning carefully the rocks around them. In a few moments, the rocks were above their heads on both sides.

"Very dangerous now," Charlie whispered to himself. *"Muy peligroso."*

They all rode with their rifles carried across their saddles, loaded, primed and ready to fire. Kravitz was rightfully very tense. Dan'l could smell the cats now, too, almost as strongly as Charlie could, and he realized they must be lying in ambush. They figured four were not too many now that they were rested. Anyway, they did not like being driven out of their newly established territory.

It was Dan'l who heard the low growling first. It came from his side of the trail, and when he attracted Charlie's attention, Charlie heard it, too. Kravitz and Salazar were searching the rocks hurriedly, but saw nothing. Salazar, too, had caught the tension of the moment.

"Forward quietly," he said in a half-whisper. "We do not want to scare them off."

Charlie turned and gave him the kind of look he would have used on an escapee from a lunatic asylum. And then the cats came from nowhere.

The big male hurled itself at Dan'l from that side of the trail. It happened so fast that Dan'l barely had time to raise the muzzle of the long gun and squeeze the trigger. The gun exploded loudly in the rocks and echoed and re-echoed while the hot slug tore through the cat's underbelly, behind its chest. The bullet did not even slow the jaguar down. The cat hit Dan'l in the chest and face, and he felt great claws raking him across the shoulder and arm as he went plummeting off his horse.

The female had lunged upon Salazar at the same moment. He let out a muffled yelp, and tried to get his gun up, but failed. The female took him down off the horse with her, grabbing at him as if he were an antelope she wanted to keep from running. When they hit the ground the jaguar bit hard into his skull, killing him with one deadly bite. Salazar's eyes and jaw flew open, and blood spurted onto the cat's muzzle and chest.

Charlie had judiciously leapt off his horse, and Kravitz's pony kicked and bucked until he was thrown over its head and to the ground. In just seconds all four mounts were running off in different directions in panic.

Dan'l had hit the ground violently, the heavy cat on top of him, the iron smell of its pelt in his nostrils. He had the fired rifle up between himself and the snarling cat, and his strength was failing fast. He had never dealt with such frenzy, not even with grizzlies. And such quickness. It was overpowering. He wanted to get to his knife, but could not release his hold on the rifle, or he would be dead in seconds.

Charlie fired his Charleville, hoping to hit the animal and not Dan'l, and struck the big cat in the side, up near the shoulder.

The jaguar screamed so loud it hurt Dan'l's ears, jumped high in the air, then turned and hurled itself off Dan'l and onto the kneeling Indian.

In the meantime, Kravitz had gotten up onto one knee also, and now aimed his gun at the female cat, still ravaging Salazar, and fired one quick shot. The lead struck the cat behind its right ear. It leapt up, too, and fell onto its side, thrashing for a moment.

The male was now on Charlie, going for his neck. Charlie was doing the same as Dan'l, but had little strength against the cat. Dan'l drew his skinning knife, threw himself onto the jaguar's back, and plunged the knife into its neck, at the base of its skull.

The animal leapt high for the second time, throwing Dan'l onto his back again, then started to pounce toward him. Halfway through the attempt, it collapsed onto its side and died there, within reach of Dan'l's bloodstained hand.

The three men lay there, trying to suck air into their lungs, trying to make sense of what had happened. The big male twitched once more, and they all jumped back. But it was dead. Dan'l had severed its spinal cord.

Kravitz was the only one unscathed by the cats. But even he had sprained his shoulder in the fall from his mount. He got up now and went over to Salazar. He took one look and shook his head.

"Shit," Dan'l said quietly. He sat up and made a face. He had a deep gash across his chest, and several other, lesser ones on his torso and arms. There was a great deal of blood, and he needed bandages. Charlie had two shallow wounds on his side and belly, but did not seem to be bothered by them. He came and looked at Dan'l, raising his rawhide shirt. "This one will need a poultice and bandage."

"Salazar had some stuff on his mount," Kravitz said heavily. "I'll go try to find the horses while you look after Dan'l, Charlie."

Dan'l squinted in pain when he moved. "Hell,

I been worse grizzly-bit. Don't make no bother about me."

"Just stay put here," Kravitz told him.

Then he went off on foot looking for the horses.

Chapter Seven

They limped back to the column bivouac in early afternoon.

The body of Juan Salazar was thrown over the rump of Kravitz's horse, and Dan'l's chest wore a thick poultice bandage. Charlie wore a lesser one on his side, and the shirts of both men were torn to shreds.

Colonel Rivera was stunned when he saw Salazar's body, then furious. Officers and noncoms gathered around him, and he examined Salazar's corpse, then turned directly to Dan'l, his face livid. "I tried to tell you this was a useless exercise! Chasing two mountain cats! Delaying our march! Now look what has happened, damn you! I have lost one of my best officers to this foolishness!"

Dan'l was slumped on his saddle, and Rivera now saw the bandage through his ripped shirt. "What happened to you?"

"The same as happened to all of us," Dan'l said heavily. "We went through a few minutes of hell. Them animals was man-eaters. They would've attacked the column. Over and over. Now they're dead."

"Damn foolishness," Rivera spat out in Spanish. "Such damn foolishness!" He paced the ground, watched closely by the men around him. "I knew it! I knew I should not take outsiders!" He switched to English, turning back to Dan'l. "I knew you were trouble."

"He risked his life to save mine," Charlie said in good Spanish. All the soldiers gathered around heard the words clearly, and they all looked toward Dan'l.

Now Kravitz was angry again. "We done what had to be done, Colonel. We're just as sorry about Salazar as you."

Rivera glared at him.

"Now," Kravitz said slowly. "These two need medical aid. When you get finished with your assessment." He said the last word acidly. He himself had his left arm in a cloth sling, made from part of Salazar's shirt.

Rivera calmed down and saw the serious eyes of his men on him. "Yes, yes, of course. Medic!"

In the next hour, Salazar was buried hastily, Dan'l was given a better bandage for his chest wound, and his and Charlie's other wounds were tended. Dan'l's chest wound was not as deep as he had thought, and he expected it to heal fast, if he kept infection out of it. It would hamper his movement, though, and would make riding painful for a few days.

Both Dan'l and Charlie were issued blue uniform tunics before the column headed out again, in mid-afternoon, and Rivera was forced to appoint a successor to Salazar in that company. Kravitz suggested Dan'l.

"Protocol dictates that if another captain is available, he should take command," Kravitz stated flatly to Rivera in front of Dan'l and Rivera's other three captains. "Dan'l Boone holds that temporary rank. Given to him by the governor."

Rivera frowned curiously at Kravitz. "What? Appoint a civilian to command one of my cavalry companies? You must be joking, Kravitz."

"He is presently not a civilian, Colonel," Kravitz argued. "And he has certainly shown his ability to fight."

Dan'l made a sour face. "Let it go, Kravitz. I don't want it or need it."

"There, you see?" Rivera said. Actually, he was in a dilemma. The sergeant under Salazar, who would also be considered for a field promotion under ordinary circumstances, was not really competent to lead a company in battle. It was Torreon, the drinker.

But he would consider it an embarassment if

he appointed Dan'l, after opposing his coming on the expedition.

"I agree with Kravitz."

Rivera turned in surprise, and saw that one of his captains had spoken. The same one who had sided with Kravitz and Dan'l about going to Spanish Wells first.

"Ah. Yes?" Rivera said caustically.

"He has shown leadership qualities," the captain said in Spanish. His name was Delgado, and he was quite young.

Rivera could not believe it. He looked at the other two captains to get their reaction, and one was nodding in agreement with Delgado.

Rivera tried to hide his surprise. "I see," he said stiffly. He turned to the wounded Dan'l. "I realize you have served in the military, Mr. Boone, if we may call your home militias that. But have you served ever in any command position?"

Dan'l sighed. "In the Carolina Militia, yes. And later in the Continental Army. General Washington commended me for saving official documents and maps from falling into the hands of the British."

At that summary, there was a muttering of awe among the assembled officers when Kravitz translated for them.

Rivera stood there, not knowing what to do. Dan'l had obviously cleared himself of charges of inexperience. And then there was the hard-drinking, incompetent Sergeant Torreon, the one who had been drubbed soundly by Dan'l in the cantina. Rivera finally swallowed his pride, and turned to Dan'l.

"Very well, Mr. Boone. Or should I say, Captain Boone? I give you command of Company B."

Kravitz and the officers smiled.

"It's your decision, Colonel," Dan'l said.

"Yes. It is. Are you fit to ride?"

"I reckon I am, Colonel."

"Then we will move out immediately. To Spanish Wells." He smiled a small, taut smile. He had salvaged some authority, retained some dignity, at least. "Gentlemen, get your troops ready."

Dan'l took his position at the head of his company when they rode out, after Rivera announced his command. They all accepted him without question, and some were secretly pleased that the Kentuckian, the great Indian fighter, the one the Apaches were calling Ancient Bear, would lead them into battle.

The only one showing any reservations was Torreon, who was still nursing bruises put on him by Dan'l, and whose friend Gomez had missed the expedition because of Dan'l. But his attitude changed swiftly when, in late afternoon, before Dan'l rode out to the scouting position to find Charlie, he placed Torreon in charge and said he trusted him to do a good job. From that moment on, Torreon became one of Dan'l's loyal soldiers.

The column made its detour from Devil's Canyon about that time, and by early evening, with Rivera keeping them on the march, they arrived at Spanish Wells.

The sun was still up in the sky when they arrived there, and they were stunned by the complete destruction. No whole building had survived. With the column stopped outside the site, Rivera, his captains, and Kravitz entered the ruins of Spanish Wells. There was only desolation, and they saw no sign of life.

"They were all killed," Rivera offered, his mount guffering quietly in the setting sun. "But where are the corpses?"

It was at that moment that Pedro Rueda came stumbling out of the ruins, carrying a burnt musket.

"Don't shoot!" he called out weakly. "Don't shoot!"

Two captains had already drawn their side arms.

"Pare!" Rivera said sharply to them. "A survivor!"

Rueda looked drawn and emaciated as he came toward them. *"Gracias a Dios!"* he mumbled, dropping the musket halfway to them. "You have come! I knew you would!"

He turned and waved at the ruined building he had emerged from, and after a moment Elvira Lucas came out into the soft sun, with three children beside her.

"Good God!" Dan'l muttered.

"There are five of us!" Rueda said to Rivera. "Please. We need good water. And food."

Elvira just stood there in the sun for a moment, looking at the officers and the massed soldiers out at the edge of the ruins. She could not believe it for a long moment. She had lost hope. They had survived on polluted water, but she was very weak, as were the children.

"Where are the dead?" Rivera asked Rueda.

"We buried them. In a mass grave." Rueda pointed toward the far outskirts of the ruins, where a mound of dirt and rocks stood. "They are there."

"Those bastards," the young captain named Delgado said bitterly. "The dirty Apaches!"

"It is this way everywhere around here," Rueda told them. "They killed all settlers for a hundred miles."

"To avenge his defeat at Santa Fe," Rivera said grimly. Elvira now walked out to them, keeping the wan-looking children beside her. They looked frightened.

Rivera turned triumphantly to Dan'l and Kravitz. "Now do you see?" he said loudly to them. "This is why we came to Spanish Wells. These people need us. They need us now."

"Thank God you are here," Rueda said pitiably, understanding a little of Rivera's English.

Elvira was there now. She was fluent in Spanish, and used it now. "You are Colonel Rivera of Santa Fe, I presume?" She looked very weak, and her face was dirt-smeared. Her blondish hair was unkempt.

Rivera's chest expanded at the thought that this woman would know who the commander at Santa Fe was. He glanced toward Kravitz before he replied. "Why, yes, madam. At your service."

"We could probably have lasted another week, if we conserved our energy. But thank God we did not have to, Colonel."

Kravitz and Dan'l exchanged a knowing look, while Rivera avoided their eyes. "Well, who knows? You might have been dead tomorrow, drinking this water. But you are quite safe now. Captain Delgado, take these people aboard one of the supply wagons and feed them."

"Yes, sir," Delgado said briskly.

The officer dismounted and led the survivors to the column, a hundred yards away. Rivera watched them go for a moment, then dismounted, and so did Dan'l and the other officers, followed by Kravitz. They led their horses into the ruins and looked around.

"This is the Apache," Rivera said bitterly. "Very efficient. No loose ends, ordinarily."

Dan'l kept looking off past the buildings, hoping they would not be ambushed. All seemed quiet out there on the shimmering horizon.

"We will encamp here tonight," Rivera said at last. "In the morning, we will discuss the best time and manner of attacking Yellow Horse's stronghold."

"I suggest we send a scout out to make sure he's still in the canyon," Dan'l said. "He might just be planning an offensive of his own. He must know we're here."

Rivera smiled. "He knows, all right."

"I'll volunteer to go," Dan'l told him. "I could take Charlie with me."

Rivera sighed. "The Apache prides himself on arranging impregnable defenses. Yellow Horse will wait for us in the canyon. He wants us to expend our strength by throwing ourselves against an impenetrable perimeter."

"He might also send some warriors to test our firepower," Dan'l said. "A couple of us might find that out, if we could get past his sentries."

"No, he will not venture out, even in a small force. Not at this time, under these circumstances." He turned from Dan'l, making it clear that that discussion was finished. "Let's prepare to make camp, Captains."

Kravitz caught his gaze. "Colonel. Do you intend to take the survivors with us to Devil's Canyon?"

Rivera frowned. "Of course. They travel with us now."

Kravitz glanced at Dan'l, who said, "They might be safer here, Colonel. We can come back this way when it's over."

Rivera screwed up his swarthy face in dismay. "First you want to pass these poor people by—act as if they are not here—and leave them to die in this wilderness. And now you suggest we abandon them here with a little food and water, now that they think they have been rescued? *Increible, Capitan!* Do you not find this suggestion cruel?"

"I find it sensible, Colonel," Dan'l answered. He was becoming more and more irritated with the pompous, incompetent Spanish officer. "But you're the boss."

"Yes." Rivera said. "Yes, I am. Now see to your duties, Captain Boone."

Dan'l touched a hand to his brow. "Anything you say, Colonel."

In the village of Yellow Horse, there was raw excitement in the air. Runners had come back telling of the approaching Spaniards, and they had found out that Dan'l was in the fighting force. The runners could not get around the whole perimeter of the column, but they knew there were over a hundred cavalry coming. That, and the fact that Dan'l was with the small army, worried Yellow Horse.

On that early evening when the Santa Fe expeditionary force was encamping at Spanish Wells, and Rueda and Elvira Lucas were getting their first real meal in a week, Yellow Horse met again with his shamans and his son, Running Dog, to talk strategy. He had already called his top warriors together, and planned a defensive stand in the canyon. Now Yellow Horse was deciding whether to listen to Running Dog, and send out a war party the following morning to harass the Spaniards and test their firepower. That would be important to them when the big attack came against their village.

The fire in the center of the big tipi was burning more brightly this time, but the two shamans had shed their straw masks in favor of very fancy headgear. One wore the head of a grizzly bear, with just his face showing in its open mouth. The other had a tall cap atop his weathered face, adorned with fancy beads and feathers. Both of their faces were painted with war paint.

Yellow Horse wore no special clothing or decorations. Sometimes, when the occasion was as serious as this one, he would come to a palaver almost naked, and let others do most of the talking. Running Dog wore only a fancy breechcloth and high moccasins, and the usual armbands with trailing ribbons. But he carried a long war lance across his knees, with its painted shaft and eagle feathers secured to it with brightly colored cloth.

"Long ago we waged war on Santa Fe, and won," Yellow Horse finally said to those present, after a long silence. "We will drive the white man out again. But first we must defeat this army sent to attack us in our homes."

Running Dog took a buffalo-calf tobacco pouch from his belt, and tamped some of its contents into a short, personal pipe. But Yellow Horse looked over at him sternly, and he put it down. Protocol was strict in these meetings.

Nobody smoked unless the chief smoked. Nobody walked between the chief and the fire. Only the chief could initiate the conversation, and then it must stay on the subject he introduced.

Running Dog did not put much importance on protocol, though, and had to be reminded occasionally by his father. Around his waist he wore the red-dyed elkskin sash of the society of warriors, called Crazy Dogs, which was the most elite group outside of the shamans.

Outside the tipi there were the sounds and music of *gahe* dancers, who were dancing for a victory against the Spaniards. The last time they had taken a Spaniard prisoner, on their first expedition against Santa Fe, these same dancers had tied the poor fellow to a post over an open fire, and while he began screaming in agony, they'd shot his body full of arrows. Then they'd cut his chest open, caught his blood in a buffalo-stomach paunch, and cooked his heart and eaten it. Later they'd studied reflections in the pool of blood in the paunch, to see their future in it.

"We will send them to their Spanish hell!" Running Dog declared. It was all right for him to speak now, since Yellow Horse had first spoken. "We will boil their white bodies in cooking oil, and eat their livers with the desert bean!"

The shaman with the bear headdress began chanting quietly, and then the other one joined him in a musical prayer to White-Painted

Woman and Pahy, the Sun God. The shaman with the tall buckskin cap wore a thick bead necklace with a polished yew medicine cross suspended from it, to make his powers of magic more potent.

Some black powder was thrown into the fire by the man with the bear head. The fire sizzled, and white smoke curled upward. "Aiiiy!" the shaman called.

"What do the spirits show us?" Yellow Horse asked, his eyes tightly closed.

"The smoke reveals two great armies battling," the bear-man replied in a singsong voice. Both he and the other shaman had been careful not to pray to the god called Ancient Bear in the last few days. That was now considered inappropriate.

"We know that," Running Dog said testily.

"Will our village survive?" Yellow Horse asked.

The other shaman said, "Ancient Bear is with this army. His power prevents our seeing into the smoke clearly."

"If Ancient Bear wishes to destroy the village, it will require all of the medicine we can call down to prevent it," the bear-man said.

"Then I will kill him!" Running Dog exclaimed. "This is a man, not a god. He has no power over me."

"He may be protected by his soldiers," the bear-man told him. "Even if you get to him, Running Dog, you had better pray that White-

Painted Woman and Killer of Enemies are on your side, and will assist you in Ancient Bear's defeat."

"I do not need the power of ancient gods to kill this impostor from the East." Running Dog raised the war lance from his knees. "I require only this, and my strong arm."

Yellow Horse opened his eyes and scowled at his son. "By the Holy Spirits! Do not blaspheme in this place, you impudent boy! You will accept all the medicine you can obtain from any source, to defeat this force that is assembled against us. Tonight you will pray to all the ancient spirits. Do you understand me?"

Running Dog hesitated, allowing himself to regain some calm. He finally lowered his eyes. "Yes, my father."

Yellow Horse nodded to his advisors.

The shaman with the tall headdress now spoke again. "It is well that Running Dog has no fear, because someone must seek out Ancient Bear and try to kill him. It may be impossible to do so, but it must be tried if Yellow Horse wishes to continue as the great chief of the combined bands of Apache."

"If Ancient Bear is not killed," the other shaman said very slowly, "this entire village will be destroyed, and the Apache will be decimated, so that Ancient Bear may start a new society afresh, with his chosen few. He will bring down the thunder and lightning, and rage among us like the grizzly, and he will tear our hearts out and devour them in his anger."

Running Dog muttered something, but Yellow Horse ignored it.

"Then it is written in the smoke," Yellow Horse said solemnly. "We will resist the return of Ancient Bear. We have declared him enemy, and we call upon all the magic of the ancient spirits to defend our tribe against his onslaught. So be it."

"So be it," the shamans echoed in unison.

After supper at the bivouac, Rivera called his captains and Kravitz into his tent, reiterated his belief that they were safe at that site and that Yellow Horse would not bother them there, and announced that he was posting twice the usual number of sentries until dawn. Dan'l and Kravitz kept their silence this time, because Rivera had made it clear he was not open to further suggestions.

Rivera's command tent was the only one thrown up that evening. The four companies of soldiers were asked to sleep on groundsheets, with their boots on, because of their proximity to Devil's Canyon. Many small fires were lighted, though, throughout the camp, since Yellow Horse knew their location, anyway. The soldiers sat in groups around the fires, told each other stories of previous battles, and tried not to think about what was coming for them.

Dan'l and Kravitz bedded down near each other, up against an adobe wall at the edge of the burnt-out ruins. Dan'l had seen that his company was fed and taken care of, and then left Torreon with them. Dan'l and Kravitz talked for a short time about tactics, and after a while Kravitz went off to see how Scarface Charlie was doing. Charlie was understandably tense about being so close to Yellow Horse. If he was captured by the Apaches, things would go very badly for him. The Apaches were not kind to one of their own who sided with the enemy, and they considered Charlie an Apache.

Kravitz had been gone for just a few minutes when Dan'l looked up and saw Elvira Lucas approaching him. For a moment, silhouetted by the fires in the growing darkness, she looked just like Rebecca, the wife he had left back in Missouri.

"Ah, there you are," she said as she came up to him. "I was told I'd find you over here."

Dan'l rose and grimaced in pain from his chest wound. "Well. Good to see you, ma'am. I reckon the kids is snugged down for sleep about now?"

"Please don't stand," she said. "I heard about your wound." she sat down against the wall, pulling her ankle-length dress to her shoes. Dan'l sat down beside her.

"Yes, the children are fine. I asked Mr. Rueda to watch over them while I took a short walk. It is a beautiful night, isn't it?"

Dan'l looked up at an almost-full moon. He realized that the camp was more visible in its light, and disliked having to look at it from that military perspective.

"Yes, ma'am," he said.

"When I heard there was an American with the troops, I just had to talk with you," she said to him with a pretty smile. "I hope you don't mind."

"Not a bit, ma'am," Dan'l said. She seemed a comely woman to him, and he wondered what she was doing out here in the Spanish Southwest, by herself with two children.

"Somebody said you're from Kentucky," she said. "I've never been there."

"Well, me and mine live in Missouri now. But I spent a lot of my life in Kentucky and Carolina."

"My husband took me and the children to New Orleans from Charleston," she said. "Charleston was a lovely town, but I guess it's been damaged by the Revolution. That's why we went south. To get the children away from all that."

"It was hell for a while," Dan'l admitted. "But it all come out good. What took you out this way, ma'am?"

"Robert brought us here. For a free land grant out of Mexico City. I liked Santa Fe, and wish we'd stayed there. But Robert thought the land was better down here. We didn't know about the Apache."

"What happened to Robert?" Dan'l asked.

"He took a fever last year. I nursed him day

and night. He looked like he was over it. Then he just went real sudden." She looked up at the moon seriously, as if trying to read her future in the mysteries of its surface.

"I'm right sorry to hear that, ma'am."

She sighed. "I been working at the trading post, trying to keep things going. I'd decided to try to get back to New Orleans. Then this happened. I guess we're lucky we're not all dead."

"Right lucky," Dan'l agreed. He felt a little awkward with her.

"You say your family is in Missouri," she said. "I might ask what you're doing here, too."

Dan'l smiled. "I brung some investors out. I got this thing inside of me, ma'am. I got to see what's on the other side of the hill, I reckon. I always been that way."

She returned the smile. "And you volunteered to go find Yellow Horse?"

"That's right."

"I find you a remarkable man, Mr. Boone."

Dan'l looked over at her. It was good to see a fair-haired woman out here in the territory of Spaniards and mestizos. "I reckon you to be a remarkable woman, Miss Elvira." He glanced down at his thick hands for a moment. "Listen. Rivera wants you with us, God knows why. We got some fighting to do, and it'll get dangerous for you and the kids. You keep well to the back of it, ma'am. You hear me?"

Elvira held Dan'l's serious look, and found

that she liked him. "Why, yes. I can do that, Mr. Boone."

"You keep way out of it."

"Captain Delgado said you're an experienced Indian fighter," Elvira said after a long moment. "Was that in Kentucky?"

"Yes, ma'am. And call me Dan'l."

"All right, Dan'l. Do you think this army can subdue the bloodthirsty Yellow Horse? Or must I fear a defeat?"

Dan'l regarded her soberly. "We got the wherefore to get the job done," he said.

She sighed again. "I'm pleased to hear that. I worry so over the children. If it weren't for you, we'd still be out here alone, of course."

"Don't give me no credit for your quick rescue, ma'am," Dan'l said, regarding her sideways. "I wanted to pass you by. Go right to Yellow Horse and get the job done. Then come and look for survivors here at Spanish Wells. You can thank Rivera for being with us now."

Elvira thought about that for a moment, while Dan'l studied her face in the moonlight. It was a strong, beautiful face, with blue eyes and a full mouth. Her blond hair was disheveled, but that did not detract from her attractiveness.

"You were probably right," she finally said to him. "This bivouac is dangerous, isn't it?"

Dan'l was surprised. "Yes, ma'am. It is."

"We could have held out for another week," she said. "We might have lost our faith in rescue, but that wouldn't have mattered. In the long run."

Dan'l grinned. "Like I said, you're a remarkable woman."

She smiled nicely. "As I said about you, you're a remarkable man."

It was just after the troops' post-dawn meal the following morning, while Rivera still relaxed in his tent, shaving with cold water, that they came.

There were only thirty of them, and they had no guns. Yellow Horse was saving the few he had for the big battle. These warriors came with bows only, and did not attempt to penetrate the defenses of the camp. They rode in wide circles, barking out their staccato war cries, and sailing their arrows into the bivouac wildly. Always moving. Never giving an easy target.

Because Rivera had been so sure they would not be attacked, and because he had withdrawn two thirds of his night sentries at dawn, the troop was taken completely by surprise.

Except for Dan'l.

After he had finished eating ahead of the others, he had ridden out past the sentries, toward Devil's Canyon, and had seen them coming. It was he who had raised the alarm.

He came thundering into the bivouac on the mottled appaloosa, yelling loudly.

"Apaches! Apaches! Form your perimeters!"

Absolute chaos followed. Men were washing

mess kits, and pulling on tunics. Some were bridling mounts. None were ready for the assault, including the Taos Indians with them.

Colonel Rivera came out of his tent with his face soaped for shaving, a razor in his fist, no shirt on.

"What? What is it?"

Dan'l dismounted and came running up to him, his face grim. "It's them! They're right behind me!"

Rivera could not believe it. But just seconds later, they were there, yelling and whooping, and the deadly arrows began to fall into the bivouac.

Dan'l found Elvira and the children at a nearby wagon with Rueda. Kravitz was with them, looking stunned, loading his rifle.

"Get them under that wagon!" Dan'l yelled to his friend. "Stay with them!"

"It's done, Dan'l!"

"Rueda! You stay put, too!"

"*Sí*, Capitan Boone."

The Spaniards were firing rounds off at the circling Apaches, but not hitting much of anything. Rivera was armed, with shaving soap still lathered on his swarthy face, and was aiming at the galloping Indians. He fired and hit an Apache, and the warrior fell from his horse, hit through the head. Dan'l had hit a warrior, too, and knocked him off his racing mount. Now he crouched in the open, priming the Annely pistol he had been issued, and fired again and again as arrows flew past him. He saw soldiers hit around him—in the side, the chest, the leg—and still the Apaches circled, some of them not firing at all. Counting. That was what they were doing, Dan'l realized. Counting guns.

"Return fire!" Rivera shouted crazily. "Make them pay for coming here! Knock them off their horses!"

Dan'l raced to the troops of Company B, which he commanded. *"Aprisa!"* he shouted at them. "Load and fire!" He walked among them, arrows whizzing past him. "Make a circle! Protect each other's backs!" All of this was translated by Torreon.

They followed his orders, and knelt in a loose circle, so that they were all facing the enemy and protecting their comrades. They were beginning to hit Indians with hot lead.

The rest of the command was still disorganized, running about, trying to find cover where there was none, except for the wagons parked on one perimeter. Elvira, Rueda, and the children huddled under one of them, lying flat, trying to keep from getting hit, either by Indians or Spanish firepower.

"Close ranks!" Rivera yelled. He had seen how effective Dan'l's troops had been in their closed formation. "Close your ranks up! Defend your—"

An iron-tipped arrow struck him in the side like a bolt of lightning. Dan'l heard him cry out dully, and turned to see him go down.

"Son of a bitch!" Dan'l grated out. He ran to the supine colonel, examined the arrow sticking out of his side, and dragged him to the nearest wagon, out of the heavy fire. He leaned him up against the wheel of the vehicle.

"Don't go anywhere, Colonel. I'll be back."

Rivera looked up into Dan'l's square, bearded face. *"Gracias, Capitán."*

Dan'l turned, aimed at a circling Indian, and fired. The Apache went flying off his mount. Then, at a signal from a warrior in charge, they all galloped off as suddenly as they had come.

It was over.

Yellow Horse would now know the strength of his enemy.

Dan'l lowered his side arm and looked around. There were a number of dead and wounded. Out beyond the bivouac area, there were over twenty dead and almost-dead Apaches. A sergeant from another company was out there, finishing off the injured. Dan'l watched somberly. He knew this was the way things were done out here. But he did not like it.

He went to the wagon where he had left Elvira and the children. They had crawled out from under the wagon, but Elvira was holding the little mestizo boy to her bosom, and tears were streaming down her face. She looked up at Dan'l.

"My Toby and Janie are all right," she said quietly. "But little Robi is dead."

Rueda was sitting on the ground beside her, shaking his head slowly. Neither of them had known the boy for more than the few days since the attack on the settlement, but Elvira had come to think of him as one of her own.

"Goddamn," Dan'l murmured.

"It was a ricochet bullet," Elvira explained. "He never knew what hit him."

Dan'l was angry, but knew that anger did nobody any good. "We'll get him buried with the others," he said.

He walked slowly over to Rivera. A couple of officers were already there, and they had removed the arrow from Rivera's side.

Dan'l knelt down beside him and looked at the wound. He had seen worse. "How bad is it?" he asked Rivera.

Rivera held his hand over the wound. "I will be all right. It did not hit anything vital."

Dan'l nodded. "That's good." He did not say that he had warned Rivera of this. He did not say that the survivors from Spanish Wells had been subjected to great danger, and that one of them had been unnecessarily killed. But he wanted to.

"You may have saved my life, Boone," Rivera said to Dan'l, and all of the old arrogance was gone. He did not feel arrogant anymore. "And you were right. We should have gone directly to Devil's Canyon."

Dan'l shrugged. "Knowing what we got ain't

going to beat us necessarily. I'll arrange a burial detail, Colonel."

Rivera squinted up at him. "Please do, Captain."

"We ought to have an infirmary, too. Set it up and mount a guard on it when we leave. You ought to be in it."

Rivera shook his head. "No. I'll be ready to ride. I suspect we should move to Devil's Canyon immediately. Do you agree?"

Dan'l nodded. "I would."

Rivera let out a deep breath, and winced. "Help get the column ready to move, Captain."

Dan'l rose to his feet. "Incidentally. One of the kids is dead. Stray bullet."

Rivera hissed through his teeth. *"Que terrible!"*

"My thought exactly," Dan'l growled.

Chapter Eight

It took a while to bury the dead.

In the meantime, Dan'l and another captain assigned a detail to erect a canopy from two wagon covers, and the wounded were placed on bedrolls under the canopy for treatment.

There was only one man present, in Company A, who had any medical training, and he began digging out arrowheads and closing wounds immediately. Elvira, who saw how overwhelmed he was, volunteered to assist him, which meant that she and the children would remain behind when the column left for Devil's Canyon.

Dan'l knew they could not be ready to leave before early afternoon, so he and a couple of sergeants helped with the wounded, too. He found himself working beside Elvira, and he was surprised to find how competent she was. Her woman's touch was much appreciated by the wounded, and several of them told her so.

Dan'l was carefully removing an iron arrowhead from a private soldier when Elvira spoke to him from over another wounded man close by. They were both working from a kneeling position, since all the wounded were still on the ground. A sergeant was still trying to find a group of folding cots that had been brought along for officers.

"It looks like Janie will be all right," Elvira said to Dan'l without looking over at him. "She's only five, and has no idea what's going on, thank God. But eight-year-old Toby asked me what happened to his new friend Robi. I had to tell him."

Dan'l made a last pull and extracted a wicked-looking arrow point from the soldier's chest. The dark-haired fellow was biting down on two lead balls from his ammo pouch. He now spat them out, and grinned weakly up at Dan'l.

"*Mil gracias*," he said.

"*De nada*," Dan'l told him. He was learning a few words of Spanish, but not enough to speak to any of them at any length.

He looked at Elvira. "I guess he's got to know about this sometime, ma'am. Living out here."

"I won't come back down here," Elvira said. She was tying a bandage around a soldier's biceps, and he was smiling up at her pleasantly, not understanding any of what she was saying to Dan'l. "No matter what happens with Yellow Horse."

"It ain't much of a place to raise kids," Dan'l offered.

"Do you have any children, Dan'l?" she asked him tentatively. Asking, really, if he was married.

"Yes, ma'am. Several. Back in Missouri. And a right purty wife, too."

He did not turn to see her reaction. He kept working on the soldier's wound, sterilizing it now as best he could.

"I see," she said after a moment.

Dan'l decided to fill the silence. "She didn't want to come to Missouri. She thought she'd made Kentucky her home. But she'll go anywhere I ask her to. Damn fine woman."

Elvira looked over at him now, and he was staring off into the encampment, thinking. Rebecca had not wanted him to come on this trip west, either. She thought she might not see him again. But his deep need had overwhelmed her, and she had relented. Not many women would have put up with him. He knew that well. Rebecca was one in a million.

"Then I guess you've . . . made a fine marriage," Elvira said, watching his face.

Her words brought him back to the present. "Oh, yes, ma'am. I couldn't done no better if I looked a hundred years. Ain't hardly nobody else would've stayed with me, and that's the truth of it."

"I just find that hard to believe, Dan'l," Elvira said quietly. She had met a lot of men out on the frontier, before and after her husband's death, but none of them were quite like this Dan'l Boone. She had never met a man, including her deceased husband, who radiated such masculine magnetism.

Dan'l was embarrassed. "Excuse me, ma'am. I want to talk to your friend Rueda."

Dan'l rose and walked over to the closest wagon, where Rueda was trying on a Spanish tunic and examining a rifle that had been given to him. He understood English well, so Dan'l did not need Kravitz for translation.

"I see you been outfitted, Rueda," Dan'l said as he walked up to him.

"*Sí*, I have volunteered to fight Yellow Horse," Rueda said grimly. "For my little friend Robi."

"You mean, go to Devil's Canyon?"

"*Exacto*."

Dan'l let out a long breath, and stared at the ground for a moment. "Rueda. I come to ask you to stay with Elvira. Here at the bivouac."

Rueda frowned. "Stay here? No, senor. I fight with the soldiers. The fire is in my belly."

"Listen to me, *compadre*," Dan'l said slowly. "Colonel Rivera is leaving only a handful of men here to protect the wounded. And Elvira and her children. Do you understand?"

"Yes. I understand. Of course there will be

some danger to them. But there will be more in the canyon."

"You won't be needed in the canyon," Dan'l said to him. "Not as much as you're needed here. She don't know any of these men. She spent several days of hell with you. You'd be a big comfort to her. It's a good thing she's doing. You can help with the wounded, too. They need you. Elvira needs you."

"But Robi. I let him die," Rueda said, his face screwed up in pain. "I must do something to avenge him."

Dan'l placed a hand on his shoulder. "You fought well. We all let him die. Together—us at the canyon, and you here—we can make Yellow Horse pay for these deaths. Please help us, amigo. In the right way."

Rueda looked into Dan'l's eyes. *"Muy bien, compadre.* I will stay."

Dan'l was glad. Elvira deserved it. She was one gutsy woman.

The burial detail was completed by noon, and many of the wounded had already been tended. Rivera had a thick bandage on his rib cage, under his bright tunic, and Dan'l found him at a map table, planning their route to the canyon. Scarface Charlie stood beside him, pointing out a geographic feature, and Kravitz also stood nearby.

"The burial is done, Colonel," Dan'l announced as he strode up to the small group, under a small green canopy. "We can march on your command."

"Ah, good, Captain Boone. And the wounded are being taken care of properly?"

"Your medic and the Lucas woman is doing a great job, Colonel. She'll stay and keep on with it."

"Fine. I've already assigned a detail to watch over them. We'll march within the hour. I'll advise the other captains to form up ranks."

"We can be there in just over an hour," Charlie said.

Rivera nodded. "We will fight the battle today."

"I have been trying to dissuade the colonel from going," Kravitz said to Dan'l. "We have his plan of attack, which we will execute to the letter. His presence is not required. He cannot fight with that side wound."

Rivera drew his side arm and brandished it. "This will do my fighting for me." He laid it on the table, and his face grew serious. "My presence *is* required, Kravitz. Good or bad, I am the leader of this garrison. The men know me, and are familiar with the sight of me at their fore. They need me out there. I hope this does not sound boastful, but they look for me out there. I must go."

Dan'l nodded in agreement, surprising Kravitz. "I thought it over, Colonel, and you're right. None of us can lead this army like you can. I'd feel the same way, if I was their commander."

"Damn it, Dan'l!" Kravitz complained.

Rivera smiled at their disagreement. "It is all right, Kravitz. You are concerned with my welfare, and I appreciate that. But Boone knows it is the welfare of the column that is uppermost in importance. He has had the weight of command on his shoulders before he ever came here."

Kravitz caught Dan'l's serious look. "I know. I am sorry, my friend. You are undoubtedly right."

Dan'l shrugged. "I reckon we both are."

"Charlie, prepare to move out," Rivera said crisply, rising from a chair at the table, his left arm in a sling. "Kravitz, get my other captains over here."

"Yes, sir," Kravitz replied. He had noticed the change in the colonel, since Dan'l Boone had joined this expedition, and he was pleased at what he saw.

When they were gone, Rivera met Dan'l's gaze, and held it for a long moment. "I wanted to tell you, Captain Boone. In case I am not able at a later time. I feel very fortunate that the governor recruited you for this trek."

Dan'l was surprised by the remark. "I'm mighty glad to hear that, Colonel."

"Every time we have disagreed, you have been right," Rivera went on. "I needed your experience. Your . . . expertise."

"You do all right yourself," Dan'l said.

Rivera made a face. "I know I am not the best

commander in the territory. I am not a fool, Boone. My uncle is very close to Viceroy de Galvez. That is how I received this appointment."

Dan'l did not know what to say.

"It is my knowledge of my . . . insufficiency that has made me stupidly hostile toward you, whom I sensed at once to be everything I want to be."

"Colonel—"

"No, you do not have to deny any of it. Maybe in ten years, if I survive, I may have some of your know-how, Boone. In the meantime, I will keep trying to learn. If you should ever seek a permanent commission with my command, I will recommend it to the governor."

"That's real good of you, Colonel."

"Of course, you would have to learn some Spanish." Rivera grinned.

Dan'l grinned, too. "I reckon you do as well as a lot of officers of higher rank, Colonel," he said. "And I seen you fight, at Santa Fe and here at Spanish Wells. I don't suppose there's a better soldier in your outfit."

Rivera extended his hand and Dan'l clasped it.

"That means much to me, Captain," Rivera said. "*Gracias.*"

"*Por nada,*" Dan'l replied.

The column broke camp less than an hour later, and headed toward the village of Yellow Horse, in the red-butte Devil's Canyon.

It was still mid-afternoon when the small army arrived at the mouth of the canyon. A wind had blown up, and dark clouds had gathered behind them. Dan'l kept looking toward the sky. He had never seen a sky quite like it in Kentucky.

Rivera held up his hand for the long column to halt. He had been in this area before, but was not familiar with the geography. The canyon might have an escape route at its rear somewhere. He had no way of knowing. Scarface Charlie had never been in the canyon, and had not been able to determine its terrain from his brief scouting for the column.

There were boulders sitting in the floor of the canyon, also, so the village itself, about a mile inside, was barely visible. No Apache army could be seen from where Rivera sat his mount, but he knew they were there. Probably in about the same numbers as his own expeditionary force.

Rivera sat his mount stiff-backed, with his captains surrounding him, staring into the canyon, the warm wind at his back making his clothing flutter. Kravitz and Charlie also were up at the fore with him.

"Just as we thought. They wait for us," Rivera said into the wind. "But where are they?"

Charlie looked very old and very Indian on his spotted pinto. He put a dark brown hand up to hold his black hat on. "As soon as we enter the canyon, they will be there," he prophesied. "On the canyon rims, on both sides of us. They will have the high ground, and they will make good use of it. When they have attacked us from both sides, catching us in their crossfire, Yellow Horse will send his troops right down this canyon floor, right at us. I hope we are ready."

One of the horses guffered nervously, and Rivera's black stallion pranced in a small circle. Dan'l looked back at the threatening sky behind them. The weather was changing dramatically.

"It looks like a storm is brewing," Dan'l said.

"It is a blue norther," Captain Delgado said from beside him on his horse.

Dan'l turned to him. "A blue what?"

"It's a particular kind of storm," Kravitz said, looking at the sky. "Peculiar to the dry country. Big winds, but very little rain, if any."

Charlie was looking, too. "Big winds, big trouble."

Rivera squinted into the wind, which was blowing some sand now. "In the winter, men have frozen stiff in it. Still in their saddles. Bad ones drive women mad."

Dan'l thought of Elvira, back at the bivouac. He was glad he had talked Rueda into staying with her.

"This one will come in a hot wind," Rivera went on. "The wind will howl until you can't hear yourself talk, and you may not be able to see thirty feet. Unfortunately, the animals will be terrified."

"Now what do we do?" Charlie asked.

One of the captains spoke up. "We go now! To beat the storm. It will take well over an hour to reach us." He said to Rivera, "We can have Yellow Horse on his knees by then."

Kravitz looked at the sky, and ran a hand over his mouth. Nature had its ways of intervening in the most important human enterprises.

Zigzag lightning crackled through the boiling sky on the far horizon, illuminating the blue-blackness. But there appeared to be no rain.

"I have seen hail in them as big as small cannonballs," Kravitz said worriedly. "We could also just wait it out. Yellow Horse pays it just as much respect as we do."

"Yellow Horse is secure in his hole," Charlie offered. "He will not be tempted to attack us because of delay."

Dan'l felt a gust of wind pull at his broad-brimmed Quaker hat, and squinted into the canyon, where he could see nothing.

"Is that true about Yellow Horse?" he said to Charlie.

Rivera looked over at him.

"*Como?*" Charlie said.

"What Kravitz said. About Yellow Horse being as scared of this thing as we are."

Charlie thought about that for a moment, while they all looked toward him.

"Well. It depends on what his shamans are telling him right now. And his *gahe* dancers. The Thunder Spirit is much feared, but sometimes it comes to help the Apache. The dancers will be shaking hand rattles from gourds, or buffalo scrotums. They will have visions. The visions will tell them whether the storm will help or hinder."

"And what's the most likely?" Dan'l asked.

Charlie grinned a crooked grin. He had stayed sober all through the trek, and had gained Dan'l's utmost respect.

"I think they will take it as a bad omen," Charlie said slowly. "And with Ancient Bear leading the white army into battle, they probably think you called down the spirits to make this storm, and are controlling it."

Dan'l nodded and turned to Rivera. "Colonel, I think we should attack *in* the storm."

Rivera frowned curiously at him. "During it?"

"Yes."

"I don't know, Captain. I don't know if our troops can fight through such a thing. It looks like a big one."

"It will be as tough for the Apache as for us," Dan'l told him.

"Visibility will be almost zero," Kravitz said. "Some of the animals will go crazy. You might not control them in a charge. I say we should probably go now, Dan'l, before the storm arrives."

The wind was rising. Sand was being picked up in it, and they could feel it on their skin.

Dan'l turned back to Rivera. "I don't agree. We got a big advantage, Colonel. Let's use it. If they see us coming at them in the middle of this storm, knowing I'm with you, it might just scare the hell out of them. Their superstition about Ancient Bear might work against them. What does it matter that it ain't real? That it's all swamp gas? They don't know that."

Charlie sighed inaudibly.

"You might have something, Boone," Rivera said thoughtfully. He moved his left arm and made a face. Dan'l, too, could feel his own wound hurting from the fight with the big cat, and hoped his restriction of movement did not get him killed in the coming battle.

"I say we delay here till it hits us with its full force," Dan'l concluded. "Then ride in with it. If nothing else, it might catch them by surprise."

"It is a wise plan," Charlie offered from his mount.

Rivera was convinced. "Very well. Captains, get your people dismounted."

A couple of them exchanged dubious glances. A thickset one beside Captain Delgado said in Spanish, "Colonel, look at our men. They are already apprehensive of the storm. I don't know if we can even get them re-mounted in the middle of it."

Rivera nodded. "I know. But we will try. It should be upon us soon. Keep the men in tight formation, securing the reins of their animals. We don't want to lose many horses."

"Maybe the horses will be more manageable galloping into the canyon," Delgado suggested, "than just sitting here bombarded by the storm."

"We will hope so," Rivera said. "Get at it, Captains!"

Kravitz turned his mount to ride off with the others. He grinned at Dan'l as he passed by him.

"I hope you know what you are up to, Kentuckian. This looks like a wild one. I knew a Mexico City dandy that got caught in one for the first time a while back. His hair turned white overnight. He returned to civilization hurriedly, and has never been seen in the territory again. The Apaches' dogs sometimes lose control and end up biting their own innards, killing themselves. A mountain man, a few years ago, was killed by a skinny little cottonwood branch caught in the wind of a norther. Lanced him through and through, like an Apache war spear."

"You make it sound right nasty," Dan'l said with a slow grin.

Then he rode back to his company.

Behind them, the storm rolled forward like a black curtain from Hades.

Chapter Nine

The harsh wind was rising quickly.

Black, boiling clouds rolled overhead, close enough that it seemed the men could reach up and touch them.

Sheet lightning now rippled through the clouds, momentarily casting white light across an afternoon that had gone almost midnight-dark. In that quick light, pale, scared faces stared straight ahead toward the canyon, the mouth of which had been obscured from them as if a big door had been closed on it.

As the winds mounted, howling in their ears and tearing at their clothing, some light rain pelted their faces for a few moments, but then the air was dry again, with sand from the ground beginning to hit them like needle pricks.

Horses in the big column guffered and whinnied nervously, their reins held tightly by each soldier, who either stood hard against his animal's flank, or crouched or knelt on one knee. Waiting for it to get worse.

And they knew it would.

Dan'l and Kravitz waited together at the front of Company B, which was situated on the right flank of A Company, just outside the mouth of the wide canyon. Those two companies would be the first in, and the other two would follow close on their heels. It would be a cavalry charge the likes of which this territory had never seen.

Somebody tried to erect a canopy over Rivera, but it would not stay put. He sat huddled on a small, straight chair, all by himself for the moment, between the two lead companies, an orderly kneeling by his side. Rivera was wrapped in his own deep thoughts. It was important to him to win this fight against Yellow Horse. Not just for Alvarado, or Viceroy de Galvez. For himself. To restore his own image of himself, as a leader of men.

Up nearer the canyon mouth stood a lonely figure in the wind. It was Scarface Charlie, watching the sky, waiting to tell Rivera that the storm was almost at its height. He was facing into the biting wind, trying to keep his balance.

"How much longer is he going to wait?" Kravitz called to Dan'l above the sound of the wind.

Dan'l glanced at him. He had taken his hat off

and stuffed it into his belt. His graying hair blew in all directions, and his lined face looked hard.

"It won't be long now," Dan'l said. "We want to go at the worst, to get maximum effect."

"You don't think this is enough effect?" Kravitz said with a crooked grin.

Dan'l grunted. "It's as bad as I ever been in already. But Charlie knows his stuff."

They were kneeling out in front of the huddled men and horses, their own mounts held steady by two private soldiers, off to one side. Dan'l's appaloosa was surprisingly calm, just prancing a little when a severe gust swept past.

Dan'l pointed to the right of the canyon mouth. "We'll go in hugging that wall over there. That way we won't be riding into our own people in A Company. We probably won't be able to see much until we get right in the village. But Yellow Horse's rim troops won't be able to see to fire down on us, neither."

"That will afford some cover," Kravitz agreed. "Maybe the tactic is not as crazy as it sounds." He tried a wry grin.

"Believe me, I ain't no more sure than you that it's right," Dan'l admitted.

"My father always told me that there is no best tactic, that conditions change so fast in battle that tactics must be flexible and change with them. I suspect he might have liked your present plan," Kravitz said.

Dan'l cast a sideways look at him.

"He was in the Polish Cavalry," Kravitz explained. "Fought in Silesia in the War of Austrian Succession. He said that Genghis Khan made the first important use of cavalry. I suspect those troops were much like these of Yellow Horse."

Dan'l closed his eyes against a blast of sand. "I reckon so. I wouldn't know about any of that. I ain't never read any of them history books." He met Kravitz's eyes. "I ain't read any book."

Kravitz could not believe it. The Indian fighter of legend, the great hunter and guide who could speak several languages, the man who had saved Carolina state documents from the British when the Continental Army was being overwhelmed, was admitting he was illiterate.

"You . . . can't read?" Kravitz said.

"Not much," Dan'l said. "Maps. Little things from newspapers. But not much. Ain't never found the time to learn."

Kravitz sighed, then smiled. "Well. I doubt that the Mongol could read much, either. But it didn't keep him from conquering the world."

Dan'l huddled against the roaring wind, and looked behind him. Men were pacing, and horses were getting uncontrollable. He looked back at Charlie, and wondered himself if the half-breed was waiting too long.

"I bet that bastard Running Dog don't read," Dan'l said quietly.

"He's a cold-blooded killer, Dan'l. And I hear he doesn't put much credence in spirits and gods. He'll want to get you in his sights, you can count on it. To show Yellow Horse that you are mortal."

"He better find me before I find him," Dan'l growled. He still remembered the atrocities Running Dog had committed at Santa Fe, and he thought of the women and children slaughtered at Spanish Wells.

"Look!" Kravitz said suddenly, pointing at Charlie.

Charlie had walked over to Rivera, and was gesturing animatedly at the sky. And almost like magic, the wind suddenly began howling fiercely, almost knocking Charlie over. There was now a lot of dirt and sand in the air, and it was so dark that it was difficult to see twenty or thirty feet.

Rivera stood up stiffly and turned toward his troops, where his captains waited anxiously, bracing against the new savagery of the wind, trying to keep their mounts under control.

"We are going!" Rivera shouted, raising his saber into the air. "We are going in! Mount up!"

Kravitz turned to Dan'l. "I will be riding with A Company. Good luck, hunter!"

"Same for you!" Dan'l yelled into his face.

Some men had turned their mounts loose in these last minutes, and were huddled on the ground, shaking fearfully, as superstitious as the Apaches about this storm. The Taos Indians, who had been distributed among the companies for the attack, all seemed to take it fairly well.

The sergeants and corporals moved through the ranks, prodding the faint of heart to their feet, and helping them get mounted. Within a few minutes the entire column was mounted, Charlevilles prepared, sabers at their fingertips.

The men hunkered down on their horses, trying to fathom the craziness that was taking them into the teeth of the Apaches through this.

"Forward—ho!" Rivera shouted.

The blistering wind carried his words away. Most did not even hear them. But they saw him wave his saber.

In a terrorizing wind that threatened to blow them out of their saddles, grit and dust abrading their skin and clothing like rough sandpaper, the first companies moved at an even pace into the mouth of Devil's Canyon.

The other companies followed right behind them.

At first they went at a walk, the horses relieved not to be standing still in the storm. Some of their nervous energy was released just by moving.

They moved ahead that way eight abreast—four in each company. Ahead of them was a wall of dust, swirling and blowing. It got into their eyes, ears, and nostrils. It got down the necks of their tunics, and blew up their sleeves.

A horse panicked near Dan'l, and broke into a bucking gallop, running up against the can-

yon rocks nearby and throwing its rider off.
That made several others buck and kick for a
couple of moments.

They moved two hundred yards into the canyon, and still saw nothing. No Apaches in front
of them, and the rims of the canyon on either
side were occluded by the storm.

Rivera gave another signal, and the first companies spurred their mounts into a trot. Now
the horses were doing better. Some had the idea
they were running from the storm, and were
glad to be released from the tension of staying
put and gritting it out.

The men were much the same. Any movement, any action, was better than just stoically
abiding the violence around them.

Suddenly Dan'l spotted the shape of the village coming dimly at him, getting more and
more distinct. Tipis and wickiups hovered like
ghosts off the canyon floor.

"We're there!" he yelled, hoping that Rivera
could hear him.

Now Rivera saw the ephemeral images, too.
He raised his saber again. "Attack! Attack at full
gallop!"

Almost simultaneously, an arrow flew out of
the roaring wind and thumped into the chest of
a soldier near him.

Dan'l heard the sound of it above the screaming wind, turned, and saw that it had hit Sergeant Torreon, the one who had forgiven him
for the beating in the Santa Fe cantina. Torreon

slid off his horse and the mount kept on going. Another arrow sank into the horse of a private soldier, and the horse went down, falling on its rider and crushing him. Dan'l saw the same was happening in Company A.

"Attack!" Dan'l commanded. "Attack now!"

The other captains were repeating the command, too, and a moment later the lead companies of cavalry were charging wildly into the wall of dust and dirt.

Soon the other companies were coming up fast behind them, and the small army thundered into the canyon like demons from hell, the wind and dust whirling around them, shrieking in their ears, driving them into frenzy. As they plunged into the depths of the canyon, the village gradually took shape in the storm, as did individual Indians behind low stone barricades, firing rifles and arrows at the attackers.

Most of the attackers had slid their rifles back into their saddle scabbards, because they could not see to shoot. Instead, as they exploded into the big village, they began wielding their sharp-edged sabers.

The Apaches were thunderstruck by the mid-storm attack. They reacted as fast as they could, but many warriors were not even ready for defense. Suddenly the Spaniards were there, coming out of the dust like an adjunct of the storm itself, roaring at them intent on destruction.

Yellow Horse heard the alarm and burst forth from his tipi, war paint covering his square face. He had been sure the Mexicans would delay their attack until the storm had abated, and was taken completely by surprise.

His son was not. He was out at the stone and wood barricades, screaming at his warriors to fight back, to keep the attacking army at bay.

In seconds, though, the Mexican cavaliers had breached the low wall of defense, knocking parts of it down and jumping their mounts over it elsewhere. Behind that redoubt stood and crouched over a hundred first-line Apaches, but they hardly slowed the ferocious attack. Several men of Company B went down, though, with arrows protruding from them and lead tearing up their insides. Kravitz had a revolver in one hand and a saber in the other, fighting wildly. In a quick glance Dan'l saw Charlie lying in the dust with his throat cut from ear to ear.

There was general chaos. Several Taos warriors were shot by Mexican soldiers, mistaking them for Apaches. Rivera was yelling loudly, turning and wheeling on his charger. Dan'l fired and hit an Apache in the left eye. Another shot exploded the heart of a valiant defender, throwing him backwards as if jerked by a rope. Dan'l looked around darkly for Running Dog, but could not find him.

Just then Dan'l felt an arrow slam into his left calf. He reached to pull it out, but it had passed on through, just taking a small amount of flesh with it. Another arrow tore at his shirt, exactly where his head had been a split-second before.

He saw the crimson running down his high boot, but it was not bad.

When he looked up, an Indian was running crazily right at him. He re-primed quickly and fired just as the warrior reached Dan'l's horse and grabbed for its reins. The bullet tore through the man's throat and severed his spinal cord, and he dropped like a stone.

The entire column of cavalry was in the village now, wreaking havoc in the dust and wind. Apaches were slashed open, many decapitated in one savage cut. Women tried to get out of the way, but were cut down, too. The Mexicans felt no moral restraints, and Dan'l understood why, but hated it. He wheeled his mount in the midst of his men, shouting at them.

"Not the women and children!" he yelled. But it was in English, and in a howling, eye-squinting wind, and nobody seemed to pay any attention.

As he reined his mount tightly, trying to get off another shot, a couple of nearby Apaches saw him and stopped fighting.

"Ancient Bear! It is Ancient Bear!"

The word spread, and soon many of the Indians had stopped fighting, and were staring hard at Dan'l, with abject fear in their faces.

"Ancient Bear!"

The cavalry took advantage of this lapse, and cut the stunned Apaches down. It was turning into a massacre, much worse than the one at Spanish Wells. Suddenly Yellow Horse appeared in front of Dan'l, magnificent in his headdress and war paint. He held a long lance under his arm.

"Ancient Bear, you must die!" he called out to Dan'l, barely audible above the wind.

He had just started a charge against Dan'l, the lance out in front of him, when Dan'l raised his pistol and fired it at the Indian's chest.

The shot struck Yellow Horse just beside the heart, ruptured his aorta, and broke posterior ribs on exiting.

Yellow Horse flew off his mount and hit the ground just beside Dan'l, very dead.

A lot of Apaches saw their chief go down, and that added to their panic. The yelling from their side abated, and those who had thus far escaped the sabers and gunfire of their attackers were running toward the far end of the canyon.

Rivera appeared beside Dan'l, red-faced, yelling in Spanish at the top of his lungs, "They're beaten! Don't let them escape! No prisoners!"

But many of the women had already fled, followed by the warriors still able to escape. Just a few, Dan'l saw through the now-abating storm. Most of them lay dead around him. Cavalry horses were stumbling over the many corpses.

"Don't let them—" Rivera was hit hard by an arrow in the shoulder and knocked off his horse. The horse almost kicked him in the head, and then ran off. Dan'l swore under his breath, holstered his gun, and started to dismount to help Rivera. But Running Dog came between them, mounted on a white horse, his diamond-hard eyes focused on Dan'l.

"You killed a great Apache chief, damn you!" Running Dog was yelling in his native tongue, and Dan'l could not understand a word. "Now I will avenge him, you dirty impostor!"

Running Dog came at Dan'l with a war hatchet raised above his head, intent on splitting Dan'l's skull open. Dan'l recognized him immediately, and his face went hard.

"You bastard!" he growled. He wheeled his mount, trying to get his pistol re-primed.

Running Dog came at him with blood in his eye. Dan'l could not get the weapon cocked before the warrior reached him, and now the tomahawk was within striking distance. But Dan'l's mount reared in the excitement of the moment, and Running Dog's horse slammed into it, and the Apache was thrown over its head. He thudded up against Dan'l's side and his wounded leg, then hit the ground. Dan'l tried to control his animal, but fell off the far side of it.

They were both on the ground.

Running Dog swore at Dan'l and hurled the hatchet from a supine position. It sailed past Dan'l's right ear and sank into the chest of another unseated soldier, felling him.

Dan'l finally aimed the gun and fired. But his mount bumped him and the shot went wild. Now Running Dog was on his feet, and a cavalry horse without a rider came running between him and Dan'l. Running Dog caught it by its reins, threw himself aboard away from Dan'l, and rode in a gallop down toward the far end of the canyon, where a small opening allowed a few Apaches to escape.

"It is not finished!" Running Dog screamed into the dying wind, looking over his shoulder at Dan'l. "You are a dead man, I promise you!"

Dan'l was as frustrated as Running Dog. "Stop that one!" he yelled out desperately. "Shoot him!"

But Running Dog was gone, galloping through the escape opening at the end of the canyon, with the remnants of his once-great army.

"It is too late, Captain," Rivera said, getting clumsily to his feet. "But we got Yellow Horse. You did. And we decimated his army. They will never again be a threat to Santa Fe."

Dan'l went over to him. "Hold still." He pulled the end of the arrow on through Rivera's shoulder, and Rivera almost fainted. Dan'l held onto him. "There, that's better."

"You were hit, also," Rivera said. He had seen him limp when he came over.

"It ain't bad," Dan'l said.

They looked around. A few Apaches were still running about at the end of the canyon, but the fight was over. Though a few shots rang out yet, the chaos had subsided.

There were soldiers lying dead and wounded around them, but they were nothing in comparison to the Indians. The ground was littered with dead and wounded Apaches. It was worse than anything Dan'l had ever seen, even at Fort Duquesne.

"Tell them to cease fire, Colonel," Dan'l said wearily.

Rivera looked at him curiously.

"There are still twenty or thirty warriors and old men left down there at the end that can't get out to escape. They'll want to surrender. And there's still women in them tipis. Some with kids."

Rivera hesitated, then nodded slowly. "All right. We will do it the Kentucky way," he said with a small grin. He turned toward the troops between him and the far end of the canyon.

"Cease fire! Cease fire!"

The shooting stopped, and sabers were lowered. Men looked toward him quizzically.

"There will be no more killing!" Rivera yelled in Spanish.

The wind had died down. The storm had passed over them. Dan'l looked around at the carnage, and realized they had used the storm to good advantage.

"Thanks," he said to Rivera.

Dan'l helped the colonel to his mount.

"Por nada, amigo," Rivera said. "You have earned the right."

That seemed to say it all.

Chapter Ten

When the returning troops arrived in Santa Fe, they were treated like conquering heroes. Cactus blossoms were scattered on the streets before them, and great crowds met them with garlands and wild cheering. The news of their great victory had preceded them back.

Dan'l was surprised at all the celebration. He had never had this when returning from Fort Duquesne or other battles in Carolina. He did not like all the attention.

He and Rivera had had medical treatment, such as it was, before starting back, and their wounds were healing well. The garrison infirmary received them and all the other wounded, and medications and fresh bandages were applied. A few men were hospitalized with rather severe wounds.

Elvira Lucas, Rueda, and the two children, survivors of Spanish Wells, were received with much fanfare and given a personal audience with the governor. Elvira could not stop talking about the heroism of the soldiers, and particularly Dan'l Boone.

Dan'l and Rivera became instant heroes, no less so to their own troops. The governor was advised that Dan'l had been given command of a full company after Salazar's demise, and had performed in a way that brought honor to the command.

Dan'l tried to ignore all of it. The night of his arrival back, Jameson and Douglas came to him at his garrison quarters and demanded that he prepare to return to St. Louis as soon as he was physically able. They were happy that the Apache had been subdued, but wanted to get back to their families, and get on with their lives.

Dan'l could not blame them. They had been rather patient about all this, and he figured he owed them an early departure.

The Taos Indians who had fought with them had been incorporated into the four Mexican companies at Spanish Wells, and they had fought well against their traditional enemies. Now the few survivors returned to Taos Pueblo with their heads held high. They had helped end the reign of terror of Yellow Horse.

The very next day Governor Alvarado called Rivera, Kravitz, and Dan'l into his private office to congratulate them personally. After smiling greetings all around, they took their seats while Alvarado, dressed up in sash and cummerbund, lauded their victory.

"What you have accomplished for this territory is not measurable," he said from behind his desk. "I have heard of your heroics, gentlemen, from our captains. You have made me very proud. You have the gratitude of this office, and of Viceroy de Galvez, who will hear of this great victory with the first courier we can get ready to go south."

They sat there rather uncomfortably. Rivera wore two thick bandages, on his shoulder and rib cage. Dan'l had one on his lower leg, as well as his chest, and he walked with a small limp. Kravitz had a bandage across his forehead, where he had received a glancing blow from a war hatchet. But none was seriously injured.

"Incidentally, I am sorry about our half-breed," Alvarado went on. "I know he was a good soldier."

Dan'l wondered why the governor could not bother to even say his name. "Yes, he was," he said.

Alvarado smiled warmly at him. "Colonel Rivera has made a special report about you, Captain Boone. He is very impressed with your leadership abilities."

Dan'l shrugged and looked down. "Just doing

what comes naturally, Governor," he managed.

"I can't tell you how pleased we are that you volunteered for this mission," Alvarado added. "I get the feeling it would not have gone as well without you."

"That's the damn truth," Kravitz offered.

Rivera smiled, not minding that Dan'l got so much credit. "Mr. Boone was invaluable to me," he acknowledged. "I would like to have him here on a permanent basis."

Alvarado raised his dark but graying brows. "Ah. What do you think of that, Captain Boone? What an asset you would be for us, with your vast experience! I could make your commission a permanent one with just a stroke of a pen."

Dan'l smiled slightly. He could not imagine why anybody would think he wanted a military career. "Mr. Governor, I'm real honored by the offer. But soldiering ain't for me. I turned down a commission in the Continental Army, too, offered by General Washington. I guess I'm too much of a loner to suit up with a garrison every morning of my life. But I thank you for thinking of me."

"Well, you know your own mind, I'm sure," Alvarado said. "But the offer stands open, my friend. If you change your mind after you get back to Missouri, just let us know. There will always be a place for you in Santa Fe."

"I'm much obliged," Dan'l said.

Alvarado came around the desk with something in his hand. "Would you mind rising for just a moment, Mr. Boone?"

Puzzled, Dan'l got to his feet, feeling the pain in his leg as he did so. "Yes, sir."

"In a few days," Alvarado said, "we will have a grand ceremony at the garrison HQ, to honor the heroes of this great victory. But I am told that you might not be here then, since your investors are eager to get on their way back."

"That's right," Dan'l said.

Alvarado nodded. "Therefore, I must take this opportunity to make this presentation while I still have you here in Santa Fe." He showed Dan'l the sunburst medal he held in his hand, then reached forward and pinned it to Dan'l's rawhide shirt.

"Oh, Jesus," Dan'l muttered.

"Mr. Boone, or Captain, as the case may be, I herewith invest you with the Military Order of Extreme Merit, for your imaginative leadership and your outstanding courage in the subjugation of the Apache at Devil's Canyon and Spanish Wells."

Alvarado touched his forehead in a salute, and Rivera rose and gave Dan'l a very proper, crisp salute that moved Dan'l. Kravitz rose, too, and shook his hand.

"Congratulations, Dan'l," he said.

"Hell, I feel like a girl at her first dance," Dan'l said, looking down at the medal hanging from a multi-hued ribbon. "I sure do thank you, Governor. And it was a real pleasure serving in your command, Colonel."

"The pleasure was mine." Rivera smiled.

"I'll be gone in a couple of days," Dan'l told them. "But I like what I seen here. I'll probably be back, maybe with more Missourians. People that might want to settle here."

"Nothing could please us more," Alvarado said. "Remind them that land grants for ranch land, here and in Tejas, are practically free. Our government wants immigrants to our territories. Especially the new Americans."

"I think they might be here sooner than you think, Governor," Dan'l suggested.

"Please, gentlemen. Sit down," Alvarado said.

Dan'l thought it would be finished by now. He resumed his seat, between Rivera and Kravitz. Alvarado went back around his desk, sat down, and folded his hands in front of him before he spoke.

"Mr. Boone, you may have some trouble on your way back to Missouri."

Dan'l hunched his broad shoulders. "I reckon I'd be surprised if we didn't."

"Chief Morning Star has sent a courier. I don't know how they find these things out so fast. But he says the Apaches believe the Ancient Bear prophecy has been fulfilled."

Dan'l smiled slightly. "Oh?"

"They are convinced you are Ancient Bear. That you led a great army against them, calling down the furies from the sky. That you have recruited the Thunderbird as your own demon, and also have the power to bring down the wrath of other deities upon the remnants of the tribe."

"Goddamn savages," Kravitz grumbled.

"It is primitive stupidity," Rivera agreed.

Dan'l just shook his head. "I thought Running Dog didn't believe any of this."

"Running Dog no longer rules the Apaches," Alvarado said. "If the Taos have their facts straight, he has been ostracized from them, apparently *because* he does not believe."

"Good. Maybe he'll starve to death," Dan'l said.

"The remaining Apaches have moved south. They believe you are ruling them from some other plane of reality, and watching over them unseen. They pray to you."

"Hell," Dan'l said.

"Running Dog has gone off with a few renegades. He has made a blood vow to kill you, to prove your mortality." He leaned forward onto his desk. "This is very important to him. It involves his whole future."

"I understand that," Dan'l said. "The only Apache that knows the truth about me is a black-hearted bastard. Ain't that sweet?"

"There is also the matter that you killed his father. It would have been better if one of our soldiers had, frankly. It will give his renegades a reason to ride with Running Dog, whatever they believe about the Ancient Bear legend."

"In the Shawnee tribe," Dan'l said slowly, "Chief Blackfish announced to his people that anyone who brought him my scalp would go directly to Indian heaven. They tried to get me underground for years, Governor. But here I am, as you can see. I ain't afraid of the likes of Running Dog."

"He undoubtedly knows you will be heading back East with a small party," Alvarado continued. "He cannot afford to let you finish the trip alive. He is desperate to regain his standing with his people. He can only do that by killing you, and bringing your head to them."

"It would be good if Dan'l could have a military escort," Kravitz suggested. His lean face looked weary from the ordeal they had endured. But he was tough, like Dan'l.

"I would be pleased to lead a detachment to St. Louis with Boone," Rivera said. "I owe him much, Governor."

Alvarado smiled. "You are in no condition to go on such a trip, Colonel. And I need you here. I could send a few men under one of our captains. But none speak enough English to be understandable. Too bad Cabeza is no longer with us."

"I could go, I speak English," Kravitz offered.

Dan'l shook his head. "Every man in your garrison needs rest, Governor. And you need them here. We come across Indian country without no escort to get here. I reckon we can do the same going back. Both Jameson and Douglas got a couple aides, as you know, and they all shoot pretty good. And the drivers that got the wagons here can both handle a gun. We'll be all right, Governor."

"Well," Alvarado said. "I very much hope so."

Dan'l found Jameson at their special quarters early that afternoon, and announced to him that if the investors' entourage could be ready, they would leave in two days' time. Jameson said they were all very ready to depart, except that one of the drivers who had brought a wagon there had left Santa Fe and could not be located. Dan'l said he would find somebody, but Jameson said that was not all of it. The other driver, an older fellow who hailed from Fort Pitt, was not feeling so well, and a medic thought he had mountain fever. Dan'l went to the infirmary to visit him, and found out that he was getting worse.

Dan'l decided that he, too, was lost to the expedition.

That evening, Dan'l met Kravitz at the cantina and mentioned that he had to hire a couple of wagon men before he could leave.

Kravitz looked into Dan'l's deep blue eyes. "Dan'l, I drove a wagon for pay years ago. I would like to go with you."

Dan'l regarded him narrowly. "Your life is here, Kravitz. It's a long way back from St. Louis, and I might not be coming this way again for a long spell." He swigged some mescal. "Anyway, I can teach a couple of them aides to drive, I reckon."

"Accountants? Clerks? I don't think so, Dan'l. You'll need experience, if you get into any trouble."

"You got mines here, and land. You got an import business yourself."

"My business is up for sale," Kravitz said. "I made that decision before I laid eyes on you. And the mines don't need me. Frankly, I need a change. I been thinking of going East for a while. Going with you just fits into plans I have already made."

Dan'l grinned sourly. "Like hell."

Kravitz smiled. "Well, the timing is a bit off, perhaps. But I would be doing this, Dan'l."

Dan'l looked at him.

"It is also in the back of my head," Kravitz went on slowly, "that I like what you're doing for a living. Once in St. Louis, I might try to become a part of it. If you'll let me."

Dan'l shook his head. He really liked Kravitz. Maybe as much as he had liked John Findley, who had filled his head with stories about Kentucky when Dan'l was still a Carolina farmer, or Sergeant Jake Medford, who had been to Fort Duquesne with him and later became his fast friend. Kravitz had the same kind of background as Dan'l, and the same way of looking at things. He was also the only one at Santa Fe who felt close enough to him to call him by his first name.

"You do have a lot of crazy in you," he finally said to the Polish immigrant. "But are you sure you ain't doing this just to get my butt back to St. Louis in one piece?"

"I suspect you are perfectly capable of taking care of your own butt," Kravitz said. He looked down. "I guess you will make me say it. I . . . like being with you, Kentucky hunter. You make me remember why I came to America in the first place."

Dan'l sighed. "Running Dog might get in our way. He's my problem, not yours. You could pick a better party to go back with, if you really want to go."

"I wish to go now. With you," Kravitz replied.

"Hell, all right. Be here at the garrison day after tomorrow. At dawn. You'll drive the lead wagon."

Kravitz grinned at him. "I'll be there."

Dan'l left the cantina shortly thereafter, and returned to his private room at the garrison, having to pass sentries at the big gate. It was dark when he went in and began undressing. He had just pulled a new rawhide tunic off, revealing a still-thick bandage across his muscular, hairy chest, when a knock came at his door. He went to answer it without replacing the shirt.

Rueda stood there. And just behind him, Dan'l could see Elvira Lucas.

"Buenas noches," Rueda said. "We are sorry to bother you, Senor Boone. May we speak with you briefly?"

Elvira came forward. Dan'l and Rivera had complimented her on helping treat wounded men on their campaign, both before and after the big battle. She had been very friendly with Dan'l on the way back to Santa Fe.

"Good evening, Dan'l." She had come to call him by his first name, too, at Dan'l's insistence. She stared hard at the big bandage, and the muscular look of him, and wished it was she who had met him when they were both young, instead of his wife. "We won't keep you long."

Dan'l hesitated, then waved them in. "All right. But I'm getting ready for bed."

They came in past him, and he closed the door. Then he went and got the shirt and put it back on. He grimaced when he moved his arms.

"Are you all right, Dan'l?" Elvira asked. She looked very pretty that evening, with her blond hair combed and her face radiant.

"Oh, sure," Dan'l said. "I'm healing real good. What can I do for you?"

Rueda spoke first, because he felt it was his responsibility. "Mr. Boone. We wish to accompany you to St. Louis."

Dan'l frowned. "What?"

At that point, Elvira jumped in. "The two of us and the children, Dan'l. We won't be any trouble. And Mr. Rueda has some money he had hidden on him. We hope it will be enough to pay for our passage."

Dan'l sat on the corner of a wooden table nearby. "This ain't no stagecoach line, ma'am. Everything is bought and paid for by my investors. You ought to wait till a real wagon train goes east. I hear there's a couple a year."

"Not really," Elvira said. "Anyway, we want to go with you. We know you, and we want to go now. This is no place to raise these children, Dan'l. I know that now. I want to take them into Tennessee. Maybe Carolina. Get them a good education."

"It won't be so bad here now, with Yellow Horse defeated," Dan'l reasoned. "They got a good school here in Santa Fe, too, I hear."

He did not want them to go. It was one thing to acquiesce to Kravitz's request, because he would prove to be an asset if there was real trouble. But now he had a woman with two children asking. If Running Dog came at them, Elvira and her children could end up very dead.

"I want them to go to some civilized school back East," Elvira told him. She stuck her chin out defiantly. "I'm going, Dan'l. With or without you. But you can spare us the problem of arranging a way of doing it. We'll go alone, if it gets down to that."

"*Absolutemente*," Rueda said firmly.

"You couldn't go it alone out there, ma'am," Dan'l said somberly. "It just ain't done."

"If we have to, we will," Elvira insisted. "But you can spare us that ordeal, Dan'l. You can take us with your party. I can do some cooking for you. We won't get in the way."

Dan'l sighed. "Do you know that Running Dog vowed to kill me?" he asked. "That we might run into him on this return trip?"

"We heard that," Elvira said. "But you're talking to the survivors of Spanish Wells, Dan'l Boone. Do you think Running Dog can scare us now?"

"Yes, do you?" Rueda challenged Dan'l.

Dan'l looked the middle-aged man over. He looked soft. "You ever drive a supply wagon?" he finally said.

Rueda squinted at him. "Wagon?"

Dan'l sighed.

"He doesn't understand the word," Elvira said.

"A wagon, to carry things," Dan'l repeated. "With horses pulling it."

"Ah. *Un carretón*," Rueda said, his face brightening. "*Sí*, I have driven. For a Spanish Wells trader."

"Do you think you could drive a big *carretón*?" Dan'l asked. "Could you manage two horses in harness?"

"Oh, *sí*," Rueda enthused. "*Es no problema*."

"I reckon that's a yes," Dan'l said.

"I think he will be very good, Dan'l," Elvira ventured.

Dan'l scratched his thick, unruly beard. "Hell, all right. I'll take the four of you. If Jameson and Douglas agree. You don't have to pay nothing. If Rueda drives a wagon and you do some cooking."

"Oh, thanks, Dan'l!" Elvira cried out, her eyes moist. She came and hugged him, and embarrassed him.

"It's all right, ma'am," he said. "Just remember when we're out there, this ain't no Sunday outing in New Orleans. You and the kids will have to keep out from underfoot, you understand?"

Elvira was not offended. "I understand."

"Good. I'll talk to my people."

"You will not be sorry, Mr. Boone," Rueda promised.

"I reckon that remains to be seen," Dan'l answered.

They did not reply to that. With a brief good night, they left his quarters.

Not far east of Santa Fe, hidden in a deep, narrow gorge, Running Dog made a secret, smokeless camp with his dozen renegade Apaches.

Earlier that day, two of his warriors had captured a Taos courier who had just come from Taos Pueblo, and was on his way to a village to the east, to take a message to a cousin of Morning Star. Running Dog had tied the captive to a slim cottonwood tree, and begun cutting parts off him, until the Taos had told him all he knew about Dan'l's impending departure from the settlement.

Then Running Dog had cut the captive's jugular, held a gourd to the wound to catch the blood, and tried to read the immediate future in reflections in the thick, crimson liquid. The body of the Indian had later been covered with stones, deep in the end of the gorge, to keep it from attracting vultures.

The moon rode high over their camp that night, and even though the temperature had fallen, Running Dog would not let his men have a fire. In mid-evening he washed out the gourd and placed it on the ground between them, where they sat in a small circle on the floor of the gorge in the moonlight, surrounded by mesquite and palo verde. Running Dog took his narrow war knife from a rawhide sheath, and placed the bowl closer to himself.

"Come closer," he commanded his men.

They came into a tight circle, squatting on their haunches. They were all naked to the waist, including Running Dog, wearing only breechcloths and high moccasins. Running Dog had a headband that held three feathers of a golden eagle.

"You all know I have taken an oath to White-Painted Woman," he began, "to kill this impostor that has led the Mexicans against us, and killed my father in his prime of life."

"Yes, we know," several said in unison.

"You are all still Dog Soldiers," he went on. "You are warriors of the tribe. As such, you will be called upon to help avenge our shameful loss at Devil's Canyon, and the death of Yellow Horse."

"The impostor must die," one of them said.

Actually, most of them were disappointed to learn that Running Dog's top priority was to kill the one called Ancient Bear. They had thought they would be out looking for isolated ranches, and miners, and robbing them. But they had resolved to be patient, to see Running Dog through this mission he had set for himself.

Their long, black hair moved in a slight breeze coming through the gorge.

"This man Boone will not leave this territory alive," Running Dog told them. "If he does, we will fall into greater disgrace than those who failed to stand their ground at Devil's Canyon. Do you all understand that?"

There was a general nodding and mumbling. They had accepted Running Dog not only as their leader, but as chief of all the remaining Apaches in the south.

Running Dog made some lines in the dirt at their feet, which the moonlight illuminated. "This is the way they will come. Along here. Toward La Justa, which is just a few ranch buildings. We will wait until they are well past that point, so they are far from the garrison at Santa Fe. Then we will attack them and kill everyone."

"Yes. Everyone," a hard-faced warrior agreed. He was thinking of the loot that would probably be involved.

"Direct all your efforts toward Boone," Running Dog ordered. "But do not kill him. Please understand this. It must be my honor. I have promised White-Painted Woman."

They all mumbled agreement. They would disable him and leave him to Running Dog.

Running Dog turned the knife around, held his arm over the gourd bowl, and suddenly sliced into his own left wrist. Blood dripped into the bowl.

"You will now take this oath with me. To avenge our defeat with the death of this white impostor, and free the spirits of our dead at Devil's Canyon to allow them to join our ancestors in the Netherworld, where White-Painted Woman reigns supreme with Killer of Giants, and keeps the real Ancient Bear and Owl-Man Spirit buried in the depths of the Old Place."

"Yes, yes," they agreed.

Running Dog no longer believed in these deities, but he knew that most of them did, and he understood the importance of making the deities a part of his argument to go after Dan'l.

He passed the bowl around, and the knife with it. Each warrior in turn cut a place on his wrist or arm, and dripped his lifeblood into the bowl. Finally the bowl came back to Running Dog.

"Now our blood has run together," he told them. "And has bound us as brothers in revenge and justice. Now the wrath of Killer of Giants will descend upon us if we do not keep our promise to kill this paleface from the East."

"Let it be so," one of the older ones said.

Running Dog took a sip of the mixed blood, then passed the bowl around again. Each Dog Soldier sipped of the mixture, some not very eagerly. When it came back to Running Dog, he held the almost-empty bowl aloft.

"May our blood unite to strengthen our will!" he said solemnly, with his eyes closed. "May this Boone be dead before five moons have risen!"

"May it be so!" they all replied.

Running Dog lowered the bowl to the ground, and stared at it for a long moment, thinking of his triumphal return to the People of Three Buttes, his father's tribe.

"I will flay his skin from his body," he said quietly. "I will pull his eyeballs from their sockets. I will cut his lying tongue from his mouth. Then we will cook his vital organs into a stew and consume it until it is gone."

A couple of them exchanged looks. They did not like this Ancient Bear thing.

"It is a thing," the older warrior finally declared, "that must be done."

Chapter Eleven

When Dan'l and his two-wagon party set out on that dim gray morning, he was surprised to find a small group of well-wishers in the plaza as the party emerged from the garrison headquarters. The governor himself was in the group, looking puffy and sleepy, along with a couple of his close aides. Rivera stood beside Alvarado, ramrod straight, wide awake, as if he had never gone to bed.

Dan'l, at the head of the train with Kravitz, stopped his mount before the governor and Rivera.

Rivera was nervous. He looked up into Dan'l's face. "The most dangerous part will be the first hundred miles or so," he said. "After that, Running Dog will have to look out for Kiowa."

Dan'l smiled. "We'll be careful."

Alvarado stepped forward and touched the appaloosa's muzzle. *"Vaya con Dios,"* he said. "It has been an honor."

A few minutes later, they left Santa Fe behind them, and as the misty shape of the Mission of San Miguel faded out of sight behind them, Dan'l could not help wondering if he would really see it again. He had rather liked the town. It had stood in the midst of a harsh wilderness since 1610, surviving hostile Indians, disease, and the weather, and it had produced some hardy pioneer Mexicans who were not unlike those settlers of Kentucky who were still carving a civilization out of the wilds back East.

The small expedition spent an uneventful first morning out, passing through dry, high-butte country. Dan'l and Kravitz rode out ahead of the wagons a half mile, watching for trouble, but there was none. Behind them was the wagon of Will Jameson, where he and two assistants rode, the younger of whom had volunteered to drive the wagon until Kravitz would take over in rougher terrain. Sam Douglas, his glasses clouding up with dust, rode in his follow-up wagon, with Rueda driving it. His older aide had decided to stay in Santa Fe at the last moment, so it was just the other, younger one who rode with him, along with Elvira and her two children. Tethered behind this second wagon were two unsaddled riding horses. All the supplies of the expedition were stacked inside the two wagons. There was no meat. That would have to be shot along the way.

The children were no trouble. Well disciplined by Elvira, and having already gone through hell at Spanish Wells, they accepted their cramped quarters well, and offered a minimum of complaints to their mother. Douglas's aide, a fellow named Blakey, took a liking to Elvira, and spent the morning asking her about herself. Elvira paid scant attention, occupied with seeing after her children and peering ahead to see if she could see Dan'l and Kravitz.

"Will we be there tomorrow, Mama?" little, blond Janie asked as the wagon rumbled along.

Elvira and Blakey exchanged a smile.

"That's dumb, Janie!" eight-year-old Toby exclaimed. "It could take a month to get to St. Louis."

"That's right, Toby," Blakey told him. "It was a bit longer than that coming."

"I don't like this," Janie said. "Can't we ride on a horsie, like Mr. Boone?"

"After we get out in the hills, only Mr. Boone will be riding," Elvira said. "We all have to ride the wagons."

"We could walk," Janie suggested.

"Only if Mr. Boone says it's all right," Elvira said.

"*Que estupido!*" Toby muttered. Both children were fluent in both Spanish and English.

"I'll speak with Mr. Douglas," Blakey told the children. "If he says you can walk alongside the wagons, it will be all right. He owns this wagon."

Elvira gave him a long frown. "Dan'l is in charge, Mr. Blakey," she said curtly. "Please don't undermine his authority with the children."

The aide was surprised. "Just as you say, Miss Elvira."

Suddenly the wagon rumbled to a stop. It was late morning already, and Elvira was glad to have a rest, even if it was brief. Pedro Rueda, up on the buckboard, turned and looked back through the canvas cover toward them, past stacks of supplies.

"We are stopping here."

Up ahead, Dan'l and Kravitz had reached the brink of a steep hill, and were looking down its rocky incline. Dan'l shook his head. "I been looking forward to this all morning as a problem. On the way here, we had to detour five miles to get around this. Now we got the same thing going back. Except it's downhill. The horses could never hold the weight of these wagons once they started down. We'll have to head south around this. It'll take the rest of the day to do it."

"And maybe part of tomorrow morning," Kravitz agreed.

Rueda had climbed off the second wagon, and was now approaching them, together with Jameson and Douglas. Jameson, looking lanky and fatigued, wore a scowl.

"Oh. We're here again. I remember this place."

"Maybe we could put the horses in back of the wagons," wiry, spindly Douglas offered, wiping at his spectacles with a handkerchief. He would never make another trip west. He hated the traveling too much.

Dan'l shook his head again. "They ain't strong enough, even four of them. They'd lose their footing."

"We could use the other horses, the spares," Jameson suggested.

"There's no harness for them," Dan'l reminded him. "No, I think the safest thing is to go around, like we done before."

"We had this situation when I rode with a supply train to Tejas one year," Rueda said, standing on the very brink of the hill and looking down. "It was very steep. Our guide suggested an old Indian trick. We unloaded the wagons, and drove a thick post in the ground at the brink of the drop-off. We looped a big rope around the post once and then tied it to the harness of four horses. On solid, level ground, the horses could be made to lower a wagon slowly down the hill. Then we packed the supplies on their backs, a little at a time, and guided them down on foot. It worked."

Jameson's long face brightened. "Hey, that could work, Boone. And we don't need to plant a hitch post. Look over there."

He pointed to a twisted, gnarled tree, some

kind of evergreen, that stood on level ground thirty yards away. "No post could be stronger than that tree. It's been hanging onto that dirt and rock for a couple hundred years or more."

Dan'l went over to it with Kravitz and looked it over. Its trunk was almost a foot thick; and its roots looked deep.

"It might work, Dan'l," Kravitz told him. "It could save us a half day."

"We got enough rope to drop a wagon down that whole slope?" Dan'l asked Jameson.

Jameson nodded. "If we put my stuff with Douglas's, I'm sure of it."

"Please, I will supervise it, I have seen it done," Rueda said. "Let us try it, Mr. Boone."

It all sounded dangerous to Dan'l. But it was obvious they all wanted to save the time.

Elvira walked up to them, accompanied by the three aides. "What is it?" she asked Dan'l. "Will there be a delay?"

"Not long," Jameson told her. When he had heard Elvira could cook, he had been the first to accept her presence with the expedition. Douglas had agreed grudgingly, bowing to Dan'l's wishes. "We're going to unpack and lower the wagons down this incline," Jameson added.

Dan'l looked over at him sourly.

"That decision has not been made yet by Mr. Boone," Kravitz said pointedly.

Dan'l sighed. "It's all right, Kravitz. I guess we can give it a try. Trouble is, once we get partway through it, it'll be pretty hard to backtrack."

"It will work, Mr. Boone," Rueda assured him.

"Then let's get at it," Dan'l said.

The next hour was spent unloading the wagons. The children kept running off, and Elvira was kept busy with them. But finally the supplies had been off-loaded, and the wagons unhitched, and Jameson's had been set up near the brink of the precipice, between the tree and the edge. Then Kravitz and Dan'l, with Rueda's help, tied the big rope to the rear of the wagon, wrapped it around the tree once, and fastened the other end to the harness of the four wagon horses, facing away from the brink.

"That should do it," Rueda said energetically. "Now we must only guide the horses backward, a little at a time, after the wagon rolls over the edge."

Soon they were doing just that. Elvira and the children were sent off to a small cluster of mesquite, and sat there in the shade with the aides while the work was being done. On the way out from St. Louis, the aides had never involved themselves in much physical work, and the investors did not require them to. Now it was the same.

"All right, let it start down!" Dan'l called out to Rueda at the head of the four-horse team.

The horses were guided backwards, and the wagon headed down the hill, with Kravitz beside it, guiding it over stones and out of ruts.

Slowly, bumping wildly, it was lowered down. Fifty yards. A hundred.

"Keep it coming!" Kravitz yelled up to them, sweating now in the sun.

"Give us some more rope!" Dan'l yelled at Rueda.

The horses backed up too much, and the wagon bumped crazily downward for ten feet or more, and almost tipped over. But it righted itself, and kept on its downward journey. In another few minutes, it sat on rather level ground at the bottom of the descent.

"It worked!" Kravitz called up. "Let's do it again!"

They pulled the rope back up, and positioned the second wagon at the brink. Kravitz had returned up the grade, and helped with the operation on top. When the wagon was ready, Rueda volunteered to take it down this time.

"Are you sure?" Dan'l said. He knew Rueda was not as strong as Kravitz.

"Yes, Mr. Kravitz deserves a rest," Rueda insisted.

"What a wonderful idea!" Elvira called to them. "It's good we have Mr. Rueda with us, isn't it?"

"Yes, very nice," Jameson told her impatiently. "Maybe we could go a little faster on this one, heh? We still have to get all these supplies down there."

"Maybe one of your employees would like to help," Dan'l said caustically to Jameson.

His two aides were chatting lightly under the shade of the small mesquite trees, while Blakey, Douglas's assistant, was entertaining the two children.

Jameson looked toward the aides, who had not heard Dan'l's remark. "Hell, they'd only get in the way, Boone. They're good for nothing but writing contracts and computing interest rates."

But Rueda did not want to wait, anyway. "All right, Mr. Boone!" he called out, beside the wagon. "Let's take it down!"

Dan'l walked the length of the long rope, several hundred yards, to the horses in harness. Kravitz was standing there, holding them in place. "I've got them. Go take a rest," Dan'l told him. Kravitz was still red-faced and sweaty from taking the wagon down and then climbing back up the steep grade.

Kravitz hesitated. "All right. I'll go help Rueda get it started down."

Rueda and Kravitz rolled the wagon over the edge, and the rope went taut. Dan'l slowly guided the team backwards, letting the wagon slip down the grade.

Rueda was more nimble than he looked, and guided the vehicle around some large rocks, yelling for more slack when he wanted it to roll forward, and pushing it when it needed a boost to get over a hump in the grade.

"All right! More rope!" he called up.

The wagon bumped and careened sideways

for a moment, then righted itself, with Kravitz yelling for Dan'l to hold the horses steady. Then it hit a boulder, despite Rueda's guiding hand, and would not roll over it.

The rope slackened some more, but the wagon moved and stopped. "Just a moment!" Rueda called up. He went out in front of the wagon, with Kravitz looking on from above, and began shoving on the small boulder, to move it out of the way.

"Wait!" Kravitz shouted. "Don't get in front of the wagon! We must take up the slack in the—"

Suddenly, but with agonizing slowness, or so it seemed to Kravitz, Rueda moved the big stone. But his body was still right in front of the left front wheel.

"Dan'l!" Kravitz shouted. "Take up the slack!"

But it was much too late. The wagon, freed of the obstacle, rolled forward with all its weight, and caught Rueda under its wheel. The wheel knocked him down, and then rolled right over his chest, crushing his ribs in on his heart and lungs.

The wagon kept on moving faster, and its rear wheel bounced over Rueda's abdomen, almost cutting him in half.

When the wagon reached the end of the rope's slack, its momentum snapped the thick rope at a weak point, and the wagon kept on going.

It bounced and rambled on down the hillside,

kicking up rocks and dirt. Fortunately, it had only a hundred yards to go to get to level ground, so it reached that area upright. It careened drunkenly into a stand of low-growing ironwood, crashed almost all the way through it, and finally came to a stop with two wheels in the air, one of them busted, the vehicle supported by the dense brush.

The broken wheel spun crookedly for a long moment, then stopped.

Up on the bluff, Dan'l felt the quick release of tension from the rope, and when the team plunged forward he had to rein it in. Then he saw Kravitz waving wildly, heading away down the slope.

"What happened?" the pale Douglas called out from the shade.

"Oh, hell!" Jameson was sputtering.

Blakey, Elvira, and one of the Jameson accountants came running toward the brink, where Jameson now stood. Dan'l beat them there, though, and saw Kravitz sliding down the hill toward Rueda, who was supine on the ground.

"Son of a bitch!" Dan'l growled.

"What is it?" Elvira asked him. "Is Mr. Rueda hurt?"

Dan'l ignored her and skidded down the slope after Kravitz. In moments he was there, raising a small cloud of dust. Kravitz was bending over Rueda.

Kravitz looked up at Dan'l and shook his head

slowly. "The wagon rolled right over him," he said dully.

Dan'l knelt on the other side of Rueda, looking him over. There was not much blood, but Rueda looked like a broken doll. Crimson seeped from his mouth and his nose. His eyes were glazing over.

Up on the brink, Elvira cried out to the children, "Stay back, Toby! Janie! Stay where you are!"

Blakey went back to tend them, but the other men all looked down toward Rueda, stunned.

"We must get the—other wagon down," Rueda was saying in thick Spanish.

"Lie quietly," Kravitz said.

"The rope. Knot the rope. The cargo—"

A rivulet of blood surged from his open mouth, and Rueda breathed his last.

Dan'l let out a long breath.

"I'll be damned," Kravitz muttered.

Jameson came stumbling down the hill, and stopped beside them, kicking up more dust. "Is he all right?"

"What the hell do you think?" Dan'l said icily.

Kravitz closed Rueda's open eyelids. "He's dead," he told Jameson.

"Good heavens!" Jameson exclaimed.

Dan'l looked into his eyes. "It's all right," he said. "It waren't one of your accountants. That's all that matters, ain't it?"

Jameson's face grew red. "You and the drivers were hired to do the physical work on this trip, damn it! Don't try to make me feel bad about your Mexican friend! If he didn't know what he was doing, you should have been on the wagon!"

Kravitz saw the anger boil up into Dan'l, and he quickly rose and stepped between them. "I think you should drop the matter, Mr. Jameson. We'll take the body on down the hill. Maybe you could start taking the harness off the animals up on top."

Jameson cooled down. "Of course we'll help. This is an emergency, isn't it?"

Dan'l and Kravitz took Rueda down the hill, got shovels off the busted wagon, and buried him in a shallow grave, just off the trail. When Elvira got the news, up above, she could not stop crying. She had planned on helping Rueda get a job in St. Louis. She had valued his friendship. He had helped her and her children survive at Spanish Wells.

The children seemed to take the news stoically. Douglas and the aides expressed regret out of courtesy, but their main concern was about losing a good driver. It was agreed that Blakey would try his hand at driving, since the other man had not performed well when he'd substituted temporarily for Kravitz, and Dan'l was needed as a guide and scout out front.

When the horses had hauled all of the supplies and equipment down, a spare wheel was put on the broken wagon. It took most of two hours to finish that and get the wagons reloaded. But they had saved many hours over going around the hill.

Somehow, though, that no longer seemed important.

Kravitz said a few words over Rueda's grave, and then they were ready to continue. Elvira stood over the grave for several minutes after the others returned to the wagons. Dan'l finally came to get her.

"It's odd," she said to him. "I only knew him for a little while. But he was my best friend."

"I liked him," Dan'l said. He took her arm. "Come on, ma'am. We can make some distance before the day's over. Rueda would've wanted it."

Elvira nodded. "Yes. He would."

They headed out again, away from the base of the bluff, heading directly east. Dan'l rode out ahead of the wagons, while Kravitz and Blakey drove them. They rumbled along on fairly level ground into mid-afternoon, and everything went well.

Then Dan'l spotted them, on the crest of a nearby butte.

A small hunting party of Comanches.

He had been told how to distinguish them from the Apaches and Kiowa by their headdress and lances. He rode back to the wagons and made the announcement.

Jameson and Douglas were terrified. All the way out from St. Louis, they had avoided running into Indians.

Dan'l looked again at the butte. "They're coming down," he said. "To pay us a visit."

Jameson, Douglas, and Elvira had gotten off the wagons, and were standing there looking very nervous.

"I'll issue guns to our people," Jameson said. "We'll start shooting as they approach. Take them by surprise. There are only four of them."

Kravitz made a face. "Mr. Jameson—"

But Dan'l interrupted him. "Nobody does any by-God shooting unless I say so," he growled at Jameson. "Keep your guns stashed. I'll handle it."

"Our lives are at stake!" Douglas said loudly, shoving his dusty glasses up further onto his nose.

"Let's kill as many as we can," one of Jameson's men said from inside the lead wagon, behind Kravitz, who was on the wagon seat, reins in hand.

"If anybody fires a weapon, I'll shoot him," Dan'l announced.

"Why, you impudent bastard!" Jameson said angrily.

Dan'l glared at him. He glanced toward the base of the butte, and saw the Comanches coming. "You put me in charge of this outfit, by Jesus. You want to get rid of me? Maybe you can make it to St. Louis on your own."

Jameson's bluff was called. But he was still fuming. "All right. We'll do it your way this time. But don't let that medal Alvarado pinned on you go to your head. This isn't Santa Fe."

Kravitz shook his head. "You don't know when to quit, do you, Jameson?"

Dan'l ignored him, though. He saw the Comanches were just fifty yards away, and coming. "Here they are," he said.

The one riding in the fore wore a headband bearing several eagle feathers. They were all naked to the waist, and rode the same small ponies as the Apaches. But their hair was knotted and braided, and they did not wear the high-top moccasins. They did not look as wild as the Apaches. But their powerful tribe had scared off all settlers in their territory. They stopped twenty yards away.

"I can speak some of their language," Kravitz said to Dan'l. He got off the wagon, and walked out in front of his group. He put a hand up as a friendly greeting, and the lead Comanche did the same, but with a sober face.

"Greetings to our Comanche friends," Kravitz said to them in their language.

The Indians came on up to the wagons. Dan'l was still mounted, like the Comanches. The two investors, Elvira, and now Blakey were on the ground beside the lead team of wagon horses. Dan'l rested his hand on his Annely revolver, but realized it was not primed. The Indians had no firearms visible. They all had bows slung on their shoulders, and quivers of arrows attached to their riding blankets.

"Your greetings are returned," the young,

muscular-looking warrior said to Kravitz. He had a square, aquiline face, and his breechcloth was ornately decorated. His mount guffered quietly. "Where do you travel?"

Kravitz put a smile on his long face. He was dressed like Dan'l, in rawhides and high boots, but his crumpled, dusty hat was not as wide-brimmed as Dan'l's Quaker one. He, too, wore an Annely on his belt.

"We travel east, to the Great River. We will not stop in your territory. We will appreciate your hospitality as we pass through."

The Comanche nodded gravely. He looked beyond Kravitz, to the wagons and the horses, and then over to Dan'l. His gaze held on Dan'l for a long moment. "This is the party of Ancient Bear, is it not so?"

Kravitz grunted. "This man is so called by the Apache, yes."

Dan'l heard the reference to him, and figured they were talking about him.

"We do not believe in this legend," the Comanche said.

"Nor do we," Kravitz told him.

"We Comanches have no fear of this man."

"I understand."

"I see you have several fine horses. Also, I suppose, supplies on your wagons."

"Yes."

"As a gesture of friendship, we ask for four horses. And flour, if you have it. We like the white face's flour."

"What are they saying?" Jameson demanded.

Kravitz turned to Dan'l, ignoring Jameson. "He knows you're Ancient Bear, but denies you any god-like qualities."

"Good," Dan'l said.

"He wants four horses and some flour. And we can pass peacefully."

"That's outrageous!" Jameson said loudly.

"Shoot them down like dogs," Douglas offered. His hand went to a gun on his hip, then he recalled what Dan'l had told them.

Dan'l looked toward the two spare mounts, trailing after the second wagon. "Tell them they can have the extra mounts," he said to Kravitz. "And one sack of flour."

"Hell!" Jameson muttered.

"Tell them that that's our one and final offer," Dan'l added easily. "Then give our best wishes to their chief and their people. Tell them it's a great honor to meet with the famous and brave Comanche."

"For God's sake," Jameson sputtered.

Kravitz turned to the Indians and translated for Dan'l in broken Comanche. When he was finished, the lead warrior gave Dan'l a long, serious look. Finally he said, "It is agreed. We accept your fine gifts in friendship."

The tension dissolved, and the two horses were untethered and delivered over to the Comanches. Dan'l personally brought a sack of flour, and threw it over the rump of one of their mounts. A couple of them smiled for the first time.

Their leader looked down at Dan'l. "Running Dog is in this area, looking for you. To kill you."

Kravitz translated, and Dan'l nodded acknowledgment.

"He will probably do so. Unless we find him first," the Comanche said meaningfully.

Dan'l listened to Kravitz's version.

"We will watch for him," he said.

The Comanche held his steady gaze. "Go in peace," he said to Dan'l. Then they rode off with their booty. In a few moments they disappeared around the end of the butte.

"Do you mean to do that every time we run into Indians?" Sam Douglas asked Dan'l.

"You gave that stuff without our permission!" Jameson said.

"What's the matter with you two?" Elvira suddenly said. "Do you think we had any choice? You didn't make this much fuss about Rueda, for God's sake!"

That outburst seemed to subdue them. Kravitz came over to Jameson. "If you wish to survive this journey, Mr. Jameson, I suggest you listen to those who have experience in these things. Or you may not get to St. Louis."

Dan'l went over to a low-growing cottonwood tree and heaved himself onto the ground. All the men, and Elvira, followed him there, except Blakey, who stayed on the second wagon with the children.

"Looks like we better do some talking," Dan'l said to them. He leaned against the base of the tree, and they all stood around him. Kravitz came and sat beside Dan'l.

"This ain't working out so well," Dan'l finally said. "We got all these different ideas about how to handle these emergencies. And then there's Running Dog to complicate matters."

"What's your point?" Jameson asked.

"Kravitz here can get you to St. Louis. Probably better than me. I can cause the expedition trouble from here on, because of Running Dog. I can take a few supplies and go it alone. Maybe lead Running Dog away from you."

Suddenly the investors and their aides were not so blustery. Jameson spoke up first. "Hell, let's not be hasty, Boone. We can work things out."

"What you mean," Elvira said sourly, "is that you're afraid to go on without Dan'l. Isn't that it?"

Jameson and Douglas looked at each other. It was Douglas who said, "Maybe we are. We're not much good with guns. And these two are worthless." He gestured toward the two aides, one a skinny, effete-looking fellow, and the other a balding, soft-looking one. Neither replied to the insult.

"He's right," Jameson said grudgingly. "We need your gun. Whether or not that Apache finds us. Kravitz is good, but he's only one man."

Now Kravitz spoke up. "If Running Dog kills you, Dan'l," he reasoned, "he will still come after the wagons. He is an outcast from his tribe, and in Comanche country. He will go after these wagons, with their horses and supplies. If he kills you separately, that goal will just be all the easier for him. I think you are more valuable here than out there by yourself, trying to keep him away from us."

Dan'l thought about that, and admitted to himself that Kravitz might be right.

"Also," Elvira said, "that evil man will take great pleasure in hunting down us few survivors of Spanish Wells, and finishing the job he did there." She thought worriedly of the two children. "No, he will come after all of us. Not just you."

Dan'l shrugged. "It's your decision. I hope it's the right one."

"We could make a detour north," the soft-looking accountant suggested weakly. "Since Running Dog is probably approaching from the south, he might miss us completely."

"I thought of that," Dan'l said. "But we ain't got no idea where that son of a bitch is right now. He could've circled around north of here. I think the best chance we got is just heading east as fast as we can. It's dangerous enough for Running Dog to ride in here, where he might meet a Comanche or two. But past that it's Kiowa country, and there's a lot of it. I don't think he'll follow us that far."

"So you think we'll see him in the next day or two, or not at all?" Douglas said.

"That's about it," Dan'l answered.

"Then I say we get moving, and travel just as far today as the light will allow us," Jameson said.

Dan'l stood up, and Kravitz did, too. Kravitz was glad Dan'l was staying with them. He figured he might never have seen his new friend again if he had left by himself.

"Let's travel," Kravitz said.

There was no further trouble through the rest of that day. The buttes slowly gave way to hills with some greenery on them, and there was some hilly ground to get past, but the wagons took it all well. Dan'l looked for game, and bagged a rabbit, but that was it. He knew they would all be better off if he and Kravitz could find some real meat.

When they encamped in a low area that night, the men took turns standing sentry duty, and the night passed uneventfully. Elvira and the children slept in Douglas's wagon, and the three aides and Douglas slept in Jameson's. Jameson slept on the ground, alongside Dan'l and Kravitz, and took his turn at sentry duty. He seemed to have found a little common sense somewhere since Dan'l's offer to leave them, and Dan'l figured that would make it easier for everyone concerned.

When dawn came, Dan'l suggested that he and Kravitz should head out north for game. He had seen buffalo tracks heading in that direction at the end of the previous day, and also some antelope spoor. It was decided that the younger Jameson aide would take the Jameson wagon in Kravitz's absence, and the wagons would keep moving. Dan'l and Kravitz would rejoin them farther along the trail.

"What if Running Dog should come?" Elvira asked Dan'l, just as he and Kravitz were about to leave.

Dan'l scanned the horizon. "He ain't nowhere close. Not yet. I'd feel it if he was. We'll rejoin you by mid-morning."

"Hurry back," Elvira said.

As it turned out, the Apaches did not come that morning. But Dan'l and Kravitz found a different kind of trouble, anyway. They had ridden north less than an hour, when they came upon the small buffalo herd, grazing into the wind, their backs to the hunters.

"My God, look at the size of that bull," Dan'l said softly to Kravitz. "I never seen one that big. I guess they grow them more monstrous out here."

Kravitz slid his Charleville out of its scabbard. "There's a story going around in Santa Fe about a very big bull, a killer. Gored two hunters in the winter. One dead, the other crippled. Maybe killed another hunter last year. This could be that animal."

"Damn, he's a fine animal," Dan'l breathed.

"They look kind of skittery," Kravitz said.

"They'll never let us ride in on them."

Dan'l nodded. "No, we'll have to do it on foot."

Kravitz let his breath out slowly. He knew that was more dangerous. They both knew it. But they needed meat.

They dismounted, and made sure they had extra cartridges for the Charleville and Dan'l's Kentucky rifle. They picketed their mounts to a small mesquite tree. Dan'l's appaloosa whinnied nervously, and the big bull, on the near side of the herd of two dozen, looked up right at them. Dan'l could see the glistening nostrils, and the hard, brown eyes. It lowered its massive head and went back to feeding. Its horns looked like broadswords.

"Let's move up a mite," Dan'l suggested.

They crawled on their bellies, guns cradled in their arms in front of them. Dan'l pointed out a scorpion in Kravitz's path, and Kravitz guided himself around it.

They came to within thirty yards of the herd. Fifteen.

The bull was one of the closest animals, and looked like an elephant to them. It sensed their presence now, but could not find them. It stopped grazing, and looked all around the horizon again, scenting the air. But the wind kept their smell from him.

"He's getting nervous," Dan'l whispered. "We better take a cow now. We'll both aim at the same animal. That one just to the right of him. I'll take the head, you go for the shoulder."

Kravitz nodded. They aimed the primed weapons, and Dan'l counted to three in a whisper. They both fired.

The double explosion ripped the tranquillity of the moment, and the buffalo all jumped and began running, except for two. The cow dropped in its tracks, dead on impact. And the bull turned and stared right at the two hunters.

In the next moment, it charged them.

There was no time for reloading and priming. Dan'l already had his revolver out and was priming it as fast as the situation would allow. Kravitz was fumbling for his side arm, too, and finally got it out just as the enormous buffalo reached him. Dan'l saw the sweep of the big head and horns, and suddenly Kravitz was flying through the air, thrown by the bull. He came down hard on his back just as the bull turned its attention to Dan'l. It came at him now in a fury, red-eyed, snorting its anger at him.

The ground shook with its charge. Dan'l saw the wicked horns lowered, the ones that had just thrown Kravitz ten feet into the air. Dan'l waited. Until the bull was twenty feet away. Then ten.

He fired the revolver point-blank into the bull's face. He rolled off his right shoulder as the buffalo thundered past, grazing his left arm with its horn. When it got ten yards past him, it stopped, staggered in a tight circle, and dropped dead.

Dan'l was on his back, the rifle knocked from

his hands. He could feel the new pain in his left arm, and the older one in his chest, from the jaguar.

He stared hard at the buffalo. "God in heaven!" he muttered, lying there.

The dust was still clearing from its charges. Dan'l sat up and looked over at Kravitz, who was just rising to his feet, unsteadily. The horns had missed him, just by luck. But he had a wrenched shoulder and many bruises. He limped over to Dan'l with his dusty rifle. The rest of the herd was out of sight now.

Dan'l rose to his feet, and they went together to inspect the dead bull.

"Did you ever see anything like that?" Kravitz said.

"Not ever," Dan'l admitted. "That was the biggest, orneriest shaggy I ever come on."

Kravitz caught his gaze. "You saved my life, partner. He would have killed me."

"Hell," Dan'l said, waving off the remark. "Let's get these animals skinned."

Chapter Twelve

The war-painted Apache came riding full tilt into the tiny encampment, dusted to a stop, and leapt off the pinto. He strode up to Running Dog, who was crouching over a low fire. The other Dog Soldiers stood and sat around the encampment, looking surly because of impatience with their new leader.

"I found them!" the breathless newcomer announced.

Running Dog rose to his full height, lean, muscular, and dangerous. "Yes?"

"They are stopped a short distance from here, on the plain that leads out of these rocks. Ancient Bear and another man have just returned to the wagons with buffalo meat."

Running Dog scowled heavily at the warrior.

"Do not call him Ancient Bear!" he yelled into his underling's face.

The Apache received the outburst stoically. "Forgive me, Running Dog. I cannot remember his white name."

"It is Boone!" Running Dog said bitterly. "How many are there?"

"I counted seven men, including . . . Boone. But they do not look like warriors. It should be easy."

Running Dog looked off into the distance.

"There is also a woman, and I believe children."

Running Dog frowned. "That is not good. They will fight harder to defend them."

"It will be easy," the warrior repeated.

Running Dog glanced at him. During the big battle the warrior had been one of those who fled early from the canyon when he saw how badly things were going. He had not seen how ferociously Dan'l had fought there. "How would you know?" Running Dog now said caustically to the war-painted warrior.

The others had gathered around, looking fierce with their long, black hair and hard bodies.

"When do we strike them?" one asked.

"Soon," Running Dog said soberly. "Very soon."

The wagons rumbled along a flat plain, with low hills encroaching on its perimeter. They were making good time now, and Dan'l was beginning to wonder if Running Dog had abandoned his plan to attack them. Everything seemed so peaceful. Golden eagles soared overhead, coyotes watched them from a short distance, and Dan'l was enjoying the look of the country.

Dan'l and Kravitz had cut a lot of meat off the two buffalo, boiled some fat for tallow, and even kept the skins for possible trading. The skin off the big bull was the largest one Dan'l had ever seen.

That afternoon passed peacefully. Elvira sang Spanish songs to the children. The sound of it drifted through the wagons, making it all seem rather idyllic. Kravitz and Blakey were back driving the wagons, and Dan'l rode out ahead, but closer now to the wagons, in case of emergency.

Late in the day, they stopped beside a small stream that ran green and clear, and made camp. They would be heading into Kiowa territory the following day, and Dan'l hoped that would be an incentive for Running Dog to quit his chase, if he was really out there. Of course, the Kiowa were a danger, too. Most of them were friendly toward travelers, but a few had been very hostile.

Elvira cooked up a great meal that evening. Just as she was starting it, Blakey left the children, whom he was entertaining, and persuaded his boss, Douglas, to accompany him away from camp a few miles while the food was cooking.

"This is the area, I know it," Blakey told him. "See that escarpment over there? I'm sure that's where we could find fossils. Let's take a look."

Douglas was very interested in fossil-collecting, and had a fine collection back in St. Louis. "How far do you think it is over there?" he asked, wiping at his spectacles.

"We can be back by the time Elvira has the dinner ready," Blakey suggested. "I'll saddle the extra mounts."

Dan'l had just walked up to them and heard the remarks. He shook his head slowly. "I reckon you ought to just stick close to camp," he said. "You don't know what's out there."

Elvira was passing them with a tin bowl of shelled peas. "Oh, let them go, Dan'l," she said with a smile. "It's such a lovely evening." Then she was gone.

"Well," Dan'l said. "Maybe Kravitz will go with you."

But Douglas took offense. "The hell he will!" he scoffed. "We're both armed, Boone. What can happen? We'll probably be in sight of you the whole time."

Dan'l was suddenly tired of coddling these Easterners. "I can't stop you," he said curtly. "But if you ain't back in an hour, we'll have to come looking."

"Everything will be fine, Boone," Douglas assured him.

They rode out ten minutes later, with Dan'l watching them soberly.

Within fifteen minutes, the two riders arrived at the bluff, which revealed layers of shale and limestone all along its exposed face. Douglas had read that this kind of formation often contained remnants of past animal life, and he was very interested in taking a look. He and Blakey rode all along its base, and when they came to its abrupt end, they followed around it, not realizing they had put the encampment out of sight.

When they rounded another curve in the base, there were the Kiowa.

There were three riders only twenty yards away, looking as surprised as Blakey and Douglas. They had not seen the wagons, and were very shocked to run into two white men out here.

"Oh, damn," Blakey said quietly.

Douglas put a hand on his revolver, but it was not primed. The Kiowa spoke quickly among themselves, looking behind the white men for more of them. But they quickly realized they were alone.

Unfortunately for Douglas and his aide, these Kiowa were far from home, farther north, and were renegades who robbed and killed their own kind.

"Who are you?" the closest Kiowa said. "What are you doing here in Kiowa territory?"

"He's asking us a question," Blakey said, his

mouth paper dry. "Too bad we don't understand him. They might be peaceful."

"We come from a wagon train," Douglas said, trying to speak past his fear. He gestured. "Back there. Many men with guns. Do you understand?"

None of the Kiowa spoke any English. They spoke again among themselves, then the closest one came and rode completely around them, looking at their horses and their guns.

"They must come from some fort to the south," he said to his companions. "Couriers, probably. We will take their horses, their guns, and their clothes."

"Let me have the little one," a tall one said with a grin. "I think he will give us entertainment."

The shorter one beside him laughed aloud. "The palefaces make so much more noise than Kiowa."

The first one, more broadly built than the others, came close to Douglas and shouted into his face. "We are taking your horses, white face!"

Douglas drew the Annely clumsily, and started priming it, while Blakey just stared, frozen into immobility. The broad Kiowa grabbed a war club at his belt, urged his mount forward, and bashed Douglas's head in with it.

The glasses fell off Douglas's face, and blood ran down through his hair and into his eyes. He just sat there for a moment, his skull staved in, staring ahead but not seeing. Then he fell from his horse to the ground.

The tall Indian came and caught the reins of Douglas's horse before it could run off.

Blakey now went for his own gun, but the shorter Indian rammed his horse into the side of Blakey's, and knocked Blakey out of his saddle. He also fell to the ground, not far from the motionless and very dead Douglas. The Kiowas had grabbed Blakey's horse, too, and now were laughing riotously among themselves.

Blakey was bruised, but otherwise unhurt. He watched them all dismount, and picket the horses to some agave nearby. He knew he was too far away from the wagons to yell for help. He sat up warily.

"Please. Don't hurt me. Take our horses and guns. I won't give you any trouble."

"What is he jabbering about?" the tall one said. "I wish we still had the little one. He would have made more noise."

The broad one came and stood over Blakey. "Your clothes." He bent and touched Blakey's cloth shirt, then his own. "We want them. Take them off." He made a gesture.

"My clothes? I don't understand." He was an accountant out in the wild country, and none of this made any sense to him.

The broad Kiowa kicked him hard in the thigh, and Blakey cried out. "Your clothes!"

The others were gathered around him now, with razor-sharp knives in their fists. They watched him with wide grins. Blakey began removing his clothing, hoping all would be all right.

He tried not to look at the knives.

Elvira finished with the meal early, and the group began eating, sitting around with tin plates on their knees. Elvira was a good cook. The buffalo steaks were juicy, and it was just the kind of food they all needed to sustain them out on the trail. Elvira had put two steaks aside, until Douglas and Blakey got back.

They all enjoyed the meal and the tranquillity of the setting. Dan'l kept looking toward the bluff, though, wondering why Douglas and his aide were not back. Or at least in sight on their way.

Little Janie was not eating her vegetables, and needed encouragement from her mother. "I don't want any peas," she complained in her high, reedy voice. "I want dessert."

"We don't have dessert," Elvira said. "You can have dessert when we get to St. Louis."

"Why aren't we there yet?" Janie whined. "I don't like it out here. I want to go home."

Dan'l looked over at the child. She was beautiful, and reminded him of his own Jemima when she had been this age. He turned from her out toward the escarpment.

Toby's light brown hair was in his face as he chewed on the steak. "We don't have a home anymore," he said to his sister. "Don't you remember anything, Janie? The Apaches burned it down."

"You'll have a nice home in St. Louis," Will Jameson promised the little girl, from where he sat on a stool nearby. "I'll help you find one."

"Why, that's very kind, Mr. Jameson," Elvira told him.

The older Jameson aide glanced toward Elvira. "You did this meat to perfection, Miss Elvira."

The other one nodded his agreement, but was too busy eating to say it.

Elvira said, "Glad it suits you."

Kravitz put his almost-finished plate down, took a brass instrument out of his trousers, and held it in the palm of his hand. It was a handsome sun dial, made in Paris to fit into a man's pocket. Molded into its face was a compass, and a gnomon or pointer, hinged flat against the engraved dial, for convenience in storage. Kravitz raised the gnomon and stood up. He turned so that the compass read at the right heading, then observed the dial. The time was almost eight, and dusk was falling.

"They should be back," Kravitz said to Dan'l.

Dan'l nodded and put his plate down. "Maybe we better take a look."

"I'm sure they're all right," Jameson offered. "Sam loses track of time when he's interested in something." But he looked toward the bluff, too.

Elvira caught their concern, and frowned in

new worry. "Do you really think they're all right?"

"They're probably breaking fossils out of rocks," Dan'l suggested. "But we'll ride out and get them in before dark."

The two men were saddled up in moments, and rode out toward the high bluff where Douglas and Blakey had disappeared. Neither of them spoke all the way there, and Dan'l felt a foreboding grow in him as they began riding around the end of the bluff.

Kravitz saw them first. "Oh, shit," he muttered.

Dan'l came up beside him, grim-faced. "Goddamn it."

They rode up close to the two figures on the ground. Douglas lay in a dark patch of sand that his blood had colored. They could plainly see the big depression in his skull where it had been crushed. He was stripped of clothing except for his underwear.

But it was Blakey that made them stare in anger. He was completely naked, and he had been carefully disemboweled. Blood and guts were all around him, and his eyes were wide open, his jaw ajar.

He had been through hell.

Dan'l dismounted, looking about. Then he went and studied the tracks of the unshod horses.

"Indians," he said. "Probably Kiowa. Only three of them. There ain't no villages hereabouts. I'd reckon they're renegades."

Kravitz dismounted, too, trying not to look at Blakey. "I wonder if they saw our wagons."

"I don't think so. They never come around that bend. They headed off the same way they come. Anyway, they wouldn't attack us if they seen us. They ain't enough of them. We probably seen the last of them."

Kravitz sighed. "The children liked Blakey."

"He was good with them," Dan'l said.

"How the hell do we tell them?" Kravitz said. "And Elvira?"

"You got a shovel on your irons," Dan'l said. "We'll bury them right here. I don't want any of them to see this. Not even Jameson."

"I agree," Kravitz said.

It took another hour to get Douglas and Blakey under the ground, and then Dan'l and Kravitz rode back into camp somberly.

"What happened? Where are they?" Jameson asked them as soon as they dismounted. The others gathered around tensely.

"They're dead," Dan'l said.

Elvira let out a little cry. She turned to her children, playing nearby. "Toby. Janie. Get back to our wagon. Now."

Toby saw the distress in her face, and guessed what Dan'l had told them. He took his sister's hand and led her to the far wagon.

"Good God!" Jameson finally said.

"By Jesus!" the older aide whispered. His younger partner just shook his head slowly.

"It was Kiowa," Dan'l told them.

"Do you know it wasn't Running Dog?" the older aide wondered.

Dan'l shook his head. "There was just three of them. We reckon them to be renegades from up north. We don't think they ever saw our wagons."

"Are you sure?" Elvira said nervously. "They could kill us all in our sleep."

"We'll stand sentry duty," Dan'l reassured her. "Just like usual."

"Where are the bodies?" Jameson asked dully. He could not make himself believe that Douglas was dead. That he would not ever see St. Louis again.

"We thought it might be better to bury them out there," Kravitz said.

"Oh, yes. Of course," Jameson replied, in a fog.

"I tried to tell them," Dan'l said angrily. But he knew he should have argued with Douglas, should have tried harder to dissuade him. "Goddamn it."

"You couldn't have stopped him," Elvira said, watching Dan'l's grim face. "It's partly my fault. I encouraged him."

"He wasn't listening to anybody," Kravitz said. "Including you, ma'am."

Dan'l looked at their faces. "I hope this tells you all something," he said quietly. "This ain't a goddamn French tour we're on out here. And we maybe ain't seen the worst of it yet." He turned and walked away, toward the nearest wagon, while they all just stood there, silent.

There was little to add to that.

The night passed without incident, with Dan'l taking most of the sentry duty.

At dawn, when he was half awake and dead tired, the Apaches came.

Kravitz had just gotten up from his ground-sheet, and saw them first. Just specks in the distance at first, and then very quickly it became clear what they were.

"Apaches!" he yelled loudly, throwing down a plate he had been eating from. "Apaches!"

Just that one word alone had struck terror into the hearts of Southwest settlers for a century and a half, and it did so again on that rather cool, early summer morning. Everybody in camp turned and looked numbly toward the galloping riders, coming across the plain from the south. The younger Jameson aide dropped a pan of water he was carrying, and it splashed at his feet without his knowing it. Jameson was descending from his wagon, and a look of abject fear crossed his long face. Elvira made a small sound in her throat, and grabbed her children to her.

Dan'l swore under his breath, standing there with a bundle of harness in his thick hands. He had allowed himself to believe that maybe Running Dog had given up on him and returned south. But now here he was. Intent on wiping out the entire party, Dan'l was certain.

"Secure the horses at those trees!" Dan'l yelled to Jameson's aides. "Kravitz, help me pull this wagon alongside the other one!"

Jameson helped, too, and in just moments the wagons stood side by side, with just ten feet between them. With the six horses picketed securely in a stand of low aspen just a short distance from the wagons, all of the party took cover between the wagons. The men went for their guns. Elvira had just gotten the two children situated under the Douglas wagon when the Apaches arrived, whooping and making a thundering uproar. The men were still priming their guns when the Apaches were suddenly all around them.

Dan'l saw Running Dog immediately, but Running Dog could not immediately spot Dan'l. The Apaches had a couple of long guns on their irons, but had decided to use only bows in this close, hectic encounter, because they were faster-firing. The defenders were still loading and priming as the Apaches made their first sweep around the encampment, firing arrows and screaming at the top of their lungs. Because of the close quarters, the defenders opted for handguns, using Annelys and Mortimers. Dan'l got off the first shot, with arrows flying past his head, and knocked one of Running Dog's renegades off his mount, hitting him in the side of the head. Kravitz, across the ten-foot cover from Dan'l, also hit an Apache, in the low chest.

Jameson fired and missed, and so did his older aide. The younger fellow had crawled under the Jameson wagon, and was just lying on his belly there, his eyes closed against the chaos, when a stray arrow pierced his high chest and angled downward through his heart. He hardly made a sound as he expired.

"Keep firing back!" Dan'l yelled at Jameson, nearby. "Don't let them in here!"

But just at that moment one of the renegades ran his pony right between the wagons, firing an arrow as he came. He almost knocked Dan'l off his feet as he swept past, and then was gone without anybody hitting him. The arrow he shot hit Jameson in the hip, but did not go in deep. He yanked it out and kept priming his gun. Running Dog circled the wagons. When he finally found Dan'l, grim resolve came into his face. But in the next split-second, Dan'l, Kravitz, and Jameson all fired almost at once, and two Apaches were torn from their ponies. Running Dog swore loudly and rode right at Dan'l, who was re-priming against the Douglas wagon. Running Dog swung a war hatchet at Dan'l's head as he roared past. Dan'l jumped back and the weapon cut fringe off his rawhides, but missed his head and arm. Dan'l aimed after him, hoping to hit him in the back, but the gun misfired.

Now the older aide killed an Apache, and their numbers were dwindling. Dan'l aimed and fired again, and hit another Indian, who fell to the ground and cracked his head wide open on a rock. Kravitz shot another one, too, and the Apache rode off slumped over his mount, hit in the side.

Suddenly Running Dog was down to five warriors and himself, and still Dan'l stood unharmed, despite several attempts to kill him. Running Dog was frustrated and undecided what to do, until a small incident made up his mind.

An arrow came and thumped into the thigh of the Jameson aide, and he went down for a moment, dropping his revolver to the ground. Toby Lucas, beside his mother, and Janie, under the nearby wagon, saw the gun, and before Elvira could stop him, he had crawled out from under the wagon to retrieve it and kill an Indian himself.

"Toby!" Elvira screamed.

At that very moment, Running Dog had turned his mount to head between the wagons again, to make another try at killing Dan'l. But both Kravitz and Dan'l saw him, and both were re-priming and almost ready to fire. Running Dog fired an arrow at Dan'l's chest, but Dan'l leaped back and it merely grazed his side. Then both he and Kravitz were aiming at the outcast Apache prince.

It was then that Running Dog saw the boy run out from cover, down at his end of the wagons. He kicked his mount forward, leaned down and grabbed Toby by the shirt, and hoisted him kicking and yelling aboard his pony. Both Dan'l and Kravitz had to hold their fire to keep from hitting the boy. Then Running Dog was gone.

He rode away from the wagons, yelling to his men, "Enough! Follow me!"

There were some further gunshots, which hit nothing, and a couple of arrows flew into the sides of the wagons. Then the Indians raced off in the direction they had come from.

Elvira was immediately out from under the wagon, holding Janie and screaming loudly.

"They got Toby!" she yelled, crying. "Go after them, they got my son!"

The Apaches were out of sight. Kravitz came over to her. "They're gone, ma'am. We can't catch them."

"You have to try!" Elvira sobbed. "They've got my Toby!"

Dan'l walked over to her. He holstered his gun, took Elvira by her shoulders, and shook her once, hard. The yelling stopped abruptly, as she stared hard into his face.

"They won't kill him," he said quietly to her.

She searched his face for truth, and sniffled.

"They want me to come after him."

Kravitz sighed heavily. Jameson limped over to his aide, and examined the thigh wound. "That son of a bitch!" He looked down at the other aide, dead on the ground. "He killed Ashley."

"Then why don't you go find him?" Elvira

pleaded to Dan'l. "Why are you just standing here?"

"He ain't in no danger right now," Dan'l told her patiently. "We got wounded to tend here, though, and plans to make. I won't leave here without Toby."

That seemed to calm her. She turned away from him, holding Janie tightly to her chest. "Oh, my God," she murmured.

That seemed to say it for all of them.

Chapter Thirteen

A heaviness had fallen over the wagons.

With Toby gone, it was like three adults had been taken from the party.

They spent almost an hour tending the wounds of the remaining Jameson aide and Jameson himself. They were not serious wounds, though, and would not disable either man. Dan'l had a flesh wound in the right side, but did not even bother putting anything on it. After the wounds were tended, and they all drank some water, Dan'l and Kravitz buried the dead assistant. That put an even heavier gloom on the encampment.

Dan'l then gathered them around him, between the wagons. He was sweating and tired, and he felt responsible for Toby's abduction.

"Running Dog won't come back now," he announced. "His last hope is to kill me when I come for Toby."

Elvira met his gaze, then looked at the ground.

"Douglas's wagon got a wheel busted in the attack, and there ain't no easy way to fix it."

They all looked at him.

"I want you all to go on ahead in Jameson's wagon, and I'll catch you later."

"You can't go after him alone!" Elvira said. "There are still a half dozen of them."

"We'll all just stay here and wait," Jameson said. "It's important we recover the boy."

Dan'l shook his head. "You're just sitting ducks out here for any renegades that come along. If you go on, you'll get through the dangerous part in a day or two. You can't wait here."

"Then I'll go with you," Kravitz said firmly. "They'll have two men that can use guns, if any trouble comes. And like you said, they won't have to worry over Running Dog anymore. But if you go alone, it'll be suicide. And the boy won't be recovered."

Elvira met Kravitz's sober gaze, and realized he was right. "Listen to Kravitz, Dan'l," she said. "You'll have a good chance to get him with two of you. We can take care of ourselves in the meantime. I can shoot, too, if I have to."

The aide spoke up. "She's right, Boone."

"Take Kravitz," Jameson added. "I can drive the wagon."

Dan'l looked at Kravitz and stroked his beard with a thick hand.

"I'm going," Kravitz told him, sticking his jaw out.

Dan'l sighed. "I reckon you are."

Kravitz grinned.

"We'll load most of the provisions from the busted wagon into Jameson's," Dan'l told them. "We'll take some ourselves, too. We might have to chase Running Dog some. You sure you can drive a wagon, Mr. Jameson, with that bad hip?"

"Absolutely."

"And if he can't," Elvira said, "I can."

"Did the bad Indian take Toby?" little Janie said from her mother's arms.

"It's all right, Janie. We're going to bring him back. Aren't we, Dan'l?"

Dan'l wished he could really promise that. "Of course we are," he said with conviction.

"Are you sure we shouldn't just stay put till you get back?" Jameson wondered, grimacing from the hip wound.

"No, I'm convinced it's safer for you to keep moving," Dan'l told him. He lowered his voice, turning toward Elvira. "If we ain't rejoined you in a couple days, we probably run into more trouble than we could handle. Just keep on to

St. Louis. Maybe you'll see us there with the boy later."

Elvira's eyes watered up at that.

"I see one of the wagon horses run off," Dan'l said, changing the subject. "But that'll still leave you with an extra one, since you only got one wagon now. You can use it to bargain with, if you run into friendly Kiowa. You can give them half of your supplies, too, if you have to. Do you hear me, Jameson?"

Jameson nodded. "I understand, Dan'l." It was the first time he had called Dan'l by his first name.

"Good," Dan'l said. "Well, let's get the supplies loaded, and your horses in harness. Then me and Kravitz will be riding out."

"And may God go with you," Elvira said.

By mid-morning the loading was completed, and the team was harnessed to Jameson's wagon. With Jameson riding on the wagon's seat, they headed off east, waving back at Dan'l and Kravitz as they left. Then the two hunters headed south, following the tracks of the re-treating Apaches.

The tracking was easy for the first couple of hours, but at midday they ran through a very rocky area, and Dan'l was obliged to dismount and study the ground several times to pick up the trail again. Kravitz was a good tracker him-self, but he was astonished at Dan'l's seemingly magical ability to find spoor where there

269

seemed to be none. If Kravitz had been by him-self, he would have lost the trail a couple of times, and not found it again. But Dan'l had done this sort of thing since he was a small boy, and he was better than the Cherokee or Shaw-nee.

Dan'l was certain that Running Dog would not harm Toby Lucas until Dan'l had come for him, which Running Dog was counting on. The Apache figured he would have Dan'l outnum-bered and in an awkward offensive posture, which would put all the odds on Running Dog's side to end Dan'l's life once and for all.

Dan'l thought Running Dog might stop after a short retreat, and wait for Dan'l to catch them. But as the afternoon wore on, and the tracks did not halt or slow down, it became clear that Run-ning Dog had decided to ride out of Kiowa ter-ritory before encamping, and also place himself at least on the outer edge of the Comanches' domain. He did not need harassment by hostile tribes while trying to end this thing with the great impostor from the East.

At mid-afternoon they came upon a lone In-dian rider, who warily allowed them to ap-proach him. When they got close enough, Kravitz recognized him as another Comanche and signaled to him. He drew an arrow from a rawhide quiver, and held it against a short bow while Kravitz spoke.

"You come from the south," Kravitz said.

"Yes. You are hunters?"

Kravitz nodded. "We hunt men."

The Comanche frowned. He was rather young, with a broad, flat face and hard eyes.

"Apaches," Kravitz explained. "Up from the south. This is their trail that we follow."

"I know."

"Have you seen them?" Kravitz asked.

"That is my business."

"What's he saying?" Dan'l asked.

"He doesn't want to talk about Running Dog. But I think he's run into him," Kravitz replied. He turned back to the Indian. "The Apaches have killed a friend of ours. And wounded others. They also stole a white child."

"That is your business," the Comanche said.

"The Apache is your blood enemy," Kravitz continued. "He rides through your land without fear of consequences."

"If he is not gone shortly, he will pay with his life," the Comanche said.

"We can save you the trouble," Kravitz replied.

The Indian was looking at Dan'l, now, curiously. "Is this the one called Ancient Bear?"

Kravitz glanced at Dan'l. "He is so called by the Apache."

"Why does he not speak?"

Kravitz thought for a moment. "He does not deign to speak in your tongue. But he knows all tongues."

"What now?" Dan'l said impatiently.

Kravitz ignored his friend for the moment.

"He goes to retrieve the white boy."

"If he has great power, why did he allow a dirty Apache to take the boy and kill his friend?"

"The ways of gods are strange," Kravitz said. "He had to wrestle with the power of other Apache deities."

The Indian grunted. "I will tell you where the Apache camps in exchange for the long gun of Ancient Bear."

"He wants your rifle," Kravitz said to Dan'l.

"Oh, hell. We can find Running Dog," Dan'l said in exasperation. "Tell him we need our guns."

Kravitz nodded. "We must give him something, though, Dan'l. So that he may save face."

Dan'l knew he was right. He reached into a saddle wallet, remembering some iron lance points they had brought with them from St. Louis. He still had a half dozen in the bottom of the pouch. He moved his mount forward, up beside the Indian.

"Here. Our gesture of friendship," he said.

The Comanche hesitated, then took the points. He looked them over, and decided they were an honorable gift.

"That is what we offer in friendship," Kravitz said in the Indian's language. "We need our guns for the Apache."

The fellow nodded, studying Dan'l's face. "I accept your offering," he said. He hesitated. "The Apache builds temporary shelter in a gorge in that direction," he said, pointing. "You will reach it when the sun touches that high cliff."

"We are honored by your great hospitality," Kravitz told him.

"If you do not deal with them soon," the Comanche said, "we will."

"I understand," Kravitz replied.

When he was gone, Dan'l said to Kravitz, "Careful son of a bitch, waren't he?"

"He was taking a lot on himself," Kravitz said. "But maybe his directions will help."

They did. The trail left by Running Dog wound around rather aimlessly, but thanks to the Comanche, the hunters rode on a direct path toward the gorge where Running Dog had holed up.

Waiting.

At Running Dog's encampment, his warriors had erected five brush shelters along a rock face. Their open fronts faced the direction intruders would have to come.

Running Dog had trekked southwest until he was well out of Kiowa territory, and just on the far edge of Comanche terrain. He figured they would attract no attention while they waited for Dan'l to come after Toby. Which Running Dog was certain would happen.

Now, in this chosen place, Running Dog would wait for Dan'l to show himself. Then it would be over for the fake god.

Eight-year-old Toby was terrified by his captors, but was trying to be very brave. They had handled him roughly on the way there, and when he had complained, one of the warriors had slapped him hard, making tears come to his eyes. But he had not cried out. He had been toughened by what had happened at Spanish Wells.

Now he sat in one of the brush shelters, his hands and feet tied with rawhide thongs, leaning against the rock face behind him. He could watch his captors as they built a low fire and discussed their plans. He spoke a little Athapaskan himself, but not enough to understand much of what they were saying.

Running Dog stood right in front of the shelter, looking big and dangerous to Toby. He was talking to his warriors.

"Now. We will wait here for as long as it takes," he said. "He will come."

There were only five besides him now, and one of them had a side wound with a poultice applied to it. They were a disconsolate lot. They had lost seven of their group in the attack on the wagons, and not one man present, except Running Dog, thought the effort was worth the loss. In fact, most of them now were convinced that Dan'l was unkillable, and that he might actually be Ancient Bear.

"And if he does not?" one warrior asked belligerently.

"He will come!" Running Dog stated loudly, his dark eyes flashing fire.

"I do not care whether he comes," another Apache said, looking very disgruntled. "Why must we prove this white face is not an ancient god? Whatever he is, he has powerful medicine. Look what he has done to us! I say, kill the boy and forget the white face."

"Yes, kill the boy," a third one said.

In the shelter, Toby understood those few words, and felt his heart pound in his chest.

Running Dog came and yelled into the third man's face, "We will kill the boy! All in good time! After I have caught this filthy defiler of our religion!"

They all fell silent. It was best not to argue with Running Dog when he was angry.

"Our people have accepted his great lie," Running Dog went on. "That is why we find ourselves outcast. Once we have slain this puke-bag, we will take his head to our people, and show them how very human he was. Then I will resume my place as head of our great tribe, and all of you will hold positions of high honor."

That seemed to placate them. But the one with the wound finally spoke up tentatively. "What if he really is Ancient Bear?"

It was a brave thing to say, and the warrior stepped back a pace when he saw the look on Running Dog's face.

Surprisingly, though, when Running Dog replied, it was in a quiet, yet brittle, voice. "If there is anyone who still believes that ridiculous claim, I give him my permission to leave this camp at once. I do not wish to have him fight beside me."

Everyone studied that hard face and remained silent.

"Good," Running Dog said at last. "Now, listen to me. This will be completely different from the way it was at the wagons. We were forced to attack them there. They held the defensive position and the cover. That is why we failed. Here, we hold the defensive posture. Boone will have to attack us, and there will be just him, or maybe one other. They cannot leave the wagons undefended. We will have split their force, and put them on the offensive. We will have every advantage this time. And we will use it to kill this dirty defiler."

"May White-Painted Woman be with us," a warrior mumbled.

In the shelter nearby, Toby felt the urge to urinate. He called out to them pitifully. "Please. I have to pee."

Running Dog understood English to some extent, and was rather fluent in Spanish. He went into the shelter, bending down because of its low roof.

"What did you say, offspring of feces?" he asked in his own language.

Toby repeated it in Spanish. *"Tengo que orinar. Por favor."*

"Orinar!" Running Dog growled. "You will make your water in your clothing, you little

piece of shit!" He kicked Toby hard in the thigh, and Toby cried out involuntarily and felt urine flow into his trousers.

Running Dog went back out into the sun. "There are just six of us now. We will stand sentry duty continuously until he comes. You three take your turn now. Then myself and these others will relieve you. I want one man at the head of the gorge, and two up on top there. That is the most likely place for him to approach."

"Very well," they agreed.

"I do not want him dead," Running Dog warned them. "Not unless he is escaping. I want the pleasure of killing him."

"We understand."

The threesome left the encampment, and Running Dog and the other two settled down by the fire. They would relieve the others at dark.

In the shelter, Toby Lucas had wet his trousers badly, and sat in the stink of them. Thirsty, tired, with his bonds cutting into his flesh, he was miserable. His thigh throbbed where Running Dog had kicked him, and his head swirled with thoughts of how they might kill him.

He wondered if Dan'l Boone would come after him. He wished he knew his mother was all right, and little Janie. The world suddenly seemed a very chaotic, unpleasant place.

With little hope of change.

"Look. Ahead there."

Kravitz followed Dan'l's pointing finger, and

saw the wide gorge emerging from the hazy distance.

"That has to be it," Dan'l said quietly.

As Kravitz leaned forward on his saddle, it creaked under his weight, and his mount guffered a little nervously. "I agree," Kravitz told him.

"I can see their tracks. Coming in there from the west," Dan'l said, squinting toward the gorge.

Kravitz continued to be amazed at the things Dan'l could see and hear that other men could not.

"We've been hidden by cottonwoods and rocks," Kravitz said. "I doubt they've seen us."

"I wish I could be sure of that," Dan'l said. The hair moved on the nape of his neck, as it had back at Santa Fe, when he had sensed the town would soon be under attack. "I think we'll hang back here till dark. We're only going to get one chance at this."

"Do you think Toby is still alive?" Kravitz asked.

Dan'l nodded. "Yeah. He can't risk killing him. He wants me too bad."

They dismounted in a low stand of cottonwoods, and ate some hardtack and drank some of their water. Kravitz was rather surprised at Dan'l's silence, but realized he was getting ready mentally for a life-or-death struggle. As the sun set behind the trees, darkness came on quite swiftly.

Dan'l rose and walked to the appaloosa. "This is going to be tricky."

"I know."

"If they take us alive, it won't be purty. At least we got a little rest. Remember, it's me they want. If they get me, ride out. You couldn't get Toby alone. Maybe they'll take him back alive, like a trophy."

"We'll see," Kravitz said noncommittally.

They moved out then, and when they got to the head of the gorge, they looked for sentries, but could see nothing. They picketed their mounts at one side of the gorge, and peered into it, rifles loaded and primed, revolvers on their hips.

The moon was obscured by clouds. It was very dark.

"They might not know we're here yet," Kravitz whispered.

"Maybe," Dan'l said, looking up toward the top of the gorge. "I wish we could figure where they put the sentries."

"Let's go up above. At least we'll have high gun on them."

Dan'l was doubtful. "That might be where they'll expect us to go."

"Maybe so," Kravitz said. "But we could walk right into their fire down here."

Dan'l nodded, still uncertain. "Let's try the high ground."

They made sure the horses were not visible from the inside of the gorge, then started climbing. It was tough going, all rock and scrub brush, and they could not see very well. By the time they reached the crest of the gorge, Kravitz could hardly get his breath, but Dan'l was breathing regularly.

"You all right?" Dan'l asked his partner.

Kravitz grinned. "Will be as soon as I can breathe again."

They stood there, looking around. It was very quiet. Dan'l could see no one, hear nothing. But he knew there had to be sentries out. Running Dog was very thorough.

"Let's move along the brink," Kravitz said. "We have to find where they are camped."

Dan'l was not so eager to move. When you were the motionless one, the universe had to find you. When you were in motion, you were the thing attracting attention. He had sometimes sat motionless and soundless for hours on the trail in Kentucky, to let an animal come to him. Or to make sure there was not an enemy out there watching.

Kravitz headed out without waiting for Dan'l to acknowledge, so Dan'l had little choice. He followed behind, moving along the crest of the gorge. There was low underbrush, and a few trees, and boulders to hide behind. But they were not the ones hiding. They had to seek out the hiders, and Dan'l did not like that.

They crept along in the dark, looking down into the gorge. Finally, Kravitz stopped. "There!"

He pointed down to the base of the rocky cliff, where Dan'l saw the outlines of the shelters and just a hint of white smoke rising from a fire burning out.

He nodded. But the feeling at the base of his neck was back, strong. Kravitz climbed a few steps down the slope.

"Kravitz. I think we should—"

But in that moment, Dan'l saw a shadow move out of the brush and attach itself to Kravitz. Kravitz let out a small yell, and there was some thrashing about, as Dan'l headed down toward him. But then there was a thumping sound, and Dan'l saw Kravitz go down.

Just as Dan'l arrived, the Apache came into focus for him. He swung the rifle at the warrior's head, and connected, and the Indian went down beside Kravitz.

When Dan'l bent over him, there was a soft sound behind him, and he turned just in time to see a tomahawk slam broadside into his face.

Bright stars flashed inside Dan'l's skull, and then blackness swept in. He felt himself hit the ground hard, and slide downward, but then he slipped into a black abyss from which there seemed to be no return.

Chapter Fourteen

The first thing Dan'l noticed, in the deep, black place where he had gone, was the sound of ghostly voices.

It went on and on, and he listened to it without curiosity, without any kind of tension. Finally he could differentiate the voices, and realized there were more than one.

The next sensation was of the hard ground against his back, and soon after that, the sizzling pain that rocketed through his head.

Then he felt his breath sharpen and quicken, and his eyelids fluttered open.

The voices stopped when the groan escaped from his lips. He lay there looking into the dark, not able to focus on anything.

"He is regaining consciousness."

"See? He moves."

"The other one is still motionless."

Dan'l turned his head toward the voices, and saw several shadowy shapes squatting beside a low fire. Everything had fuzzy edges. No matter how hard he tried to focus, he could not do it.

One of the shapes got up, came over to him, and squatted beside him. When it spoke, he recognized the voice.

"Ah, good. You did not die. That is very good." Smiling down at Dan'l was Running Dog.

"Oh, shit," Dan'l said.

They had failed. He had allowed Kravitz to move in too quickly, too impetuously. A good hunter was always sure of the territory around him before he made any move against his quarry. It was an absolutely basic and inviolable rule.

Now they were dead. Toby was dead, too, and the wagons would have to make it through to St. Louis without his and Kravitz's help.

He would never see Rebecca again.

Or the kids.

Just because he had acted foolishly, against his instincts.

All of that flew through his head as Running Dog squatted there and peered into his face. Running Dog reached out and touched Dan'l's wild hair, and his hand came away with blood on it.

"Ah. You do bleed. Just as I suspected. You may now give up your claim to godhood."

Dan'l had no idea what he was talking about. He turned and saw Kravitz, lying near him. Kravitz groaned, and moved slightly.

"I see both are alive. The gods are smiling on us."

Dan'l looked back into that evil face and hated it. Like some white men, certain Indians were just born to do bad things. To live outside the laws of decency. Running Dog was one of them.

"It's me you want. Let the kid go," Dan'l said to the squatting Apache.

"What? Do not speak in the white tongue."

Neither man understood the other. Running Dog turned and spoke to one of the other shadowy figures. The other man went to one of the shelters for a couple of minutes, then re-emerged with Toby Lucas. The bonds had been taken off his ankles, and his eyes grew big when he saw Dan'l.

"Mr. Boone! You come for me!" He glanced toward Kravitz, who was just coming around. "Mr. Kravitz!"

Dan'l tried a grin, just for Toby. He could focus better, now. "Glad to see you're still alive, boy."

"Now," Running Dog told Toby in Spanish, "you say what he says."

"He wants to know what you're saying to him," Toby said to Dan'l.

Dan'l tried again. "You only want me," he said

to the Apache. "Let my friend take the boy back to his mother."

Toby said it in Spanish, and Running Dog listened carefully. Then he laughed very loudly. He repeated the request to his warriors, over by the fire, and they laughed, too, and made jokes among themselves.

"You will die, impostor," Running Dog told Dan'l. "Your friend will die, the boy will die." He looked grimly into Toby's scared eyes. "Tell him."

Toby translated, his brown hair hanging into his young face. He was tall for his age, and had the strong look of his dead father. His face was smeared with dirt, and his trousers were still damp and stinking from his urine.

"You son of a bitch," Dan'l said when he heard. "You ain't no man, you bastard. You're a beast from hell."

Toby was hesitant to put that into Spanish, but he did, reluctantly. When Running Dog heard, he laughed again, enjoying Dan'l's obvious discomfort.

"What happened?" Kravitz said from nearby, his tongue thick. "Where are we?"

Running Dog frowned toward him. Then he turned back to Dan'l. He spoke again, with Toby translating.

"When dawn comes, we must leave this place. My warriors have seen the Comanche. They will come soon. We will ride south and out of their land. There is an Apache village one day's ride.

They will greet me as a hero when they see I have captured Ancient Bear, and shown him to be a fraud. I will kill you with many witnesses watching, and it will be a fitting death."

"Please," Dan'l said thickly. "If you got any decency left in you, let the kid live. He ain't your enemy."

When that was translated, Running Dog shook his head. "The boy will come with us. Your friend will not."

Running Dog turned and gave orders to the warrior who had brought Toby out, and he half dragged him back to the shelter. Running Dog gave further commands, and the Apaches began erecting a spit over the low fire, a sturdy one made with large limbs from nearby aspens. Dan'l and Kravitz were left alone for a while as the moon rose in the sky overhead. Dan'l figured it was still short of midnight. He looked over at Kravitz, and wished he had come alone.

"What did he say?" Kravitz asked Dan'l. He looked bad. Crimson blood covered his face and head, and he did not seem fully aware of what was going on around him. "They're cooking something up," Dan'l said simply. "It might be for you, Kravitz. We got to get out of here. How tight is them rawhide cords on you?"

"Huh? What did you say?"

"Oh, hell," Dan'l said heavily. He worked at the cords on his wrists, but he was bound tightly. The rawhide just cut deeper into his flesh.

"They got us, didn't they, Dan'l?" Kravitz said. "Is the boy alive?"

"Yes," Dan'l said. "He's alive, all right. Can you get loose from them fittings? We got to do something here. We ain't got much time."

"I am glad about Toby," Kravitz said in a calm, serene voice. "We will be . . . all right, Dan'l."

"Kravitz! Listen to me!"

"I was captured by Kiowa years ago," Kravitz said. "Just like this, my friend. I was kept tied up for five days. No food or water. Defecated in my clothes. I kept talking to them, Dan'l. Kept talking and talking. Made friends with their shaman. They finally cut me loose, cleaned me up, and fed me like a king. I have never eaten such delicious food. Then they turned me loose with my rifle." He paused. "I will never forget that time."

"Kravitz—"

"We must keep talking to them, Dan'l. It is very important . . . that we talk to them."

Kravitz was wrong in the head, and there was nothing Dan'l could do about it. He struggled again with his bonds, and accomplished nothing.

He saw that the big spit over the fire was finished, and he had a bad feeling about it. One of the warriors was building the fire up. "Oh, no," he grunted.

In a moment, Running Dog came over to Kravitz and kicked him hard in the thigh.

"Wake up, you! You have an appointment to keep."

Two Apaches came, dragged Kravitz to his feet, untied him, and began stripping his clothing off.

"Take it," Kravitz said to them. "Take it all. Our horses are picketed up at the top of the gorge." He grunted as they tore his underclothing down. "There are guns, too." He turned to Dan'l. "We must cooperate, Dan'l. It will buy their goodwill."

"Do something, Kravitz!" Dan'l said harshly. "Run, for God's sake!"

"It's all right, Dan'l. They just want my clothing. They are all thieves at heart, you know."

He was naked now, and they had brought a long pole and were tying him to it, legs, torso, arms. A warrior dragged Dan'l back to a shelter near the fire, the one Toby now sat in. Dan'l was set upright, too, and he knew it was so he could see what they were about to do.

Kravitz was pulled off his feet, and two strong warriors carried him horizontally to the spit supports, and casually placed the pole over the fire, with Kravitz on it.

"Hey!" Kravitz yelled weakly, feeling the fire beneath him. "What is this?"

"What are they doing?" little Toby called from behind Dan'l.

"Don't look!" Dan'l said to him. "Close your eyes!"

An Apache threw some wood on the fire, and

it became much bigger and brighter. On the spit now, Kravitz was staring into the blackness of the sky, but feeling the new heat burning his back.

"Wait!" he yelled. "You don't have to do this! You can have everything!"

"Oh, shit!" Dan'l muttered, looking down.

The fire burned higher, and an Apache turned the end of the pole. Kravitz was suddenly staring into the open flames, which were licking at his chest, his belly, his face.

"No!" he screamed. "God, no!"

Dan'l could see Running Dog, on the far side of the fire, grinning evilly, watching Dan'l's face.

The screaming became louder as the spit was turned and turned, and Kravitz's body began to burn, slowly. It went on and on, and the screams stabbed into Dan'l like lances. Little Toby was yelling behind Dan'l, "Make them stop! Please make them stop!"

It seemed to last forever. But finally, with Kravitz's body twitching and jerking in deep shock, the screaming stopped. The Apache on the end of the pole kept turning it, cooking Kravitz to a deep brown. Dan'l could smell the stink of the burnt flesh, and he thought he would never forget the smell.

When they finally took Kravitz's charred corpse off the spit, Dan'l had built a hatred in his gut for Running Dog that seemed as if it might consume him.

Kravitz had been a new but valued friend. He

was the kind of man Dan'l would have been pleased to ride with on other treks. And he had gotten into all this because of Dan'l.

Behind him in the shelter, Toby was softly crying. Dan'l would have done anything to spare him what he had seen and heard.

Running Dog came over to Dan'l, grinning. He had cut something out of Kravitz. It was cooked meat. "Here." Running Dog beamed at him. "Maybe you would like to try the meat. It seems very good."

Dan'l growled like a cougar, then spat directly into Running Dog's face.

The Apache wiped at the spittle, a look of wildness in his dark eyes. He hurled a low Apache obscenity at Dan'l, and began kicking him violently in the legs, the chest, the side. Over and over. Until he was breathless with the effort.

Dan'l fell onto his side, feeling the new pain lance through him. He had not cried out. He would not give the Indian the satisfaction. Lying on his side, though, he vomited onto the ground.

"If I did not need you, you would follow the other hunter on the spit!" Running Dog hissed at him. "But your time approaches, you deceiving snake! You will receive the Death of a Thousand Cuts!"

Even though Dan'l did not understand what the Apache said, his tone was clearly threatening. "You piece of buffalo shit," Dan'l choked out. The stench of his vomit was in his face.

"Tomorrow we will reach our destination," Running Dog said harshly. "You will see the boy die first. Is that not something to look forward to?"

The Apaches threw Kravitz into a shallow grave when they were finished with him. They did not want to attract coyotes and buzzards. By then it was very late, and they went to sleep in shifts.

Dan'l could not sleep. He kept seeing Kravitz on that spit, turning and turning. Toby finally dropped off, but Dan'l heard him mumbling incoherently in his sleep, having a nightmare.

Dan'l wondered what they would do to the boy. It was not pleasant to think about.

Finally, dawn came.

The Apaches tied Dan'l and Toby to makeshift litters and dragged them along behind their horses. They also had retrieved Dan'l's and Kravitz's horses and long guns. The guns had been replaced on the horses' irons, and the horses were trailed along behind. Running Dog was wearing Dan'l's revolver on his belt, but Dan'l never saw Kravitz's side arm that day.

It was a hard, dusty ride, and the grit got into Dan'l's throat and eyes. He heard Toby cough several times, and knew the boy was having trouble, too. The travois litters just dragged on the ground, and every rock and hole jarred the prisoners.

The journey went on most of the day. No water was offered to them, and no food, and they were never freed from the litters. The Indians stopped at midday for rest and food, and the one hauling Toby complained loudly to Running Dog that the travois was wearing his horse out, and that they should just kill the boy at once. It was, after all, only Dan'l that Running Dog had decided to kill before witnesses.

But Running Dog was adamant. He wanted both of them.

The Apache that Dan'l had knocked down with his rifle in the fight on the crest of the cliff now wore a cloth wrapping around his head because of the wound Dan'l had put there, and he looked as if he would like to kill Dan'l himself.

By the time the group arrived at the small village, in late afternoon, it seemed to Dan'l as if a week had passed. He looked over at Toby when they stopped, and the boy was only half conscious, his small face covered with dust.

"Toby," Dan'l called to him. "Don't give up. Not yet."

The boy nodded numbly.

It was a poor-looking village, Dan'l noticed as they rode in. There were a couple dozen brush and hide tipis, and dirty-looking children running about half naked. The men of the village were not able to range far in their hunting, because they were just barely outside Comanche territory. When Running Dog announced who he was, they all recognized his name, and all already knew that his father, Yellow Horse, had been killed at Devil's Canyon by the Mexicans. Men, women, and children all came out and followed the war party into the village, gawking openly at Running Dog's prizes on the litters. When they stopped at a large tipi and dismounted, several children went over to Toby and jabbered at him in their own language. One poked a stick into his side.

"I have captured the one called Ancient Bear!" Running Dog announced as he dismounted. "You have all heard the stories about him." He lowered his voice. "He killed my father."

Dan'l looked over at him from his supine position on the slanting platform he was tied to.

The villagers all gathered close around him, and a few seemed very scared. "Ancient Bear!" a woman whispered.

"He is not Ancient Bear!" Running Dog said loudly. "He is just a lying white face. I have made him bleed. Just like an Apache bleeds. Now, in this village, I will kill him. With all of you as witnesses. To show you and the Apache nation that he is mortal and an impostor."

Another woman, a bolder one, came and stared hard at Dan'l, and then spat at him. She laughed loudly, and some of the others did, too. But several men looked troubled to have this possible god in their midst.

"When you have seen him die," Running Dog concluded, "I will carry his head to my people and claim my rightful place as chief of all the Apaches of this great plain."

Dan'l and Toby were untied and taken off the litters. Toby was taken to a nearby tipi and tied up again, and Dan'l saw the abject fear in his young face as he glanced back toward Dan'l at the last moment. Dan'l was led to an upright pole in the ground, in the middle of the compound, and tied securely to it, hand and foot. Then Running Dog's renegade Apaches seated themselves around a fire with the men of the village for a big palaver, with Running Dog and the local chief planning Dan'l's execution. While that was going on, children came and jabbed sharp sticks into Dan'l's legs and stomach, and women slapped and struck him with willow sticks just to see him flinch.

Dan'l closed his eyes to it all and remembered Kravitz and the way he had had to die. He looked down at his ankles, felt the rawhide biting into them, and realized the bonds were very secure there. But the Apache who had tied his wrists behind the pole had not done a good job. Dan'l felt just a small bit of play in the thong. He did not try to loosen it.

He waited.

"Tonight we will celebrate!" Running Dog announced at the fire. "Tonight we will feast and dance. Then tomorrow morning you, the Tinneh, will play the flute for Pahy, our Lord the Sun. And this interloper will be sent to the Netherworld, just as Pahy takes his throne for the new day."

Some of the villagers did not like the idea of

Running Dog appointing himself head of the Apaches, but none dared show any dissension. Running Dog had his bodyguard renegades with him, all devoted to his success.

Dan'l had been tied so well that he could not slide his wrists down the pole to sit down. He could only slump against his bonds, and that is what he did as the night came and the feasting and dancing took place nearby. The women and children had wearied of making Dan'l bleed through his clothing, and had left him. But he had many small wounds on his legs and body from their prodding and stabbing, and that weakened him further.

He felt like giving up. But there was Toby. And, back home somewhere, Rebecca and his own children.

Slumped there on the post in the ground, Dan'l fought the feeling of being a victim. He took a deep breath and remembered that he was a hunter. That was the image of himself he wanted to keep in his head. *They have made a mistake. They have allowed a dangerous killer into their midst. They have let their guard down, because he looks defeated. Humbled. But he is waiting. Until the time is right.*

It was not easy to keep those thoughts through the pain and the reality of his situation. But he had been there before. He was Sheltowee. Adopted son of Blackfish. Officer in the Carolina and Missouri militias. Survivor.

In late evening the celebration ended, and

Running Dog came personally to see that Dan'l was still secured to the pole. He was inebriated and grinning.

"Think about the morning, Boone. You will watch the boy die. Very slowly. Then will come your turn. We will see if the great hunter can accept pain." He laughed and walked away.

Dan'l had no idea what he had said, but knew it was evil. And he had seen the Apache jerk his head toward the tipi where Toby was kept.

Running Dog put two guards on Dan'l and one on Toby. One of the men watching Dan'l was a Running Dog renegade, the other a villager. Both were tough-looking warriors of a fierce tribe. They sat at a low fire, while the rest of the village went to sleep in tipis, including Running Dog. The renegade guarding Dan'l had Kravitz's rifle, primed and lying across his knees. The villager wore a long knife in his belt. Dan'l had seen both weapons, so he knew their strength. He had also seen the small corral adjacent to the village, where Running Dog had deposited Dan'l's appaloosa, without bothering to remove its saddle and irons.

Dan'l realized they would kill Toby first. Just to make Dan'l's own demise more terrible. Dan'l remembered losing two of his sons to the Shawnee, and how the first one, James, had been tortured and mutilated. He had found the boy later, and could not even recognize him as his own son. He did not know how he would be able to take watching a similar thing happen to Elvira's boy. He had come to like her and her children a lot.

Besides losing two of his sons, Dan'l had also had a daughter abducted by the Shawnee. In a dramatic two-day chase, he had followed the Indians and surprised them, and gotten the girl back before they could kill her.

Dan'l had even been taken prisoner by the Shawnee himself, and had had to effect a harrowing escape, in which he had had to travel on foot almost two hundred miles in four days to avoid recapture.

He had done it all.

And survived.

That was why the Shawnee had named him Sheltowee, comparing him to an ancient creature who held the world in place. His great strength of mind and body was revered by his enemies.

But that was in Kentucky.

Midnight came, and the village was dead quiet. Dan'l watched the guards, who talked quietly between themselves at first, but then slumped silently on their log benches.

Dan'l found that the pole was slimmer at places than at others, by moving his hands up and down as much as he was able behind him. He moved them to a thin place and felt a loosening of the thongs.

That's it, Dan'l thought. You got sloppy, you son of a bitch. You forgot who I am.

He pulled hard and made some more room.

Then he was grabbing at a knot with his fingers, and working it loose. Slowly. Methodically. Through cutting pain.

"Canst thou not beg, boy?" his father used to say to him when he was beaten with a belt. His father would not quit until Dan'l yelled out in pain, but Dan'l would not. So he had always received more punishment than his siblings.

The thongs lost their knot finally, and Dan'l patiently unraveled the rawhide from his hands. He looked toward the fire. The villager had fallen onto his side, asleep. The renegade of Running Dog was nodding sleepily.

Go careful, Dan'l told himself. There's no hurry.

His hands were now free, but swollen and bleeding. He let them find circulation for a few moments, then searched for the knot behind him that held his torso to the pole. It took some time, but he finally did. He pulled the knot toward his front and began working on it. In another half hour, it fell off him.

Now all that remained tied were his ankles. He bent and worked at the rawhide, freeing himself completely in just a few minutes.

The renegade grunted and coughed, and looked toward Dan'l. Dan'l had resumed an upright position, with his hands behind him. The Apache squinted, relaxed, and turned back toward the fire.

Dan'l stepped away from the pole and rubbed at his ankles and wrists. He hurt all over, and was afraid he might black out for a moment. But he took a few deep breaths, and turned toward the guards.

He had no weapon but his hands. In a half crouch, in the same manner as the Shawnee he had learned from, he crept silently toward the fire. He came up behind the renegade, and saw it was the one who had turned Kravitz slowly over the fire.

He grabbed him by the head from behind, one hand clapped over the Indian's mouth, and twisted viciously. The Indian grunted, and his spine snapped.

He fell limp in Dan'l's thick hands.

Dan'l let him sink slowly to the ground. The other guard, still asleep on the ground, moved slightly. Dan'l reached and pulled the long knife from the Indian's belt and woke him up. He looked up into Dan'l's grim face, surprised, just in time to see the knife descend and cut his throat open from ear to ear.

Blood fountained upward, and stained Dan'l's rawhides. The Apache grabbed at his throat, made gurgling sounds, and died there.

Dan'l looked around. Nobody was visible. Everybody continued sleeping. They had celebrated too much.

Dan'l turned and walked quickly to the tipi where Toby was kept. The flap was open. Dan'l peered inside, but could see nothing.

He stepped through the opening, knife out in front of him.

His eyes accustomed themselves to the darkness. There was Toby, bound tightly, lying awake on the ground. When he saw Dan'l, his eyes widened.

"Mr. Boone! Look out!"

Dan'l turned and saw the inside guard swinging a war club wildly at his head.

Chapter Fifteen

Dan'l had only an instant to react.

He jumped backwards, sucking his breath in, and the club missed his head and just grazed his chest and belly on the way down. Dan'l reached past it with the war knife, and jammed it deep into the guard's abdomen.

The Indian looked down at the cold steel in him as if it were a snake that had bitten him from cover. Then he looked up at Dan'l curiously. He was the other man who had carried Kravitz to the fire, grinning, on that terrible previous night.

When Dan'l pulled the blade back out, there was a hissing sound between the Indian's teeth, and he fell in a heap at Dan'l's feet.

In less than five minutes, Dan'l had killed three of his tormentors.

Dan'l bent over Toby and began unfastening the boy's bonds. In just moments Toby was free and smiling weakly. "I knew they should have killed you," he said softly.

Dan'l put a finger to his lips. "Not another word. You hear me?"

Toby nodded.

"Follow me," Dan'l told him.

They emerged into new moonlight. Dan'l just stood there for a long moment, making certain there was nobody else up and around. Then he led Toby in a wide circle around the compound, away from the fire, toward the small corral.

There were about twenty horses there, contained by a fence made of saplings. Dan'l saw his appaloosa on the far side of the corral, and they went over to it, outside the fence. It still had its saddle and gear on, including Dan'l's saddle scabbard with the Kentucky rifle tucked inside it.

It took several minutes for Dan'l to carefully unfasten two rails of the fence. The appaloosa whinnied softly, and a couple of other horses did, too. Dan'l looked toward the tipis. Nothing.

He led the appaloosa over a low rail, and outside the corral. He left the fence down, hoping some of the horses would wander off. He did not want to spook them. They would be heard.

Dan'l scanned the village. If he did not have Toby to think about, he would have gone to find

Running Dog, to kill him.

He motioned to the boy, then led the horse and Toby away from the corral on foot.

They walked the horse for a full half mile, until they were at the mouth of the gorge. Then Dan'l mounted, swung Toby up behind him, and rode off toward the northeast.

Toward the wagon train.

They did not stop. Dan'l wanted as much distance between them and the village as possible, when Running Dog discovered they were gone.

They would need it.

Two hours later the village chieftain awoke and rose in the dark to urinate in a waste ditch at the edge of the village. It was not until he returned from the ditch that he saw the two inert figures at the fire, and looked toward the pole where Dan'l had been tied.

His eyes opened wide, and he ran over to examine the dead guards. He turned and yelled at the top of his lungs, "He is gone! He is gone!"

Inside a nearby tipi, Running Dog thought the yelling was in his head at first, then realized that it was coming from outside. He jumped to his feet and dashed out into the compound, bleary-eyed. Other villagers were emerging, too, looking about wildly. The chief was just coming out of the tipi that Toby had occupied.

"They are both gone! He has taken the boy!"

Running Dog did not want to believe it. He went and examined the loosened bonds at the empty pole, and stared at them dully for a long moment. Then he threw his head back and roared at the heavens in anguish.

One of Running Dog's warriors came running up to him. "The spotted horse is taken, too. With the gun on it."

Running Dog strided without speaking to the tipi that the chief had just emerged from, and looked at Toby's untied bonds, and the dead warrior who had been with him. Then he walked to the fire, and looked down on the other two dead Indians.

"That damn hound from the black place," he moaned.

Women and children were up now, and wondering what had happened. When it became general knowledge that Dan'l was gone, there was a lot of muttering among them, and fear on their faces.

"He *is* Ancient Bear," a woman said quietly.

"Aiwee! And we have aroused his anger!"

Running Dog ignored the remarks. His remaining three warriors had gathered around him, and the village chief now came up to him. He was a rather young man, with a thin body and long face.

"You brought this man into our village and said you would prove he is mortal. You said you would kill him, and take his head to the people of Yellow Horse. We believed you."

Running Dog shook his head desperately. "He *is* mortal! But don't you see? He is a white Indian! He has great medicine, given to him by the Shawnee."

"He is smarter than you," the chief said quietly. "He may *be* Ancient Bear!"

"That is a wicked lie!" Running Dog fumed. "That should be obvious. He bleeds, he bruises, he hurts when cut. If I had chosen, he would be dead now. Do you not see that?"

"I see him gone," the chief said. "And three Apaches dead. I see he escaped from tight bindings, as if by magic. I am glad he is not here now. I do fear him."

Running Dog made a grimace of disgust. "You are all fools! Help me track him down, and I promise you this time I will kill him immediately. Give me ten of your best warriors, and I will bring you his corpse."

The chief shook his head. "I will not participate in this fiasco. One of my braves is already dead. If you wish to go after him, you must do it with your own men."

"Damn you, you are an Apache! This man killed many of my people, including Yellow Horse, my father. Will you allow him the pleasure of enjoying this victory? Do you have no Apache pride?"

"We have pride," the chief said carefully. "We gave you our hospitality, our village. We helped you guard this strange man, with no complaint that you brought him here. Now that is the end of it."

Running Dog made an ugly sound in his

throat. "All right. If we of Yellow Horse must go alone, we will. We will bring back his bloody corpse, and you will see what real Apaches can do!"

The chief raised his brows. "We wish you well. But if you bring him back here, be sure he is dead."

The sun, the spirit they called Pahy, was coloring the eastern sky a pastel hue now, and birds were beginning to sing in the gorge.

Running Dog turned arrogantly to his three remaining warriors. "It appears we must do this without assistance. Feed yourselves and prepare to ride."

One of the three, a rather short warrior who had not wanted this chase from its beginning, shook his head. "I will not go," he said.

Running Dog was stunned. "What?"

The Apache looked him in the eye. "This is foolishness. I mourn Yellow Horse as much as any of our people. But he was killed in battle, in an honorable way, by a soldier of the white face. That is all. We have avenged Yellow Horse. We must now let the matter rest."

Running Dog was livid. He drew a war knife from his belt, and came up very close to the warrior. "He is not avenged! Not while this Sheltowee is alive! You will go with us!"

The warrior was afraid of Running Dog, but he just stared hard at him, certain Running Dog would not kill one of his own.

"Let him stay with us," the chief said. "The choice is his."

Those words pushed Running Dog over an imaginary line. He thrust the knife forward, into the belly of his warrior.

The man sucked in his breath, and looked at Running Dog as if he had never laid eyes on him before. Then he sank to the ground and died.

"By the holy spirits!" the chief gasped.

Running Dog turned to his other two renegades. "Are there any more cowards among you?"

There were just two left now. One was rather tall and slim, the other one broad and stocky. They were both expert warriors, and tough as dried buffalo hide, and they still believed it was worthwhile to retrieve Dan'l, just for his excellent horse and long gun. Also, they had just seen what Running Dog did to dissenters.

"We will go," the tall one said.

The other one nodded. "Yes."

A few minutes later, they rode out.

As the sun broke over the distant hills, Dan'l stopped to allow the appaloosa some rest, and to scan the horizon for any sign of pursuers. But there were none.

"We got to watch for Comanch', too," Dan'l said to Toby, after they dismounted. Dan'l led the appaloosa over into the shade of a big, spreading cottonwood.

He picketed their sweat-streaked horse and

looked into a saddle pouch for some hardtack he had put there before heading out to find Toby. He shared it with the boy, and they sat on the ground munching it, without talking.

Finally, young Toby said, "Will he come after us?"

Dan'l looked at him. The boy had very light brown hair, and blue eyes like his mother and Janie. He was a handsome lad, and Dan'l was glad he was not back at that Apache village on this summer morning.

"He'll come," Dan'l said. "He'll be mad as a caged cougar. But he knows he has to catch us before we find the wagon."

"Then why are we stopping?"

Dan'l smiled wearily. He knew he could lie down and sleep for hours and still be tired. And he hurt all over. His rawhides were still stained with blood.

"The appaloosa needs to rest," Dan'l said. "He's carrying a heavy load." He turned to see the animal grazing in the long grass. "He's our only hope of keeping ahead of Running Dog."

"You killed them all, didn't you?" Toby said after a long moment. "All three of them?"

Dan'l nodded. "I didn't have no choice."

"Mother says you're the best Indian fighter of all time."

"If they'd started on me first, I'd be dead now, Toby."

"You'd a thought of something."

Dan'l smiled, and reached and tousled Toby's

light hair. He reminded Dan'l of Dan'l's first son, James, whom the Shawnee had killed.

"Nobody's unkillable, Toby. And we ain't through this yet. Don't forget that."

"I wish I was your son, Mr. Boone."

Dan'l was surprised by the remark, and touched. He stared seriously into the boy's eyes, then turned away.

"You got a family of your own to take care of, boy, when we get back to that wagon. You're the man of your family."

Toby liked the sound of that. "I know."

The horse had stopped sweating. Dan'l rose to his feet, and helped Toby up. "Come on. We got some more hard riding ahead of us."

Several more hours slipped past. At mid-morning, Dan'l was beginning to hope that Running Dog had not followed them after all.

Then, stopping on a hig rise of ground, he turned and saw them. Three riders. He knew immediately that it was Running Dog and his renegades.

They were a couple of miles off, but they were coming on hard. They had seen their quarry.

"Damn!" Dan'l swore under his breath.

"Is that them, Mr. Boone?" Toby said from behind him on the horse.

"It's them, all right," Dan'l said grimly. He counted again, to make sure there were just three of them. "Well, let's get riding. We got to make them rocks up ahead."

He spurred the appaloosa hard up a gradual

grade into a rocky area with head-high boulders and high rock faces, with plenty of places to hide. Dan'l rode fast through the terrain, the horse almost falling a couple of times. In less than a half-hour they came out the other end of it, onto open plains again. It was there that Dan'l reined in.

"Hop off, boy," he ordered Toby.

"Huh?"

"Get off! Now!"

Toby reluctantly obeyed, and stood on the ground looking very scared. "See them rocks over there behind us?" Dan'l said. Toby looked. "You go and hide in them. Don't come out till I get back here."

Toby swallowed back his fear. "What if you don't come back?"

Dan'l sighed. "Then you better hope a friendly Comanche comes along before you starve out here."

"You'll be back, Mr. Boone. I know it."

"Get into them rocks," Dan'l repeated.

"What are you going to do?"

Dan'l was impatient. "I'm going to try something my daddy taught me about hunting bear," he said. "When the bear turns hunter himself."

Toby grinned weakly, and ran and hid in the boulders nearby. Dan'l waited until he was sure Toby was well hidden, then spurred his horse forward. He made a big, wide turn, circling around his own trail through the rocky terrain, but just on the outside of it. He figured it was just about now that his pursuers were entering the far end of the high, rocky country.

After riding almost a mile, Dan'l cut back into the rocks, urging the appaloosa up and up, and when the going got too rough, he dismounted and picketed the animal to an agave plant, then continued the climb on foot, taking the Kentucky rifle with him. Within a few minutes, he reached a place where his own trail passed through the boulders. He could see the appaloosa's hoofprints in the hard sand below him.

Running Dog had not reached that point yet. That was good. He hoped his timing was right. If they had gotten past him, the boy would be in grave danger.

In less than five minutes, Dan'l heard unshod hoofs coming over rocks and hard dirt. Running Dog was a good tracker. He was right on Dan'l's trail. Moments later Dan'l saw all three of them come into sight in single file. They were staring at the ground, not looking right or left. They obviously thought their quarry was out ahead of them.

Dan'l loaded, primed, and cocked the long rifle. Back in Kentucky, folks said he could knock a flea off a bear's nose at a hundred yards with that special gun.

He hunkered down, out of sight. Thirty yards down below him they rode slowly past, Running Dog in the lead. Then the tall warrior, then the other one bringing up the rear. No talk among them. They knew they were close now.

Running Dog could already see Dan'l's head on an Apache lance, decorating his home village.

Dan'l waited for them to pass. *Take the last one first. Then it don't matter.* He laid the sights on the broad Apache's back.

And fired.

Down below, the Apache jerked on his pony, grabbed at the center of his back, and slumped off the animal, hitting his head on rocks.

There was immediate chaos on the trail. The shot Indian's mount raced ahead, almost knocking the tall warrior off his own horse. His horse and Running Dog's began rearing and plunging, while Running Dog searched the rocks wildly with his eyes, swearing in his native tongue. The tall warrior quickly dismounted.

"It is him! Find cover!" Running Dog yelled.

Dan'l was quickly reloading, and wishing he still had one of the revolvers, which could refire much faster. As he did so, the barrel of his rifle caught the sun, and the tall warrior saw it. Both he and Running Dog had a revolver in hand now, the guns taken from Dan'l and Kravitz.

"There!" the tall warrior announced, aiming at Dan'l. He fired, and Dan'l heard the lead fly past his ear. He raised up, fired a second time, and hit the warrior in the high chest. The renegade jumped backwards with arms flailing, and hit the ground hard. Running Dog now aimed carefully at Dan'l. There was another raucous explosion, and Dan'l felt the hot lead punch him in the side.

He was thrown violently backward, and hit the ground on his back. Down below, Running Dog quickly dismounted and issued bloodcurdling yells, throwing his arms in the air. Then he was climbing the rocks to get to Dan'l, the revolver re-primed and ready.

Dan'l felt the blood at his side. The ball had hit him under the arm and fractured a high rib, but had done no other damage. He struggled to recover the Kentucky rifle, lying nearby, but fell back onto his back, gasping for breath. He reached to his boot and found the war knife he had killed with back at the village.

Running Dog was suddenly there, staring wildly down at Dan'l, his painted face looking deadly. "Now, you damned creature from the bowels of the earth!" He aimed at Dan'l's face, no longer caring if he ruined the head for later display.

He squeezed the trigger, and there was a dull fizzing, but no explosion. He had re-primed incorrectly.

He stared down at the gun curiously.

"A man ought to stick to what he knows," Dan'l grated out dully. In a quick, fluid movement, he hurled the knife at the Indian.

The weapon turned over just once in midair, hissing as it went, and buried itself to the hilt in Running Dog's heart.

As the Apache's eyes widened, the revolver

went off finally and dug up dirt beside Dan'l's head. Then Running Dog fell onto his back. A puff of dust was raised when he hit.

Dan'l got up unsteadily and saw that the bullet had not wounded him badly. It was yet another wound that would heal. But when he caught up with the wagon, he would need some rest. He got to his feet, and stood over Running Dog. Running Dog was expiring rapidly, his eyes glazing over.

He looked into Dan'l's eyes. "You are . . . Ancient Bear," the Apache said thickly. "I recognize . . . your supremacy. Use your power . . . to save me."

He had said the last sentence in mixed Spanish and Athapaskan, and Dan'l understood the general idea.

He looked down on the evil red man, killer of babies, ravager of innocents.

"Go to hell," he said in a flat, hard voice.

Running Dog's eyelids fluttered shut, and he died.

It was still only late morning when Dan'l rode up to the place where he had left Toby, and the boy came running out of the rocks to greet him.

Dan'l was listing in the saddle, holding his hand on his side. "You stayed put. Good."

"You killed them, didn't you?" Toby asked excitedly. "You killed all of them?"

Dan'l nodded gravely. "It's done, boy. They won't be chasing us no more."

"I knew you would! I knew you could do it even if there was a dozen of them!"

Dan'l gave him a sour look. "Don't ever celebrate the death of another man, Toby."

Toby's smile dissolved. "All right."

Dan'l swung the boy up on the horse and grunted in pain.

"Are you all right?" Toby asked.

"I'll make it," Dan'l said. "Now we'll rejoin your mother and the others. They ought to be into friendly Kiowa territory by now. From there on, it ought to be an easy trek on to St. Louis. Your new home."

"When we get there, maybe I could visit you now and again," Toby suggested tentatively.

Dan'l spurred the appaloosa forward, out onto the green plain. "That might be right nice," he said.

Toby hugged him from behind, and Dan'l did not mind.

It was just like having little James with him, in those days when they were alone on the trail, breathing in the pure air of the pristine wilderness.

Acting as if there was no tomorrow.

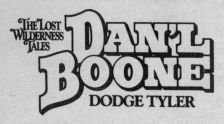

CHEYENNE GIANT EDITION:

BLOOD ON THE ARROWS

JUDD COLE

Follow the adventures of Touch the Sky, as he searches for a world he can call his own—in a Giant Special Edition!

Born the son of a Cheyenne warrior, raised by frontier settlers, Touch the Sky returns to his tribe and learns the ways of a mighty shaman. Then the young brave's most hated foe is brutally slain, and he stands accused of the crime. If he can't prove his innocence, he'll face the wrath of his entire people—and the hatred of the woman he loves.

_3839-0 $5.99 US/$7.99 CAN

CHEYENNE

JUDD COLE

Follow the adventures of Touch the Sky as he searches for a world he can call his own!

#3: Renegade Justice. When his adopted white parents fall victim to a gang of ruthless outlaws, Touch the Sky swears to save them—even if it means losing the trust he has risked his life to win from the Cheyenne.

_3385-2 $3.50 US/$4.50 CAN

#4: Vision Quest. While seeking a mystical sign from the Great Spirit, Touch the Sky is relentlessly pursued by his enemies. But the young brave will battle any peril that stands between him and the vision of his destiny.

_3411-5 $3.50 US/$4.50 CAN

CHEYENNE
JUDD COLE

Born Indian, raised white, he swore he'd die a free man.

#10: Buffalo Hiders. When white hunters appear with powerful Hawken rifles to slaughter the mighty buffalo, Touch the Sky swears to protect the animals. Trouble is, Cheyenne lands are about to be invaded by two hundred mountain men and Indian killers bent on wiping out the remaining buffalo. Touch the Sky thinks it will be a fair fight, until he discovers the hiders have an ally—the U.S. Cavalry.
_3623-1 $3.99 US/$4.99 CAN

#11: Spirit Path. Trained as a shaman, Touch the Sky uses strong magic time and again to save the tribe. Still, the warrior is feared and distrusted as a spy for the white men who raised him. Then a rival accuses Touch the Sky of bad medicine, and if he can't prove the claim false, he'll come to a brutal end—and the Cheyenne will face utter destruction.
_3656-8 $3.99 US/$4.99 CAN

#12: Mankiller. A mighty warrior, Touch the Sky can outlast any enemy. Yet a brave named Mankiller proves a challenge like none other. The fierce Cherokee is determined to count coup on Touch the Sky—then send him to the spirit world with a tomahawk through his heart.
_3698-3 $3.99 US/$4.99 CAN

Dorchester Publishing Co., Inc.
65 Commerce Road
Stamford, CT 06902

Please add $1.75 for shipping and handling for the first book and $.50 for each book thereafter. NY, NYC, PA and CT residents, please add appropriate sales tax. No cash, stamps, or C.O.D.s. All orders shipped within 6 weeks via postal service book rate. Canadian orders require $2.00 extra postage and must be paid in U.S. dollars through a U.S. banking facility.

Name _____
Address _____
City _____ State _____ Zip _____
I have enclosed $_____ in payment for the checked book(s).
Payment <u>must</u> accompany all orders.□ Please send a free catalog.